DREAMLAND

NICHOLAS
SPARKS

DREAMLAND

SPHERE

SPHERE

First published in the United States in 2022 by Random House
This edition published in Great Britain in 2023 by Sphere

1 3 5 7 9 10 8 6 4 2

A CIP catalogue record for this book is available from the British Library.

ISBN 978-0-7515-8553-7

Printed and bound in Great Britain by Clays Ltd, Elcograf S.p.A.

Papers used by Sphere are from well-managed forests
and other responsible sources.

MIX
Supporting
responsible forestry
FSC® C104740

Sphere
An imprint of
Little, Brown Book Group
Carmelite House
50 Victoria Embankment
London EC4Y 0DZ

An Hachette UK Company
www.hachette.co.uk

www.littlebrown.co.uk

FOR ABBY KOONS, ANDREA MAI,
AND EMILY SWEET

PART I

Colby

I.

LET ME TELL YOU WHO I am: My name is Colby Mills, I'm twenty-five years old, and I'm sitting in a strappy foldout chair on St. Pete Beach, Florida, on a beautiful Saturday in mid-May. The cooler next to me is stocked with beer and water on ice, and the temperature is almost perfect, with a steady breeze strong enough to keep the mosquitoes at bay. Behind me is the Don CeSar Hotel, a stately accommodation that reminds me of a pink version of the Taj Mahal, and I can hear live music drifting from the pool area. The guy who's performing is just okay; he strangles the chords every now and then, but I doubt that anyone really minds. I've peeked into the pool area a couple of times since I set up here and noticed that most of the guests have been working on cocktails throughout the afternoon, which means they would probably enjoy listening to just about anything.

I'm not from here, by the way. Before I arrived, I'd never even heard of this place. When people back home asked me where St. Pete Beach was located, I explained that it was a beach town across the causeway from Tampa, near St. Petersburg and Clearwater on the west coast of Florida, which didn't help much. For most of them, Florida meant amusement parks in Orlando and bikini-clad women on beaches in Miami, along with a bunch of other places no one really cared about. To be fair, before I arrived, Florida to me was simply a weirdly shaped state hanging off the east coast of the United States.

As for St. Pete, its best feature is a gorgeous white-sand beach, the prettiest I've ever seen. The shore is fronted by a mixture of high-end hotels and low-end motels, but most of the neighborhoods seem typically middle-class, populated by retirees and blue-collar workers, along with families enjoying inexpensive vacations. There are the usual fast-food restaurants and strip malls and gyms and shops selling cheap beach items, but despite those obvious signs of modernity, there's something about the town that feels a little bit forgotten.

Still, I have to admit that I like it here. Technically I'm here to work, but really it's more vacation. I'm playing four gigs a week at Bobby T's Beach Bar for three weeks, but my sessions only last a few hours, which means I have a lot of time to go for jogs and sit in the sun and otherwise do absolutely nothing at all. A guy could get used to a life like this. The crowds at Bobby T's are friendly—and yes, boozy, just like at the Don CeSar—but there's nothing better than performing for an appreciative audience. Especially given that I'm basically a nobody from out of state who'd pretty much stopped performing two months before I graduated from high school. Over the past seven years, I've played now and then for friends or an acquaintance who's throwing a party, but that's about it. These days I consider music a hobby, albeit one that I love. There's nothing I enjoy more than spending a day playing or writing songs, even if my real life doesn't leave me much time for it.

Funny thing happened, though, in my first ten days here. The first couple of shows went as expected, with a crowd that I assumed was typical for Bobby T's. About half the seats were taken, most of the people there to enjoy the sunset, cocktails, and conversation while music played in the background. By my third show, however, every seat was filled, and I recognized faces from earlier shows. By the fourth time I stepped up, not only were all the seats filled but a handful of people were willing to stand in order to hear me play. Hardly anyone was watching the sunset at all, and I started to receive requests for some of my original songs. Requests for beach-bar classics like "Summer of '69," "American Pie," and "Brown Eyed Girl" were common, but my music? Then, last night, the crowd spilled onto the beach, additional chairs were scrounged up, and they adjusted the speakers so everyone could hear me. As I began setting up, I assumed it was simply a Friday-night crowd, but the booker, Ray, assured me that what was happening wasn't typical. In fact, he said, it was the largest crowd he'd ever seen at Bobby T's.

I should have felt pretty good about that, and I guess I did, at least a little bit. Still, I didn't read too much into it. After all, performing for tipsy vacationers at a beach bar with drink specials at sunset was a far cry from selling out stadiums around the country. Years ago, I'll admit, getting "discovered" had been a dream—I think it's a dream for everyone who loves performing—but those dreams gradually dissolved in the light of a newfound reality. I'm not bitter about it. The logical side of me knows that what we want and what we get are usually two entirely different things. Besides, in ten days, I'm going to have to head home to the same life I was leading before I came to Florida.

Don't get me wrong. My real life isn't bad. Actually, I'm pretty good at what I do, even if the long hours can be isolating. I've never been out of the country, I've never ridden on an airplane, and I'm only vaguely aware of recent news, mainly because talking heads bore the hell out of me. Tell me what's going on in our country or around the world, talk about some issue of major political importance, and I promise to be surprised. Though it will likely offend some people, I don't even vote, and the only reason I know the governor's last name is because I once played in a bar called Cooper's in Carteret County, near the North Carolina coast, about an hour from my home.

About that . . .

I live in Washington, a small town located on the banks of the Pamlico River in eastern North Carolina, though many people refer to it as either *Little Washington* or *the Original Washington*, so as not to confuse my hometown with our nation's capital, five hours to the north. As if anyone could possibly confuse them. Washington and Washington, D.C., are about as different as two places can possibly be, mainly because the capital is a city surrounded by suburbs and is a central hub of power, while my town is tiny and rural, with a supermarket named Piggly Wiggly. Fewer than ten thousand people reside there, and in my teen years I often found myself wondering why anyone would want to live there at all. For much of my life, I longed to escape as quickly as I could. Now, though, I've concluded that there are worse places for a guy to call home. Washington is peaceful and its people kind, the sort who wave to drivers from their porches. There's a nice waterfront along the river with a couple of decent restaurants, and for those who like the arts, the town boasts the Turnage Theatre, where locals can watch plays performed by other locals. There are schools and a Walmart and fast-food restaurants, and weatherwise, it's ideal. It snows maybe once or twice every second or third year, and the temperature in the summer is a lot more moderate than in places like South Carolina or Georgia. Sailing on the river is a popular pastime, and it's possible for me to load the surfboard into the back of my truck on a whim and catch waves at the beach before I've even finished drinking my large to-go cup of coffee. Greenville—a smallish but actual city, with college sports teams and movie theaters and more-varied dining—is a quick jaunt up the highway, twenty-five minutes of easy driving.

In other words, I like it there. Usually, I don't even think about whether I'm missing out on something bigger or better or whatever. As a rule I take things as they come and try not to expect or regret much. It might not sound all that special, but it works for me.

I suppose it might have something to do with my upbringing. When I was little, I lived with my mom and my sister in a small house not far from the waterfront. I never knew my father. My sister, Paige, is six years older than me, and the memories I have of my mom are hazy, blurred by the passage of time. I have a vague recollection of poking at a toad jumping through the grass and another of my mom singing in the kitchen, but that's about it. She died when I was five, so my sister and I moved in with my aunt and uncle at their farm on the outskirts of town. My aunt was my mom's much older sister, and though they'd never been all that close, she was our only living family. In their minds, they did what was necessary because it was also the right thing to do.

They're good people, my aunt and uncle, but because they never had children, I doubt they really knew what they were signing on for. Working the farm took nearly all their time, and Paige and I weren't the easiest kids, especially in the beginning. I was accident-prone—at the time, I was growing like a weed and stumbled at what seemed to be every third step I took. I also cried a lot—mostly about my mom, I guess—though I don't remember this. As for Paige, she was way ahead of the curve when it came to teenage moodiness. She could scream or sob or pitch a fit with the best of them and spend days locked in her room while she cried and refused to eat. She and my aunt were fire and ice from the very beginning, but I always felt safe with her. Even though my aunt and uncle tried their best, it had to be overwhelming, so little by little it fell to my sister to raise me. She was the one who packed my school lunches and walked me to the bus; she made me Campbell's soup or Kraft Macaroni & Cheese on the weekends and sat with me while I watched cartoons. And because we shared a room, she was the one I talked to before I fell asleep. Sometimes, but not always, she helped me with my chores in addition to doing her own; farming and chores are basically synonymous. Paige was far and away the person I trusted most in the world.

She was also talented. She loved to draw and could sketch for hours, which is why I'm not all that surprised that she eventually became an artist. These days, she makes her living working with stained glass, handcrafting replica Tiffany lamps that cost serious money and are popular with high-end interior decorators. She's built herself a pretty good online business and I'm proud of her, not only because of what she meant to me growing up but because life has seriously kicked her in the teeth in more ways than one. There've been times, I'll admit, when I wondered how she was able to keep going at all.

Don't get me wrong about my aunt and uncle. Even though Paige watched after me, they always did the important things. We had decent beds and got new school clothes every year. There was always milk in the refrigerator and snacks in the cupboards. Neither of them was violent, they seldom raised their voices, and I think the only time I ever saw them have a glass of wine was on New Year's Eve during my teenage years. But farming is hard work; a farm, in many ways, is like a demanding, ever-needy child, and they didn't have the time or energy to go to school events or bring us to a friend's birthday party or even toss a football back and forth on the weekends. There are no weekends on a farm; Saturdays and Sundays are just like every other day of the week. About the only thing we really did as a family was have dinner every night at six, and it seems I remember all of them, mainly because every dinner was exactly the same. We'd get called to the kitchen, where we'd help bring the food to the table. Once we sat, and more from a sense of obligation than actual interest, my aunt would ask my sister and me what we'd done in school. While we answered, my uncle would butter two pieces of bread to go along with his meal, no matter what we were having, and he'd nod silently at our answers, no matter what we said. After that, our meals were marked only by the sound of utensils clicking against the plates. Sometimes, Paige and I would talk, but my aunt and uncle concentrated on finishing their meals like another chore they had to complete. Both of them were generally quiet, but my uncle took silence to a whole other level. Days would pass where I never heard him speak at all.

He did, however, play the guitar. Where he learned, I have no idea, but he was decent on the instrument and had a craggy resonant voice that drew a listener in. He favored songs by Johnny Cash or Kris Kristofferson—*country folksy,* he called it—and once or twice a week, after dinner, he'd sit on the porch and play. When I began showing an interest—I guess I was seven or eight at the time—he handed over the guitar and, with heavily calloused hands, he helped me learn the chords. I wasn't a natural by any means, but he was surprisingly patient. Even at that young age, I realized that I'd found my passion. While Paige had her art, I had music.

I began practicing on my own. I also began singing, mainly the kinds of songs my uncle sang, because they were the only ones I knew. My aunt and uncle bought me an acoustic guitar for Christmas, then an electric guitar the following year, and I practiced on those, too. I taught myself to play songs that I heard on the radio by ear, without ever learning how to read music. By twelve, I'd reached the point where I could hear a song once and mimic it almost perfectly.

As I grew older, my chores at the farm naturally increased, which meant that I was never able to practice as much as I wanted. It wasn't enough to feed and water the chickens every morning; I had to repair irrigation pipes or spend long hours in the sun, picking worms from tobacco leaves and crushing them with my fingers, which is just as disgusting as it sounds. Well before I hit my teenage years, I'd learned to drive anything with an engine—tractors, backhoes, harvesters, seeders, you name it—and I spent entire weekends doing just that. I also learned to fix or repair anything that was broken, though I eventually began to despise all of it. With chores and music taking almost all my free time, something had to give, and my grades in middle school began dropping. I didn't care. The only class I really cared about was music, especially as my teacher happened to be an amateur songwriter. She took a special interest in me, and with her help, I wrote my first song, when I was twelve. I was hooked after that and began writing nonstop, improving little by little.

By that point, Paige was working with a local artist who specialized in stained glass. She'd worked at the shop part-time while she was in high school, but by graduation she was already crafting her own Tiffany-inspired lamps. Unlike me, Paige got pretty good grades all along, but she had no desire to go to college. Instead, she worked on building her business and eventually met a guy and fell in love. She left the farm, moved out of state, and got married. I hardly heard from her during those years after she left; even after she had a baby, I only glimpsed her on the rare FaceTime call, looking tired and holding her crying kid. For the first time in my life, it felt as though no one was really watching out for me.

Add all that up—my overworked aunt and uncle, my lack of interest in school, my sister moving away, and chores I had come to hate—and it's not surprising that I began to rebel. As soon as I started high school, I fell in with a group of guys with the same tendencies, and we egged one another on. At first, it was little things—throwing rocks through the windows of abandoned houses, prank phone calls in the middle of the night, stealing the occasional candy bar from a convenience store—but within a few months, one of those friends stole a bottle of gin from his dad's liquor cabinet. We met by the river and passed the bottle back and forth. I had way too much and threw up for the rest of the night, and since I'm honest, I'll admit I didn't learn the appropriate lesson. Instead of waving off the bottle whenever it came my way, I spent countless weekends with my brain blurry at the edges. My grades remained in the tank, and I began to skip certain chores. I'm not proud of who I was back then, but I also know it's impossible to change the past.

Right after my sophomore year began, however, my life took another turn. I'd drifted away from my loser friends by then, and I heard through the grapevine that a local band needed a new guitarist. Why not? I figured. I was only fifteen, and when I showed up to audition, I saw the band members—all in their twenties—smothering their laughter. I ignored them, plugged in my electric guitar, and played Eddie Van Halen's "Eruption" solo. Ask anyone in the know, and they'll tell you it's not easy. Long story short, I ended up playing my first gig with them the following weekend, after hearing the entire set for the first time in the single rehearsal we had beforehand. Compared to them—with their piercings and tattoos and either long or spiked bleached hair—I resembled a choirboy, so they kept me stationed in the back near the drummer, even during my solos.

If music wasn't all-consuming before, it quickly became that way. I stopped cutting my hair, got illegal tattoos, and eventually the band let me start performing out front. At the farm, I pretty much quit doing any chores whatsoever. My aunt and uncle were at a loss, so they chose to ignore me, which kept our conflicts to a minimum. We even stopped eating together. I devoted more time to music, fantasizing about playing to massive crowds in sold-out venues.

In retrospect, I probably should have known it would never work out, since the band wasn't all that good. All of our songs were in the screamy, post-punk vein, and while some people enjoyed the music, I'm pretty sure most of the audiences we played to in our part of eastern North Carolina weren't dazzled. Nonetheless, we managed to find a tiny niche, and until almost the end of my senior year in high school, we played twenty or twenty-five weekends a year in dives as far away as Charlotte.

But there was friction in the band, and it grew worse over time. The lead singer insisted we play only the songs he'd written, and while it might not sound like a big deal, ego has killed more bands than just about anything. Adding insult to injury, the rest of us knew that most of his songs were mediocre. Eventually he announced that he was moving to Los Angeles to make it on his own, since none of us appreciated his genius. As soon as he stomped off, the drummer—at twenty-seven, he was the oldest among us—announced that he was quitting, as well, which wasn't a surprise, either, since his girlfriend had been pushing him to settle down for a while. As he put away his kit and loaded it in the car, the other three of us nodded at one another, knowing it was over, and packed up. After that night, I never spoke to any of them again.

Strangely, I was less depressed than simply lost. As much as I'd enjoyed performing, there was too much drama and too little momentum that might lead the band anywhere. At the same time, I had no idea what to do with my life, so I just went through the motions. I graduated high school—probably because the teachers didn't want to have to deal with me for another year—and spent a lot of time in my room, writing music and recording songs I posted to Spotify and Instagram and YouTube. No one seemed to care. Little by little, I began pitching in at the farm again, though it was apparent that my aunt and uncle had long since given up on me. More important, I started to take stock of my life, especially as I spent more time on the property. As self-absorbed as I'd been, even I could see that my aunt and uncle were getting older and that the farm was struggling. When I'd first arrived as a child, the farm grew corn, cotton, blueberries, tobacco, and we raised thousands of chickens for processing. All that had changed in the past few years. Bad crops and bad business decisions and bad prices and bad loans meant that a good portion of the original land had been either sold or leased to our neighbors. I wondered how I could have missed the changes as they'd been happening, even though I knew the answer.

Then, on a warm August morning, my uncle had a massive heart attack while walking toward the tractor. His left anterior descending artery was blocked at the origin; as the folks at the hospital explained, this kind of heart attack is often referred to as a widow-maker, because the odds of survival are incredibly slim. Maybe it was all the buttered bread he ate at dinners, but he died even before the ambulance arrived. My aunt was the one who found him, and I've never heard anyone scream and wail the way she did that morning.

Paige came home for the service and stayed for a little while, having left her child with her husband and mother-in-law. I worried that her return would create more strife, but my sister seemed to recognize that something had broken inside my aunt in the same way my sister sometimes felt broken. It's impossible to know what goes on in people's private lives, but because I'd never seen my aunt or uncle act all that romantic toward each other, I guess I'd grown up thinking that they were more like business partners than deeply in love. Obviously, I was wrong about that. To my eyes, my aunt seemed almost shrunken in the aftermath. She barely ate and carried a handkerchief to soak up her constant stream of tears. Paige listened to familiar stories for hours, kept up the house, and made sure the employees at the farm adhered to a schedule. But she couldn't stay forever, and after she left, I suddenly found myself trying to take care of things in the same way my sister had been doing.

In addition to managing the farm and making sure my aunt was eating enough, I began leafing through the pile of invoices and records on my uncle's desk. Even my rudimentary math skills let me know the whole operation was a mess. Though the tobacco crop still made money, the chickens, corn, and cotton had become steadily losing propositions. To stave off a looming bankruptcy, my uncle had already arranged to lease more land to the neighbors. While that would solve the immediate problem, I knew it would leave the farm with a bigger long-term issue. My initial reaction was to urge my aunt to sell the rest of the farm outright so she could buy a small house and retire, but she nixed that idea immediately. Around that same time, I also found clippings from various magazines and newsletters that my uncle had collected, which discussed the market for healthier and more-exotic food options, along with notes and revenue projections he'd already completed. My uncle may have been quiet and not much of a businessman overall, but he'd clearly been considering changes. I discussed those with my aunt, and she eventually agreed that the only option was to put my uncle's plans in motion.

We didn't have the money to do much right off the bat, but over the last seven years, with tremendous effort, risks, challenges, financial help from Paige, occasional lucky breaks, and way too many sleepless nights, we slowly transitioned from raising chickens for processing to specializing in organic cage-free eggs, which have a much higher profit margin; we offer them to grocery stores throughout North and South Carolina. While we still grow tobacco, we used the remaining land to concentrate on heirloom tomatoes, the kind that are popular in upscale restaurants and pricey grocery stores, and the margin on those has proved to be substantial, as well. Four years ago, the farm turned a profit for the first time in ages, and we began to lower our debt to reasonable levels. We even took back some of the leases from our neighbors, so the farm is actually growing again, and last year the farm earned more than ever.

Like I said, I'm pretty good at what I do.

What I am is a farmer.

2.

Yeah, I know. My career path sometimes strikes even me as unlikely, especially since I'd spent years of my life begrudging pretty much everything associated with the farm. Over time, I've come to accept the notion that we don't always get to choose our paths in life; sometimes, they choose us.

I'm also glad I've been able to help my aunt. Paige is proud of me, and I should know, since we see a lot of each other these days. Her marriage came to a terrible end—pretty much the worst imaginable—and she moved back to the farm six years ago. For a while we all lived in the house like the old days, but it didn't take long to realize sharing a room with my sister—as adults—wasn't something that either Paige or I wanted to do. In the end, I built my aunt a smaller, more manageable house across the road, at the far corner of the property. Now my sister and I live together, which might sound strange to some people, but I enjoy it, since she's still my best friend in the world. She does her stained-glass thing in the barn, I farm, and we eat together a few times a week. She's become a fairly decent cook, and when we take our seats at the table, I'm sometimes reminded of all the dinners we had growing up.

In other words, my life is pretty good these days, but here's the thing: When I tell people I'm a farmer, most of them tilt their heads and look at me kind of funny. More often than not, they have no idea what to say next. If I tell people that my family owns a farm, however, they brighten and smile and start asking questions. Why the difference, I'm not exactly sure, but it's happened a few times since I arrived in Florida. Sometimes after a show, people will come up to me and start a conversation, and once they realize that I'm a nobody in music, the subject eventually shifts to what I do for a living. Depending on whether I want the conversation to continue, I've learned to either say that I'm a farmer or that I own a farm.

Despite our success over the last few years, the stress of the farm can be wearying. Daily decisions often have longer-term consequences, and every choice is linked to another. Do I bring the tractor in for repairs, so I have more time to focus on customers, or do I repair it myself, to save the thousand dollars? Do I expand the offering of heirloom tomatoes, or specialize in just a few and find more outlets? Mother Nature, too, is capricious, and while you can make a decision that seems correct at the time, sometimes bad things happen anyway. Will the heaters function properly so the chickens will be warm enough in the rare times it snows? Will the hurricane pass us by, or will the wind and rain ruin the crops? Every day, I'm in charge of growing and raising healthy crops and chickens, and every day, something comes up that adds to the challenge. While things are constantly growing, other things are always decaying, and striving for that perfect balance sometimes feels like a nearly impossible task. I could work twenty-four hours a day and still never say to myself, *That's it. There's nothing more to be done.*

I mention all this only to explain why this three-week trip to Florida is the first real break I've had in seven years. Paige, my aunt, and the general manager insisted that I go. Before coming here, I'd never taken so much as a single week off, and I can count on one hand the number of weekends I forced myself to get away from it all. Thoughts of the farm intrude regularly; in the first week, I must have called my aunt ten times to check in on how things were going. She finally forbade me to call anymore. Between her and the general manager, they could handle it, she said, so in the last three days I haven't called at all, even when the urge has felt almost overwhelming. Nor have I called Paige. She received a fairly substantial order right before I left, and I already knew she wouldn't answer when in furious work mode, all of which means that, in addition to vacation, I'm alone with my thoughts for the first time in what seems like forever.

I'm pretty sure my girlfriend, Michelle, would have liked this relaxed and healthy, nonworking version of me. Or, rather, my ex-girlfriend. Michelle always complained that I focused on the needs of the farm more than my own life. I'd known her since high school—barely, since she was dating one of the football players and was two years older than me—but she'd always been friendly when we passed each other in the hallways, even though she was the prettiest girl in school. She vanished from my life for a few years before we ran into each other again, at a party after she graduated from college. She'd become a nurse and had taken a job at Vidant Medical Center, but she moved back in with her parents in the hopes of saving enough money for a down payment on a condominium in Greenville. That initial conversation led to a first date, then a second one, and for the two years we dated, I considered myself lucky. She was smart and responsible and had a good sense of humor, but she worked nights and I worked constantly, leaving us with little time to spend with each other. I want to believe that we could have worked past that, but I eventually realized that while I liked her, I didn't love her. I'm pretty sure she felt the same about me, and once she finally bought her condo, seeing each other became all but impossible. There was no messy breakup, no anger or fighting or name-calling; rather, we both started texting or calling less, until it reached a point where we hadn't so much as touched base in a couple of weeks. Even though we hadn't formally ended things, both of us knew it was over. A few months later she met someone else, and about a year ago I saw on her Instagram page that she'd just gotten engaged. To make things easier, I stopped following her on social media, deleted her contact from my phone, and I haven't heard from her since.

I've found myself thinking about her more than usual down here, perhaps because couples seem to be everywhere. They're at my shows, they're holding hands as they walk the beach, they're sitting across from each other at dinner while gazing into each other's eyes. There are families here, too, of course, but not as many as I thought there would be. I don't know the Florida school schedule, but I figure the kids must still be in their classrooms.

I did, however, notice a group of youngish women yesterday, a few hours before my show. It was early afternoon, and I was walking near the water's edge after lunch. It was hot and sunny, with enough humidity to make the air feel sticky, so I'd removed my shirt, using it to wipe the sweat from my face. As I neared the Don CeSar, a gray object surfaced and disappeared in the water just beyond the small breakers, followed quickly by another. It took me a few seconds to recognize that it was a pod of dolphins languidly moving parallel to the shoreline. I stopped to watch, as I'd never seen one in the wild before. I was following their progress when I heard the girls approach and stop a few yards away.

The four of them were chattering loudly, and I did a double take when I noticed how startlingly attractive they all were. They looked ready for a photo shoot, with colorful swimwear and perfect teeth that flashed when they laughed, making me think all of them had spent plenty of time at the orthodontist as teenagers. I suspected they were younger than me by a few years, probably college students on break.

As I turned my attention back to the dolphins, one of the women gasped and pointed; from the corner of my eye, I saw the rest of them stare in the same direction. Though I wasn't trying to eavesdrop, they weren't exactly quiet.

"Is that a shark?" one of them asked.

"It's probably a dolphin," another answered.

"But I see a fin."

"Dolphins have dorsal fins, too. . . ."

I smiled inwardly, thinking that maybe I hadn't missed much by not going to college. Predictably, they started posing for selfies, trying to capture the dolphins in the background. After a while they began making the kinds of silly faces common on social media: the *kissy face,* the ecstatic *we're-having-such-a-great-time* group shot, and the serious *pretend-I'm-a-supermodel* look, which Michelle used to refer to as the *dead-fish* expression. Recalling it made me snort under my breath.

One of the girls must have heard me, because she suddenly glanced in my direction. I pointedly avoided eye contact, focusing on the dolphins as they drifted by. When they eventually turned toward deeper water, I figured it was time for me to head back. I veered around the women—three of whom were still taking and examining their selfies—but the same one who'd glanced toward me caught and held my gaze.

"Nice tats," she offered when I was close, and I'll admit her comment caught me off guard. She wasn't exactly flirting, but she seemed slightly amused. For a moment I debated whether to stop and introduce myself, but that feeling lasted only a second. It didn't take a rocket scientist to realize she was out of my league, so I flashed a quick smile and moved past.

When she arched an eyebrow at my lack of response, I had the feeling that she'd known exactly what I was thinking. She returned her attention to her friends, and I kept walking, fighting the urge to turn around. The more I tried not to look, the harder it became; finally, I allowed myself another quick peek.

Apparently, the girl had been waiting for me to do just that. She still wore the same expression of amusement, and when she offered a knowing smile, I turned and kept going, feeling a flush creep up my neck that had nothing to do with the sun.

3.

Sitting here in my beach chair, I'll admit that my thoughts have drifted back to my encounter with the girl. I wasn't exactly looking for her or her friends, but I wasn't opposed to the idea, either, which is why I'd hauled my chair and cooler all the way down the beach in the first place. So far no luck, but I reminded myself that I'd had a pretty good day no matter what happened. In the morning, I'd gone for a run on the beach, then inhaled some fish tacos at a lunch spot called the Toasted Monkey. After that, with nothing pressing on my agenda, I eventually ended up here. I suppose I could have done something more productive than practically beg for skin cancer. Ray had mentioned there was some good kayaking at Fort De Soto Park, and before I left home, Paige had reminded me to check out the Dalí, a local museum dedicated to the works of Salvador Dalí. I guess she'd visited Tripadvisor or whatever, and I told her I'd add it to my itinerary, although sipping a cold beer and doing my best impression of a certified man of leisure felt far more compelling, at least to my way of thinking.

With the sun finally beginning to drift lower in the sky, I lifted the lid to the cooler and pulled out my second—and likely last—beer of the day. I figured I'd sip on it for a while, maybe even stay long enough to enjoy the sunset, then make my way to Sandbar Bill's, a cool place up the beach that happened to serve the best cheeseburgers around. As to what I would do after that, I wasn't quite sure. I supposed I could do some barhopping in downtown St. Petersburg, but because it was Saturday night, it would probably be crowded, and I wasn't sure I was in the mood for that. Which left what? Work on a song? Watch some Netflix, like Paige and I sometimes did? Read one of the books I'd brought with me but hadn't yet started? I figured I'd play it by ear.

I twisted off the cap, surprised that the beach was still as crowded as when I'd arrived. Hotel guests from the Don CeSar reclined in lounge chairs shaded by umbrellas; along the beach, dozens of visitors lay on colorful towels. At the water's edge, some little kids were building a sandcastle; a woman was walking a dog whose tongue lolled almost to his paws. The music from the pool area continued behind me, making me wince at the occasional off-key note.

As it happened, I neither heard nor saw her approach. All I knew was that someone was suddenly hovering above me, casting a shadow over my face. When I squinted, I recognized the girl from the beach yesterday, smiling down at me, her long dark hair framing my field of vision.

"Hi," she said without a trace of self-consciousness. "Didn't I see you playing at Bobby T's last night?"

4.

I GUESS I SHOULD EXPLAIN something else: Even though I've mentioned that I'd hoped to run into the dark-haired beauty at the beach, I didn't have a plan after that. I'm not nervous when it comes to meeting women, though I am out of practice. Back home, aside from when I play the occasional gig for friends, I seldom go out. My excuse is usually that I'm too tired, but really, if you've lived in the same small town your entire life, doing pretty much anything on a Friday or Saturday night feels a bit like the movie *Groundhog Day*. You go to exactly the same places and see exactly the same people and do exactly the same things, and how often can someone experience the endless déjà vu without finally asking themselves, *Why am I even here?*

The point is, I was a little rusty at making conversation with beautiful strangers and found myself gaping up at the girl wordlessly.

"Hello? Anyone home?" she asked into the silence. "Or have you already killed off the contents of that cooler, which means I should probably walk away right now?"

There was no mistaking the playfulness in her tone, but I barely registered her teasing as I took in the sight of her wearing a white half shirt along with faded jeans shorts that exposed part of a tantalizing purple bikini. She looked like she might be part Asian, and her thick, wavy hair was windblown in a messy-casual kind of way, as if she'd spent the day outdoors, just like me. I lifted my bottle of beer slightly.

"This is only my second of the day," I said, finding my voice, "but whether you walk away is up to you. And, yes, you may have heard me at Bobby T's last night, depending on what time you were there."

"You were also the guy with the tattoos on the beach yesterday, right? Who eavesdropped on me and my friends?"

"I wasn't eavesdropping," I protested. "The four of you were loud."

"You were also staring at me."

"I was watching the dolphins."

"Did you or did you not peek over your shoulder when you were walking away?"

"I was stretching my neck."

She laughed. "What are you doing out here behind the hotel? Trying to accidentally eavesdrop on me and my friends again?"

"I came out to enjoy the sunset."

"You've been here for hours and sunset is still a long way off."

"How do you know how long I've been here?"

"Because I saw you when you first walked by. We were by the pool."

"You saw me?"

"You were kind of hard to miss, lugging all your gear from somewhere up the beach. Seems like you could have plopped down anywhere. If you just wanted to enjoy the sunset, I mean." Her brown eyes flashed with mischief.

"Would you like a beer?" I countered. "Since you obviously came out here to speak with me?"

"Oh, no thanks."

I hesitated. "You are old enough to drink, though, right? I don't want to be the creepy twenty-five-year-old who offers alcohol to minors."

"Yup. Just turned twenty-one, actually. I've graduated college and everything."

"Where are your friends?"

"They're still at the pool." She shrugged. "They were having margaritas when I left."

"Sounds like a pleasant afternoon."

She motioned toward my chair. "Can I borrow your towel?"

"My towel?"

"Please."

I could have asked why, but instead, I simply stood, pulled it from the beach chair, and handed it over.

"Thank you." She whipped it straight, then spread it on the sand beside my chair before taking a seat. I lowered myself into my chair, watching as she leaned back on her elbows, her long, sun-browned legs stretched out in front of her. For a few seconds, neither of us said anything. "I'm Morgan Lee, by the way," she finally offered.

"Colby Mills," I countered.

"I know," she said. "I saw your show."

Oh, right. "Where's home for you?"

"Chicago," she answered. "More specifically, Lincoln Park."

"That means nothing to me. I've never been to Chicago."

"Lincoln Park is a neighborhood right next to the lake."

"What lake?"

"Lake Michigan?" she said, raising an eyebrow in disbelief. "One of the Great Lakes?"

"Is it really great? Or is it just a good or average lake?"

She laughed at my lame joke, a deep and full-throated rumble that was startling coming from such a petite frame. "It's gorgeous and . . . huge. It's kind of like here, in fact."

"Are there beaches?"

"Actually, yes. They don't have the perfect white sand or palm trees, but they can get crowded in the summer. There can even be pretty big waves sometimes."

"Is that where you went to college, too?"

"No. I went to Indiana University."

"And let me guess. This trip is a graduation gift from your parents before you have to head off into the real world?"

"Impressive," she said as she raised an eyebrow. "You must have figured that out sometime between yesterday and just now, which means you've been thinking about me." Though I didn't respond, I didn't have to. *Busted*, I thought. "But, yes, you're right," she went on. "I think they felt bad because I had to deal with all that Covid stuff, which made school pretty crappy for a while. And obviously they're thrilled I graduated, so they booked a trip for me and my friends."

"I'm surprised the four of you didn't want to go to Miami. St. Pete Beach is a bit off the beaten path."

"I love this place," she said with a shrug. "My family used to come here every year when I was growing up, and we always stayed at the Don." She stared at me with open curiosity. "But how about you? How long have you lived here?"

"I don't live here. I'm visiting from North Carolina. I just came down to play at Bobby T's for a few weeks."

"Is that what you do? Travel and perform?"

"No," I said. "It's the first time I've ever done something like this."

"Then how did you end up playing here?"

"I played at a party back home, and in a weird coincidence, the booker for Bobby T's happened to be visiting a friend in town and heard me play. Anyway, afterward he asked whether I'd be willing to come down to do a few shows. I'd have to pay my own travel and lodging, but it was a chance to visit Florida and the schedule isn't too demanding." I shrugged. "I think he was surprised when I said yes."

"Why?"

"After expenses I probably won't break even, but it's a nice excuse to get away."

"The crowd seemed to like you."

"I think they'd be happy with anyone," I demurred.

"And I think you're selling yourself short. A lot of women in the crowd were staring at you with googly eyes."

"Googly?"

"You know what I mean. When one of them went up to talk to you after your set, I thought she was going to try to grope you right there."

"I doubt it," I said. In all candor, I could barely remember talking to anyone after the show.

"So where did you learn to sing?" she asked. "Did you take lessons or were you in a band or . . . ?"

"I was in a band when I was in high school." I gave her a brief rundown of my unglamorous stint with the post-punk crew.

"Did the lead singer ever make it?" she asked, laughing. "In Los Angeles?"

"If he did, I'm not aware of it."

"Did you play at venues like Bobby T's?"

"Never. Think . . . dingy bars and clubs where the police were called after fights broke out."

"Did you have groupies? Like you do now?"

She was teasing again, but I had to admit I liked it. "There were a few girls who might have been considered regulars at our shows, but they weren't interested in me."

"Poor thing."

"They weren't my type." I frowned. "Come to think of it, I'm not sure they were anyone's type."

She smiled, flashing dimples I hadn't noticed before. "So . . . if you're not in a band and you don't perform much, what is it that you actually do?"

Naturally I said, "My family owns a farm."

She swept her eyes over me. "You don't look like a farmer."

"That's because I'm not wearing my overalls and straw hat."

She gave that rumbling belly laugh again, and I realized how much I liked the sound of it. "What do you grow on your farm?" As I described our seasonal crops and who we sold them to, she pulled up her legs and wrapped her arms around them, flashing her immaculate red toenail polish. "I only buy cage-free organic eggs," she remarked, nodding. "I feel bad for chickens who spend their whole life inside a tiny cage. But tobacco causes cancer."

"Cigarettes cause cancer. All I do is grow a green leafy plant, and then I prime and cure the leaves before selling them."

"Are those farming terms?"

"Priming means picking the leaves, and curing means allowing them to dry."

"Then why didn't you just say that instead?"

"Because I like to sound *professional*."

She fluttered her long, dark lashes and shot me an indulgent smile. "Okay, Professor . . . what's an heirloom tomato? I mean, I know they come in funky shapes and colors, but how are they different from regular tomatoes?"

"Most of the tomatoes you find in stores are hybrids, which means their DNA has been manipulated, usually so they won't spoil while being transported. The downside is that hybrids taste kind of bland. Heirloom tomatoes aren't hybrids, so each variety has its own unique flavor."

There was a lot more to it—whether or not open pollination was used, whether seeds were purchased from vendors or harvested individually, the soil's effect on flavor, climate—but only people who had to grow them cared about those sorts of details.

"That's very cool," she said. "I don't think I've ever met a farmer before."

"There's a rumor we can almost pass for human."

"Ha ha."

I smiled, feeling a buzz that had nothing to do with the beer. "What about you? How long are you staying?"

"We leave a week from tomorrow. We just got in yesterday. Not long before you saw us on the beach, in fact."

"You didn't think about renting a house?"

"I doubt the idea even occurred to my parents. Besides, I have a lot of nostalgic feelings for the Don." She made a wry face. "Plus, none of us really likes to cook."

"I guess you were on the meal plan at school."

"Yeah, but this is also supposed to be a *vacation*."

I smiled. "I don't think I saw you or your friends at the show last night."

"We didn't get there until the last fifteen minutes or so. It was pretty crowded, so we stood out on the beach."

"Friday nights," I offered. "People wanting to start their weekend, I guess." Because my beer was now warm, I dumped the contents into the sand. "Would you like a bottle of water?"

"I'd love one. Thanks."

Twisting in my seat, I checked the cooler. The ice had melted, but the bottles were still cool. I handed one to her and took one for myself.

She sat up straight, waving her bottle at the surf. "Hey, I think the dolphins are back!" she cried, shielding her eyes as she scanned the water. "They must have a routine."

"I guess," I said. "Or maybe it's a different pod. The ocean's pretty big, you know."

"Technically, I believe this is a gulf, not an ocean."

"What's the difference?"

"I honestly have no idea," she admitted, and it was my turn to laugh. Settling into a comfortable silence, we watched the dolphins riding the breakers. I still wasn't sure why she'd approached me in the first place, as she was pretty enough to have her pick of guys. Between sips of water, I stole glances at her profile with its slightly upturned nose and full lips, as delicate as a line drawing.

By then, the sky had begun to pale slightly. The crowds were finally beginning to pack up, shaking towels and collecting plastic toys, folding chairs, and stuffing items into beach bags. Yesterday, I'd seen Morgan and her friends for the first time; I marveled at the fact that I was sitting beside her the very next day. Things like this didn't happen to me, but perhaps Morgan was used to winning over strangers in an instant. She certainly didn't lack confidence.

The dolphins moved slowly down the beach, and from the corner of my eye, I saw a melancholy smile cross Morgan's lips. She sighed.

"I should probably check in with my friends before they start to get worried."

I nodded. "It's probably time for me to head back, too."

"What about all that talk about watching the sunset?"

"I'll catch it later."

She smiled, rising from her spot and brushing the sand from her legs. I picked up the towel and shook it out before draping it over my shoulder.

"Are you going to be playing tonight?" she asked, meeting my eyes.

"No, but I'll be there tomorrow at five."

"Enjoy your night off, then." Her gaze flickered toward the pool area before seeking out my own again. For the first time, I had the strange sense she was nervous. "It was nice meeting you, Colby."

"You, too."

She'd taken a step away when she suddenly turned back. "Do you have plans tonight?" She hesitated. "I mean, later in the evening."

"Not really."

She hugged her arms to her chest. "We're planning to go to MacDinton's. Do you know it? In St. Petersburg? I think it's an Irish pub."

"I've never heard of it, but that doesn't mean anything."

"You should meet us there," she urged. "Since it's your night off, I mean."

"Okay. Maybe." I nodded, already knowing I'd be there. She seemed to know it, too, and gave me a brilliant smile before starting back toward the hotel. When she was a few steps away, I called after her.

"Hey, Morgan?"

She turned but kept walking slowly backward. "Yes?"

"Why did you come out to the beach to meet me?"

She tilted her head, amusement lighting up her face. "Why do you think?"

"I don't have the slightest idea."

"Isn't it obvious?" she shouted over the wind. "I love your voice, and I wanted to meet you in person."

5.

ON THE WAY BACK, I called in a cheeseburger order to Sandbar Bill's and grabbed it to go before returning to the public parking area where I'd left my truck. Once I reached my rental condo, I popped it into the microwave to warm up, and it hit the spot. Afterward, I showered and tossed on a pair of jeans, then reached for my phone to check my messages.

There was nothing from my aunt. Recalling her scolding, I instead texted Paige to see how she was doing, asking how her latest Tiffany-replica lamps were coming along. I watched the screen for the dots, but when she didn't respond, I figured she was probably in the barn with her phone on DO NOT DISTURB.

With the sky beginning to change colors beyond the sliding glass doors, I picked up my guitar, as my thoughts drifted to Morgan. She interested me, but I knew it wasn't just her beauty that had affected me so strongly. Her confidence, especially for someone so young, drew me in. But there was warmth, too, and curiosity, and a fierce energy that I could sense even in our limited interaction. She seemed to know who she was, liked who she was, and I wouldn't have been surprised if she already had a vision of the future she wanted for herself. I tried to think of whether I'd ever met someone like her, but I couldn't come up with anyone.

Forcing those thoughts away, I found my mind lingering over a song that I'd been noodling with for the last couple of months. The rhythm—so far—had promise, but I'd been struggling with the lyrics. As memories of Morgan intruded, however, I began to try new phrases and verses, and as I adjusted the opening measures, I felt something click, like the first tumbler falling in a combination lock.

I don't know how it works for anyone else, but songwriting is a mysterious process. Sometimes a song comes so quickly, I'm a bit shocked; other times—like with this one—the final product eludes me for weeks or months. Sometimes it never feels right at all, but I'll find myself using bits and pieces in an entirely new song. With any song, however, there's always a germ of inspiration, that very first idea. It can be a phrase or a snatch of melody I can't shake, and once I have that, I begin to build. It's sort of like I'm making my way through a dark, cluttered attic, where my goal is to find the light switch on the far side of the room. As I try new things, sometimes I bump into unseen obstacles and have to retrace my steps, or—if I'm lucky—I'll take a step forward that just feels *right*. I can't tell you why it feels right—it's instinctual, I guess. After that, I try to find the next right thing, and then the next, until I finally reach that light switch, and the song is finished. I know I'm not explaining it that well, but since I don't really understand it, I'm not sure it's possible to put into words. The only thing I know with any certainty is that when I'm creating, I generally lose all track of time.

Which is exactly what happened. I had fallen into one of those creative zones when I realized the song was getting *closer*. The lyrics were about meeting someone who surprises you, and though I didn't consider it polished by any means, it was definitely a workable first draft.

By then it was half past ten, and I wasn't tired in the slightest. Remembering Morgan's invitation, I dressed in one of the two decent button-up shirts I'd brought to Florida, ditched the flip-flops for a pair of Vans, and—force of habit—grabbed my guitar, as well.

The drive to St. Petersburg took about twenty minutes, and with the help of my phone, locating MacDinton's was easy. Parking was a bit more of a challenge, but I got lucky after circling the block twice and ended up finding a spot a short stroll away. Even from a distance, it was easy to tell that MacDinton's was a popular watering hole. Outside, knots of people stood around smoking, and I could hear the music blasting long before I reached the doors.

Inside, people were jammed shoulder to shoulder, holding pints of Guinness, shots of Irish whiskey, and long-stemmed cocktail glasses. It was pretty much standing room only, and it was all I could do not to get spilled on by whomever I was squeezing past. Despite the close quarters, people had to shout to hear one another over the music.

I eventually spotted Morgan and her friends at a table near the back. They were surrounded by several guys, whom I guessed to be in their late twenties or early thirties. They were young professional types, wearing designer-label shirts and jeans and clunky watches. As I approached, I could see them calculating which girl was going home with which guy. I suspected they wouldn't be thrilled by my appearance. Right on cue, when I was a few feet away, two of them spotted my approach and began to puff up like the roosters strutting around on my farm.

One of Morgan's friends must have noticed, because she

squinted up at them, then tracked their stares to me. Eyes widening, she leaned toward Morgan. Morgan listened intently before suddenly turning to me with a wide smile.

She immediately jumped up and elbowed her way past a pair of guys, hustling toward me. That was enough to silence the entire group for an instant, but I didn't care, as all I could see was Morgan.

Gone was the beachy look that I'd seen earlier; instead, her long wavy hair was fashionably styled, and she wore just enough makeup to accent her high cheekbones. Her eyes were framed by a touch of black liner and long, mascaraed lashes; she wore a dark, luscious red lipstick that emphasized her full mouth. Her white sleeveless top was paired with a short black skirt and soft black suede boots that reached just above her knees. Her friends, I noticed, were equally stylish and groomed.

Hey there, she mouthed, waving when she was close. Even though she was almost shouting, I could barely hear her. "I wasn't sure you were going to come. When did you get here?"

"Just now. How about you?"

"About an hour ago." She put her hand on my arm, sending a warm tingle up my shoulder. "C'mere. I want to introduce you to my friends."

Back at the table, she introduced me to Stacy, Holly, and Maria. As I waved a greeting to them one by one, none of them bothered to hide their curiosity and scrutiny, making me wonder what Morgan had said about me. When Morgan pulled me down to the seat next to hers, the two guys closest grudgingly made room. One of them, shouting extra loud to be heard, announced that the last time he was at MacDinton's, a huge fight broke out near the bar, and he was one of the people who'd broken it up.

I smiled, thinking he might as well have said *Did I mention*

I'm the strong, heroic type? But I said nothing. The girls didn't seem impressed, either; three of them leaned toward one another, ignoring him, while Morgan motioned to me with her finger, prompting me to lean closer.

"What did you do after leaving the beach?" she shouted into my ear.

"I had dinner, took a shower. Wrote a song. Then I came here."

Her face lit up. "You wrote a song?"

"More like worked on a song that's been stuck in my head for a while. I finished, but I'm not sure it's fully cooked yet."

"Is that normal for you? To write one so fast?"

"Sometimes."

"Will you play it at the show tomorrow?"

"It's nowhere near ready for that."

"Any specific inspiration?" she asked.

I smiled. "It's hard to say exactly. Surprises in life, meeting you . . ."

"Meeting me?" she asked, raising an eyebrow.

"I'm not always sure where exactly they come from."

She searched my face. "I want to hear it."

"Sure. Just let me know when."

"How about now?"

I raised an eyebrow. "Now? You want to leave? What about your friends?"

She swiveled in her seat, glancing toward them; Stacy, Holly, and Maria were engrossed in conversation, ignoring the guys who were still fighting to remain of interest. Turning back to me, Morgan waved a hand. "They'll be fine. How did you get here? Did you Uber?"

"I have a truck," I said, surprised again at how quickly Morgan seemed to take control of the situation.

"Then let's go," she said. Standing, she swung her bag from the back of her seat, then leaned toward her friends. "I'll see you all back at the hotel, okay? We're going to take off."

I watched their eyes flicker between us, startled. One of the guys crossed his arms, clearly disgusted.

"You're leaving?" Maria said.

"Don't go!" Holly pleaded.

"C'mon. Stay with us!" Stacy urged.

By the way their eyes raked over me, I guessed they were concerned about Morgan leaving with a relative stranger.

But Morgan was already circling the table and leaning in to hug her friends one by one. "I'll text you guys," she said. "I'll be fine." Turning to me, she asked, "Ready?"

With her leading the way, we squeezed through the bar to the exit. As soon as we stepped outside, the cacophony dropped off, leaving my ears ringing.

"Which way to your truck?"

"Just around the corner."

After a few steps, she shot me a sidelong look.

"My friends obviously think I'm crazy for doing this."

"I noticed that."

"But I was kind of tired of that place, anyway. It was too noisy, and those guys at the table were a little too into themselves."

"Even so, do you think leaving with me is a good idea?"

"Why wouldn't it be?"

"You don't really know me."

She tossed a length of hair over her shoulder without breaking step. "You're a farmer from North Carolina. You grow tobacco, heirloom tomatoes, and raise organic cage-free eggs, and in your spare time you write music. You're here for another week and a half and you'll be playing at Bobby T's tomorrow, so pretty much everyone knows exactly where you're going to be if you try anything funny. And, besides, I have Mace in my bag."

"Seriously?"

"Like you implied, a girl can't be too careful. I grew up in Chicago, remember? My parents made me promise to be cautious whenever I went out at night."

"Your parents sound like very smart people."

"They are," she agreed.

By then we'd reached the truck, and I uttered a silent thanks that I'd wiped down the dusty seats before my trip. Keeping a truck clean on a working farm was an impossibility. As I unlocked it and started the ignition, she surveyed the interior.

"You brought your guitar with you? Like you knew I was going to ask?"

"Let's go with that," I said. "Where to?"

"Let's go back to the Don. We can sit on the sand behind the hotel, where we hung out earlier."

"Sounds good."

As I turned onto the road, I caught sight of her texting. Unlike me, she used both hands, like a miniature typist. I was more of a single-finger texter. "Letting your friends know where we're going?"

"Of course," she responded. "And your license plate," she added. "I took a picture before I got in." When she finished, she lowered the phone. "Oh, by the way, I googled *heirloom tomatoes* after talking to you today. I didn't realize there were so many different kinds. How do you know which ones to grow?"

"Research, like anything else. There's a guy in Raleigh who is kind of the world expert on heirlooms, so we met with him to find out what types grow best in our area and what flavors to expect. We spoke to other farmers who grew them, to learn the ins and outs, and then met with potential customers like supermarkets and chefs and hotels. In the end, we started with three varieties, and we've added two more."

"By *we*, do you mean you and your parents, or your brother . . . ?"

"My aunt," I said. I wondered how much to tell her, before finally deciding to just come out with it. "She's kind of like my mom. My mom died when I was little and I never knew my dad, so my aunt and uncle raised my sister and me. Then my uncle ended up passing away, too."

"Oh my God!" Morgan's shock was evident. "That's terrible!"

"It was hard," I admitted. "Thank you. So, anyway, my aunt and I run the farm. Not alone, mind you. We have a general manager and a lot of employees."

"Where does your sister live now?"

"Paige lives at the farm, too—actually, we still live in the house we grew up in—but she's an artist." I told Morgan about the Tiffany-replica lamps. From the visor in my truck, I pulled out a photo of Paige holding one of her lamps, which I had printed from my phone. When I handed it to Morgan, our fingers brushed.

"Wow! It's so pretty!" She tilted her head, studying the photo. "She's pretty, too."

"There's always a wait list for her lamps," I went on, with a trace of pride. "As you can imagine, the lamps take a long time to make."

"Is she older or younger than you?"

"Six years older. She's thirty-one."

"She looks younger."

"Thanks. I think. But how about you? Tell me about you."

"What do you want to know?"

"Anything." I shrugged. "How would you describe your childhood? What are your parents like? Do you have brothers and sisters? What's it like to grow up in Chicago, especially considering you have to carry Mace when you go out?"

She burst out laughing. "Lincoln Park is very safe. It's kind of a fancy area. Big houses, big yards, big leafy trees. Ridiculous decorations for Halloween and Christmas. I camped out in the backyard for a slumber party once, though my dad did stay on the porch all night. It wasn't until I was older that my mom and dad bought the Mace, and it had more to do with me going off to college and to frat parties or whatever."

"Did you go to a lot of frat parties?"

"A few," she continued, "but I was pretty busy most of the time. I did go to a formal, which was fun, even though I didn't really like the guy all that much. But, okay, about me: In a lot of ways, it was a typical childhood, I guess. School and some after-school activities, like most people . . ." When she trailed off, I thought I detected a hint of reticence.

"And your family?"

"My dad's a surgeon. He emigrated from the Philippines in the 1970s to study at Northwestern. He ended up going to medical school at the University of Chicago, where he met my mom. She's a radiologist, German-Irish stock from Minnesota. Her family had a cabin on a lake up there, where we spent a part of every summer. And I have a sister, Heidi, who's three years younger and looks nothing like me, and even though we couldn't be more different, I think she's amazing."

I smiled. "Your family sounds anything but typical."

"I don't know," she replied, then shrugged. "A lot of my friends' parents were doctors or lawyers, so it wasn't that big of a deal, and their families came from all over the world, too. I don't think my family stood out at all."

Where I'm from, they definitely would. "And you're the same kind of overachieving academic as your parents, I take it?"

"Why would you say that?"

"Because you just turned twenty-one and you've already graduated from college?"

She laughed again. "That had less to do with grades and SAT scores than my desire to get away from my parents. Trust me—my sister is a lot smarter than I am."

"Why did you want to get away from your parents?" I asked. "It sounds like you had a pretty comfortable life."

"I did, and I don't want to sound ungrateful, because I'm not," she hedged. "But it's complicated. My parents can be . . . over-protective."

When she paused, I glanced over at her. In the silence, she seemed to be debating how much to tell me, before finally going on.

"When I was seven, I was diagnosed with a pretty severe case of scoliosis. The doctors weren't sure how my condition would progress as I grew, so in addition to having to wear a back brace for sixteen hours a day, I ended up having a bunch of surgeries and procedures to fix it. Obviously, since my parents are doctors, they made sure I saw the best specialists, but as you can imagine, they worried and hovered and wouldn't allow me to do the things other kids did. And even though I eventually got better, it's like they still see me as the damaged little girl I once was."

"That sounds rough."

"Don't get me wrong. I know I'm not being completely fair to them. I know they care about me; it's just that . . . I'm not like my parents. Or my sister, for that matter. Sometimes it feels like I was born into the wrong family."

"I think a lot of people feel that way."

"That doesn't mean it isn't true."

I smiled. "Does that mean you're not going to become a doctor?"

"Among other things," she admitted. "Like . . . I love dancing, for instance. I started in ballet because the doctors recommended it, but I got hooked. I also learned tap, jazz, and hip-hop, but the more I got into it, the less my parents approved, even though it was good for me. Like I wasn't quite measuring up to their expectations, you know? Anyway, to answer your question, by the time I started high school, I was already itching to get out and become an adult, so I started taking classes at community college and did a summer session at IU. I took accelerated classes so I was able to graduate early. And, yes, I was pretty much one of the youngest freshmen on campus. I'd only been driving a little more than a year."

"And your overprotective parents were okay with you leaving home that young?"

"I threatened that I wouldn't go to college at all. They knew I was serious."

"You drive a hard bargain."

"I can be a bit headstrong," she offered with a wink. "But what about you?"

"What about me?"

"Did you go to college?"

"No."

"Why not?"

"I never liked school all that much to begin with, so it wasn't really in the cards."

"Do you regret not going?"

"I probably would have failed out."

"Not if you tried."

"I likely wouldn't have tried."

She smiled. "I know that school's not for everyone. And you still figured out what you want to do early on, which is more than a lot of people can say."

I considered what she'd said. "I have a knack for farming," I conceded, "and now that most of the transition work is behind us, my days aren't as long as they once were. But it's not what I grew up imagining that I'd be doing."

I could still feel her eyes on me, her delicate features intermittently illuminated by passing headlights.

"You love music," she announced. "That's what you really wanted to do, right?"

"Of course."

"You're young, Colby," she pointed out. "You still have plenty of time."

I shook my head. "It's not going to happen."

"Because of your family?" Though I didn't answer, she must have seen my expression, because I heard her expel a breath. "Okay, I accept that. Now, changing gears, since I told you about my boring childhood, what was your life like growing up in North Carolina?"

I gave her the highlights, trying to inject some humor into my dumb middle and high school exploits and responding in detail to her questions about the farm, about which she seemed endlessly fascinated. When I finished, I asked her what she liked most about college.

"The people," she said, her answer almost automatic. "That's where I met Stacy, Maria, and Holly. Others, too."

"What did you end up studying?"

"Can't you guess?" she asked. "What's the last thing I said to you on the beach?"

I love your voice. But still unsure what that had to do with her choice of a major, I gave her a quizzical look.

"I majored in vocal performance."

6.

When we reached the Don CeSar, she directed me to the hotel parking lot. Morgan flashed her room key card to the lot's security guard, and after parking I fished my guitar from behind the driver's seat and we started toward the hotel. Entering through the lower-level doors, we walked the wide carpeted hallways that zigged and zagged past high-end boutiques and an ice-cream-and-candy shop. I felt underdressed, but Morgan didn't seem to notice.

We exited near the perfectly landscaped pool area. Off to the right was a restaurant with additional outdoor seating near the beach; ahead and to the left were two pools surrounded by dozens of lounge chairs and the ever-popular bar. The restaurant, likely closed by then, still had two or three couples relaxing at their tables, enjoying the balmy breezes.

"This is the fanciest hotel I've ever seen," I said, trying not to gape at my surroundings.

"It's been around a long time. In the thirties it drew guests from up and down the East Coast, and during World War II it was leased by the military to treat servicemen struggling with PTSD. Of course, they didn't call it PTSD back then. I guess it went downhill for a while after that, and then new owners bought it and spruced it up, returning it to its former glory."

"You know a lot about it."

She elbowed me, smirking. "There's a history exhibit hanging in the hallway we just walked through."

Pleasantly surprised by the physical contact, I merely smiled. Threading between the two pools, we walked past the bar onto a wooden deck near the low-slung sand dunes. As we reached the sand, she stopped to pull out her phone.

"I'm going to let my friends know where I am," she explained, and a few seconds later, her phone dinged. "They're getting ready to leave, so they'll be here in a little while."

She suddenly reached out, holding on to my shoulder. "Stay still so I can take off my boots," she instructed, standing on one foot. "I don't want them to get ruined. But don't let me forget them, okay?"

"I'm pretty sure you'd remember the moment you realized you were barefoot."

"Probably," she said with a mischievous grin. "But this way I'll also find out whether you're reliable. You ready?"

"After you."

We stepped onto the sand, walking side by side but not quite close enough to touch. Stars spanned the nighttime sky and the moon hovered high and bright. The sea struck me as both peaceful and ominous at exactly the same time. I noticed a couple walking near the water's edge, their features hidden in shadow, and heard voices drifting from tables near the bar. Beside me, Morgan almost seemed to be gliding, her long hair fluttering behind her in the salt-scented breeze.

Just beyond the glow of hotel lights, there were a couple of lounge chairs that either hadn't been put away or someone had recently dragged out to the beach. Morgan gestured at them.

"They must have been expecting us."

We sat across from each other, and Morgan turned toward the water, poised and serene in the moonlight.

"It looks so different at night," she remarked. "In the day it's inviting, but at night, all I can think is that there are giant sharks just lying in wait for me."

"No midnight swim, then?"

"Not a chance," she said, before turning toward me. I saw the flash of her smile.

"Can I ask a question?" I ventured, leaning forward. "What did you mean when you said you majored in vocal performance?"

"That's what the major is called."

"You mean, like . . . singing?"

"You have to be accepted into the program, but yes."

"How do you get accepted?"

"Well, in addition to the taped and/or live audition, there's a keyboard requirement, so you have to know how to play the piano. And then the usual—transcripts, history of musical studies or training, performances, awards . . . all that."

"Are there actual classes, or do you just get to sing?"

"Of course there are classes—general ed, music theory, ear training, music history, just to start—but as you can probably imagine, what we do outside of class is super important, too. There are choir ensembles, rehearsals, piano practice, recitals, and concerts. The school has one of the best opera programs in the country."

"You want to be an opera singer?"

"No, but when you think about people like Mariah Carey or

Beyoncé or Adele, their vocal control—their precision, range, and power—really sets them apart. Opera training can help with all those things. That's why I wanted to study it."

"But I thought you loved to dance."

"You can love both, can't you?" she asked. "But anyway, singing was my first love, no doubt. I grew up singing all the time—in the bathroom, in my bedroom, in my backyard, wherever, like a lot of girls do. When I had to start wearing the back brace—before I started dancing—it wasn't easy for me, and not just because of my parents or the surgeries. I wasn't allowed to play sports or run around with friends from the neighborhood, and my mom had to carry my backpack to school, and I needed a special chair in the classroom . . . and . . . kids can be pretty mean sometimes. So I started singing even more, because it made me feel . . . normal and free, if that makes any sense."

When she grew quiet, I couldn't help but imagine a young girl strapped into a back brace, wanting to be like everyone else, and how hard that must have been. She seemed to sense what I was thinking, because she looked at me with an almost forlorn expression.

"I'm sorry. I don't usually share this kind of stuff with people I'm still getting to know."

"I'm honored."

"Still, I don't want you to think I'm hoping for some kind of pity party, because I'm not. Everyone has challenges, and a lot of people have them worse than I ever did."

I suspected she was speaking about the fact that I'd lost my mom, and I nodded. "So . . . singing?"

"Oh yeah," she offered. "Long story short, my parents eventually put me in singing and piano lessons so that I had after-school activities like my friends did. I think they believed it would be a passing phase, but just like dancing, the more I practiced, the more important it became to me. I sang through high school, and I've had private vocal lessons for years. I tell myself that my experience at IU was just icing on the cake. My parents may not be thrilled with my choice of major, but then again, I didn't give them a vote in that, either."

"Why wouldn't they be thrilled?"

"They're doctors," she said, as though that was all the explanation needed. When I didn't respond, she finally went on. "My parents would prefer that I have more-traditional dreams."

"So you're serious about singing."

"It's what I'm meant to do," she said, her eyes fixed on mine.

"What's next, then? Since you've graduated, I mean?"

"I'm moving to Nashville in a couple of weeks. That's another reason I wanted to graduate early. I'm only twenty-one, which still gives me time to break into the music world."

"How are you going to pay your bills? Did you line up a job there?"

"I got some money from my grandparents for graduation. And, believe it or not, my parents have agreed to help with rent, too, so I should be okay for a while."

"I'm kind of surprised that your parents would agree to that. Based on what you told me about them, I mean."

"I am, too. But my dad was terrified about me living in a place that might be dangerous, so he talked my mom into it. I don't know how long their help will last, but I'm definitely grateful for it. I know how hard it is to break into the music world, and I feel like the only way I'm going to have a chance is to give it a hundred percent effort. So that's what I intend to do, and I'll keep trying until it works. It's my dream."

I heard the determination in her tone and couldn't help but be impressed, even as I admitted she had the kind of support and opportunities of which only a handful of people could boast. "Are your friends in music, too? Holly, Stacy, and Maria?"

"No, but we have a dance group together. That's how we met. We all had accounts on TikTok where we posted videos of ourselves dancing, so we started dancing as a group, too."

"Does anyone watch?"

She tilted her head. "They're incredible dancers, better than I am. Maria, for instance, is a dance major, and she just scored an audition with Mark Morris's dance company. You've also seen what they all look like. What do you think?"

"Can I see some of the videos?"

"I still don't know you well enough for that."

"But you let strangers see them."

"It's different if I know the person. Haven't you ever felt that way? When you sing? That if there's someone you know in the audience—and want to know better—you get nervous. It's kind of like that."

"You want to get to know me better?" I persisted, teasing.

"You're missing the point."

I held up my hands. "I get it. Do you have a lot of followers?"

"That's a relative question," she said. "What's a lot? Some people have a couple hundred million followers, and there are lots of others between fifty and a hundred million. We've networked a lot, but we're not in that league."

"How many do you have?"

"Individually or as a group?"

"Both."

"Almost two million for me, and over eight million for our group."

I blinked, thinking about the 478 followers I had on all three of my social-media platforms combined. "You have over eight million followers on TikTok?"

"It's crazy, right?"

"It's hard to believe," I said, not bothering to hide my disbelief. "How did you even get something like that off the ground?"

"A lot of work and even more luck. Stacy is a genius when it comes to building followers, and Holly is a video-editing goddess. We started by posting to one another's accounts. Then we performed routines at campus events, and a lot of students followed us. After that, we found dance groups at other colleges that were doing the same thing that we were, and we linked up with those accounts, as well. And then, last November at a basketball game . . ." She hesitated. "You know basketball is really popular in Indiana, right? Anyway, the game was being broadcast nationally, and Stacy happened to know one of the camera guys. We were wearing T-shirts that had our TikTok account on the front, and the network went to one of those crowd shots during a time-out. The cameraman zoomed in on us as we performed one of our routines on the sidelines. And after that the camera kept returning to us during breaks, to the point that even the network announcers mentioned our TikTok name! Then a clip ended up on ESPN, a few influencers took note, and almost immediately our account began blowing up. Thousands of people, tens of thousands, hundreds . . . and it just kept snowballing from there."

"Do you make money with that?" I asked, fascinated.

"We do, but only recently. Figuring out how to monetize it requires a lot more work, and there are decisions about brands and whether the company is honest or whether it's something we'd be willing to promote. Stacy and Holly do most of that, too. I didn't really have time for that, but the other three have started to make some money with it—and because they do all the work, it's only fair. They could use it, too. Stacy is going to medical school this fall, and Holly has student loans. Ironically, she got a job with ESPN, if you can believe that. She wants to be a broadcaster."

"And Maria?"

"Well, that depends on her audition with Mark Morris, but her mom is a choreographer who's done some work on Broadway, so Maria choreographs all of our dances. Her mom actually sent my recordings to some managers she knows in Nashville, so we'll see how that goes."

In my limited experience, meetings seldom led anywhere—even the band I was in had meetings with potential managers, albeit minor-league ones—but I wasn't about to tell her that.

"Sounds exciting," I said. "I'm sure your presence on TikTok and Instagram will help get their attention."

"I guess," she offered. When I raised an eyebrow, she continued. "Honestly, I have mixed feelings about the whole social-media game and the constant effort to build followers."

"But having an existing fan base can only help launch your career, right?"

"Maybe," she said. "Our fans are almost all girls following us because of our looks and our dance moves. And I'll admit that we play up our sexiness in the way we move and dress. It's what sells."

When she paused, I asked the obvious. "But?"

She sighed. "I want to be known for my singing, not because I'm a hot girl who can dance, you know? And then there's the fact that social media isn't necessarily a good thing for teenage girls. There's so much editing that what they're seeing isn't exactly real, but it's hard for people to separate the fantasy. It's not as though we just walk out and dance without practicing or that we don't spend a lot of time perfecting our hair and makeup and outfits before we film. So what's the point in being regarded as an influencer—or, God forbid, a role model—if it's all kind of fake?"

I said nothing, impressed she'd considered those things. I'll be honest: I hadn't. But then again, hardly anyone followed me, so what did it matter?

"Anyway, we'll see how it goes," she said, dismissing the subject with a wave of her hand. "Now I want to hear the song you wrote."

I opened my case, taking a minute to tune my guitar and recall all the changes I'd made earlier. When I was ready, I launched into the opening stanzas, injecting additional energy to the chorus as I sang to her.

Morgan stared at me, a rapt smile playing on her lips. Watching her sway unconsciously in time with the music, I realized again how much she'd inspired the song. Not just the lyrics but the music itself; there was a bright energy and momentum to the song's driving chorus, much like her.

When I finally silenced the guitar, she leaned toward me. "That was beautiful," she breathed. "You're amazing."

"It still needs work," I said. I'd never been comfortable receiving compliments, but I already knew it was a song that I would eventually add to my rotation, if only in honor of my memory of her.

"What was that one you sang last night? The one about feeling lost?" She hummed a fragment of the top melody. "Could you sing that one, too?"

I knew the song she meant; the lyrics had come to me after a particularly hard day on the farm, and it was full of angst and uncertainty. It was also a crowd favorite, something I could probably play in my sleep, so I went right into it. After that, I rolled into another song that I'd written years ago—one with echoes of

Lady A—then kept going. Morgan would sway or tap her foot in time to the music, and I found myself wondering whether she'd finally ask me to play something that she'd be willing to sing.

But she didn't. She seemed content to listen, and I felt myself drawn into the music in the same way she seemed to be. Each song carried with it a memory, and with the moon bathing the shore in its milky glow and a beautiful woman sitting across from me, it struck me that there was no better way to end the evening.

When I finally set my guitar off to the side, light applause drifted down from the hotel. Turning, I saw six or seven people clapping and waving from the deck.

Morgan tilted her head. "I told you your voice was special."

"It must be an easy-to-please crowd."

"Did you write all those songs yourself? Without anyone?"

"Always."

She looked impressed. "I've tried to write my own music, and I can put together really good bits and pieces, but I usually have to partner with someone else to finish it."

"How many songs have you written? On your own, I mean."

"Twelve or so? But I didn't start until a couple of years ago. I'm still learning."

"Twelve is still pretty good."

"How many have you written?"

I didn't want to tell her the whole truth, but I offered part of it. "More than twelve."

She laughed, knowing exactly what I'd done. "While you were singing, I kept thinking about you in your high school band days. I find it hard to imagine you with long hair."

"My aunt and uncle weren't too fond of it. The few occasions when my sister saw it on FaceTime, she absolutely hated it. More than once, she threatened to drive back home and cut it all off when I was sleeping. And the scary thing is, I was afraid she was actually going to do it."

"Really?"

"When she gets something in her head, it's sometimes impossible to change her mind."

Just then, I heard someone calling Morgan's name. Glancing up, I saw Stacy, Holly, and Maria stepping off the low wooden deck onto the sand, making a beeline for us.

"I think they think they're coming to rescue me," Morgan whispered.

"Do you need rescuing?"

"No. But they don't know that."

When they reached us, I watched them quickly assess the situation, no doubt still trying to figure out why a girl who was as pretty as Morgan would have left with a guy like me.

"Were you just singing out here?" Holly asked.

Morgan jumped in to answer. "I insisted. He wrote a new song and I wanted to hear it. How did it go at MacDinton's?"

They gave a unified bored shrug. "It was all right," Stacy said. "Once the band took a break, we could actually hear ourselves and that was nice, but then they started up again, so we figured it was time to call it. It's getting late."

There was something almost parental in the way she said it, and when Morgan didn't respond right away, I cleared my throat.

"I should probably get going, too."

I started to put away my guitar, regretting the end of the evening. If Morgan and I had more time alone, I might have tried for a kiss, but Morgan's friends seemed to read my mind and had no intention of allowing us a final moment of privacy.

"That was fun tonight," Morgan said.

"Definitely," I agreed.

She turned toward her friends. "You ready?"

"Don't forget your boots."

She seemed amused that I'd remembered, offering up a brief wave before starting toward the hotel with her friends. I waited for them to reach the deck, where Morgan retrieved her boots, slinging them over her arm. In time, I heard their voices fade as they disappeared into the hotel.

Once they were gone, I headed in the same direction but quickly realized my mistake. The door was locked—it needed a room key to unlock—so I went back to the beach and eventually found a small path that led around the side of the hotel, then finally to the parking lot.

On the drive back to the apartment, I thought about Morgan. She was rich, classy, intelligent, driven, popular, and obviously gorgeous. Like her friends, I wondered what she could possibly see in a guy like me. On the surface, we weren't alike in the slightest. Our lives were entirely different, and yet, somehow, we just seemed to click. Not necessarily in a romantic way, but spending time with her had been easier than even my comfortable routines with Michelle.

Later, while lying in bed, I found myself wondering what Paige would think of her. I suspected they'd hit it off—I was pretty sure Morgan got along with everyone—but Paige always had uncanny instincts about people. It was clear why I was attracted to Morgan, but I kept coming back to the mystery of why, despite our vastly different lives, spending time with her felt almost like coming home.

PART II

Beverly

7.

WHEN SHE WAS YOUNG—EIGHT OR NINE, she guessed—Beverly and her mom rode the bus to New York City. Most of the ride took place at night, and Beverly slept with her head in her mom's lap, waking to the sight of buildings that were taller than anything that she'd imagined. The bus station was thronged—more people than Beverly had ever seen at once—and that was just the beginning of a trip that remained vivid in her memory despite the passage of time. Her mom wanted the trip to be special, so she arranged for *Things to Do*. They saw *The Starry Night* by Vincent van Gogh at the MoMA, which was an *Important Painting by a Famous Artist*, and afterward each of them had a slice of pizza for lunch. In the afternoon, they visited the American Museum of Natural History, where she stared at the re-created skeletons of various creatures, including a blue whale and a Tyrannosaurus rex that had teeth larger than bananas. She saw craggy meteorites and diamonds and rubies and they visited the planetarium, where she stared upward at a computer-generated sky with lines that depicted the constellations. It was just the two of them—a *Girls' Trip*, her mom had called it—and it had taken her mom more than a year to save up the money to do the things that rich people did when they went to the *Big City*. Though Beverly didn't know it, it would be the only trip they would ever take together. There would come a time when Beverly and her mom didn't speak at all, but on that trip, her mom talked practically nonstop, and Beverly found comfort in the warm palm of her mom's hand as they left the museum and walked to Central Park, where leaves flamed in oranges, reds, and yellows. It was autumn, the temperature more winter than summer, and the chilly breeze made the tip of Beverly's nose turn red. Her mom carried tissues in her handbag, and Beverly used them one by one until they were gone. Afterward, they had dinner at a place where the waiter was dressed as though he were about to get married. The words in the menu made no sense to Beverly. Her mom told her it was a *Real Restaurant*, and though the food was all right, Beverly wished she'd had another slice of pizza instead. Later, to get to their hotel, they had to walk almost an hour. Standing near the lobby entrance were two shifty-eyed men smoking cigarettes, and once they were inside, her mom paid cash for the room to a man in a dirty T-shirt who stood behind the counter. Their room had two beds with stains on the covers and it smelled funny, like a sink that had backed up, but her mom remained as excited as ever and said it was important to experience the *Real New York*. Beverly was so tired she fell asleep almost immediately.

They spent the following day at Times Square, which is where the *Tourists Went*. Beverly stared up at flashing electric signs and massive billboards. They watched people dance and saw some dressed in costumes like Mickey Mouse or the Statue of Liberty. Theaters advertised shows, but the only one Beverly recognized was *The Lion King*. They couldn't go, because the tickets were priced for *Rich People*, so instead they spent much of the day browsing in stores that sold knickknacks and souvenirs, without buying anything except a single packet of M&M's, which Beverly split with her mom. They each had two slices of pizza for lunch and hot dogs from a food cart for dinner. On one of the side streets, Beverly thought she saw Johnny Depp, the movie star, and there was a line of people taking photographs beside him. Beverly begged for a photo with him, as well, but her mom said that it was a wax statue and wasn't real.

On their last evening in town, they visited the Empire State Building, and Beverly's ears popped as the elevator soared skyward. On the observation deck, the wind was blowing hard and people crowded together, but Beverly was finally able to squeeze her way to a spot that offered an unobstructed view of the city. Beside her was a man dressed in a pirate costume, and though his lips were moving, she couldn't hear him.

Far below, Beverly could see the glow of headlights and taillights on the streets; practically every building she saw was lit from within. Though the sky was clear, there were no stars overhead, and her mom explained that city lights washed them away. Beverly didn't understand what her mom meant—how could stars be washed away?—but she didn't have time to ask, because her mom took her hand and led her to another area of the observation deck, where in the distance, they could see the Statue of Liberty. Her mom told her that she'd always wanted to live in the *Big City*, even though she'd said the same thing half a dozen times already. When Beverly asked her why she hadn't moved there, her mom said, "Some things aren't meant to be."

Beverly could no longer see the pirate, and she wondered if he was still saying words that no one else could hear. She thought about Fran and Jillian, her friends from school, and wondered whether they would trick-or-treat together for Halloween. Maybe, she thought, she could dress as a pirate, but more than likely she would go as a cowgirl again, just as she had the year before. Her mom already had the hat and the plaid shirt and the toy gun and holster, and Beverly knew if she asked about dressing like a pirate instead, she'd be told that they couldn't afford it.

Her mom was talking and talking and talking, but Beverly didn't bother to listen. Sometimes, when her mom talked, Beverly knew that whatever was being said wasn't important. From another spot on the observation deck they saw the Brooklyn Bridge, which looked small enough to be a toy. By then they had been on the deck for nearly an hour, and when Beverly eventually turned toward her mom, she saw tears on her cheeks. Beverly knew not to ask why her mom was crying, but she found herself wishing that her mom had been able to live in the *Big City*.

All at once, Beverly heard screaming and shouting, and she was bumped so hard she nearly fell over. She grabbed for her mom's hand, and the two of them were suddenly caught up in the movement of the crowd like fish trapped in a strong current. To stop meant being trampled, even Beverly knew that, and they stumbled forward. Beverly could see nothing but the bodies around her—elbows darting, bags swinging. The screaming grew louder, with more people joining in, everyone on the observation deck moving quickly in the same direction, everyone caught in the same riptide, until Beverly and her mom were finally spit out the back and able to catch their balance.

"What's happening?"

"I don't know."

Above the roar, Beverly could hear individual cries of "Don't!" and "Come back!" and "Stop!" and "What are you doing!" and "Get down!" She didn't know what any of it meant, just that something bad was happening. Her mom knew it, too; she was on her toes, trying to see over the crowd, and then, just as suddenly, the crowd stopped moving. For a few seconds, everything was still and no one moved at all, and it was the most unnatural thing Beverly had ever experienced—until the screaming started up again, this time even louder.

"What happened?" Beverly heard someone shout.

"He jumped," another man shouted.

"Who jumped?"

"The guy who was dressed like a pirate!"

There were barriers and fences, and Beverly wondered if she had been mistaken in what she'd heard. Why would the pirate jump? The other buildings were too far away to reach.

She felt her mom squeeze her hand again and tug.

"Let's go," her mom said. "We need to leave."

"Did the pirate jump?"

"What pirate?"

"The one I stood next to when I first got here."

"I don't know," her mom said. She led them through the gift shop, toward the elevators, where a line had already formed.

"They grabbed for him, but no one could stop him," Beverly heard the man standing next to her say, and when she stepped into the elevator, Beverly thought about the pirate, and thought about falling, and she wondered what it was like to go down and down, lower and lower, until there was nowhere left to go.

8.

BEVERLY SAT UP IN BED, blinking in the darkness, knowing it had been less a dream than a memory, except that this time she'd been falling, too, hand in hand with the pirate. As always when the dream resurfaced, she woke to the hammering of her heart, with shaky breaths and her sheet damp with sweat.

I'm not falling, she thought, *I'm not falling,* but even so, the physical sensation was slow to pass. Her heart continued to race, her breaths rapid, and even as the dream began to fade, she knew she wasn't herself. The world felt off-kilter and foreign. She forced herself to concentrate on the details of the room as they emerged in vague and darkened shadows. She saw a window with thin shades drawn, the soft white sky of dawn seeping through. She saw her clothing piled on the floor. There was a lamp and a glass half filled with water on the bedside table next to her. Across the room stood a chest of drawers with a full-length mirror hanging beside it. Little by little, she began to make sense of her surroundings.

It was morning. She was in the bedroom of the house she'd

just rented, and her six-year-old son, Tommie, was asleep in the room across the hallway. She had only recently arrived in town. *Yes,* Beverly thought, reminding herself. *My new life. I'm beginning my new life,* and only then was she able to push the covers back. She got out of bed, feeling a thin silky rug beneath her feet, a pleasant surprise. The bedroom door was closed, but she knew the short hallway beyond it would lead to the stairs and that, on the main floor, there was a living room and a small kitchen furnished with an old Formica table surrounded by four scuffed wooden chairs.

Beverly slipped into the jeans and T-shirt that had been heaped on the floor and wondered how long she'd been sleeping. She couldn't remember what time she finally went to bed, other than that it had been really, really late. But what had she done? The memories of the night before were nothing but dream smoke, blurring at the edges and black in the middle. She couldn't remember what she'd had for dinner or even if she'd eaten at all, but she supposed it didn't much matter. Starting over always carried with it stress, and stress made the mind do funny things.

She crept from her bedroom, peeked in on Tommie, and saw him jumbled under the covers. She quietly made her way down the stairs to the kitchen. As she poured herself a glass of water from the faucet, she remembered a recent night when she'd snuck from her bedroom, moving quietly and without turning on a single light. She was already dressed when she roused Tommie. His small backpack was loaded and hidden beneath his bed. She helped him get dressed and they crept down the stairs. Like Tommie, she carried only a backpack, for ease and speed. She knew that neighbors might remember a woman and child hauling rolling suitcases along the sidewalk in the middle of the night; she knew that her husband, Gary, would seek out those neighbors and they would tell him what he needed to know to find her. In Tommie's backpack were his favorite Iron Man action figure and *Go, Dog. Go!*, a book she still read to him every night. She'd also packed two T-shirts, a second pair of pants, socks, underwear, toothbrush and toothpaste, and hair wax for his cowlick. In her backpack were the same sorts of items and other things, along with a smattering of makeup, a brush, sunglasses, an Ace bandage, and a wig. Near the front window, she didn't bother looking for the black SUV with tinted windows that had been parked along her street for the past three days. She already knew it would be there, even if parked in a different spot. Instead, after she helped Tommie with his jacket, they slipped out the back door. She made sure not to let the screen door bang or squeak, inching it closed as slowly as possible. They crossed the damp grass to the wooden fence that bordered their lawn, and Beverly helped Tommie climb over into the neighbor's backyard. Through all of that, Tommie had said nothing. He wobbled when he walked as though still partially asleep. They exited through the neighbor's gate and stayed near the hedges until reaching the street that ran parallel to her own. There, she hid behind a car parked on the street and peered in both directions. She saw no black SUV with tinted windows.

Where are we going? Tommie finally asked her.

On an adventure, she'd whispered.

Is Daddy coming with us?

He's working, she'd responded, which was true, even if it didn't really answer his question.

It was the middle of the night and quiet, but the moon was half full and the streets were illuminated by lampposts at the intersections. She needed darkness and shadows to remain invisible, so she cut across lawns and driveways, sticking close to the houses. In the rare moments when she heard a car coming, she led Tommie to whatever nearby secluded spot she could find—

behind bushes or trellises and even an old RV. Occasionally, a dog would bark, but the sound always came from a distance. They walked and walked, but Tommie didn't whine, didn't so much as whimper. Residential streets gradually gave way to commercial ones, then, an hour and a half later, to an industrial area, with warehouses and a salvage yard and parking lots surrounded by chain-link fencing. Though there was no place to hide, the streets were empty. When they eventually reached the bus station, the entrance smelled of cigarette smoke and fried food and urine. They went inside. In the restroom, Beverly pinned her hair up with bobby pins and donned the wig that turned her from a long-haired blonde to a brunette with a pixie cut. She wrapped a long Ace bandage around her chest, making her breasts smaller, pulling it tight to the point that it was hard to breathe. She donned a baseball hat, and though it was still dark, she put on her sunglasses. Tommie didn't recognize her when she emerged. She had told him to sit on one of the benches and explained that it was important not to wander off, and it was only after she removed her glasses while directly in front of him that his eyes widened in recognition. She walked him to an even more isolated bench in the corner of the terminal, one that was out of sight from the ticket window, and told him to sit quietly.

There were only a few people milling about in the station when she went to the ticket window and took her place in line behind an elderly woman in a heavy brown cardigan sweater. When it was her turn, she stood before a man with bags under his eyes and a long side patch of stringy gray hair that he swept over his bald spot. She asked for two tickets to Chicago, and as she handed over the money, she mentioned casually that she and her sister were going to visit their mother. She didn't want the man behind the Plexiglas to know she was traveling with her son, but apparently he didn't care one way or the other—he barely seemed to notice her as he handed her the tickets. Beverly returned to a bench kitty-corner from Tommie, where she could keep an eye on him but it wouldn't be obvious that they were together. Every minute or so she would glance at him, then toward the entrance, searching beyond the glass for the black SUV with tinted windows, but thankfully it never appeared. She also studied other faces in the terminal, trying to memorize them, seeing if anyone was paying attention to a little boy sitting all alone, just in case. But no one seemed to care.

Dawn arrived, a bright late-spring glare. In time, the engine of the appropriate bus began to idle beneath one of the aluminum canopies out back. With her stomach in knots, she sent Tommie ahead so he could pretend to be boarding with a man in a bomber jacket, a father and son traveling together. Through the windows, she watched Tommie follow the man toward seats near the rear of the bus. Others boarded, then she finally stepped aboard, walking past the thin, dark-haired bus driver. She took a seat in the second-to-last row; on the opposite side, in the next row up, was an older woman crocheting, moving the needle like a conductor standing in front of an orchestra. Tommie remained in his seat ahead of her until the bus started moving, just as she'd instructed, and when they reached the highway, he joined her. There, he leaned his head against her shoulder while she continued to watch the people on the bus, forcing herself to remember them and trying to figure out whether any of them had noticed anything amiss.

She reminded herself of how careful she'd been. Gary was out of town, doing whatever secret thing it was he did for the government. They'd also left on a Saturday, and on each of the four previous weekends she'd made sure not to leave the house or even let Tommie play in the yard, establishing a pattern that would hopefully buy time. Using money she'd secretly saved over a period of six months, she set up automatic timers on the lights, which would come on and then go out in the evenings. With any luck, the driver in the black SUV wouldn't know they were gone until the school bus showed up on Monday morning.

The bus rumbled along, and as the hours slowly passed, Beverly thought that every minute meant another mile farther from the home she needed to escape. Tommie slept beside her as they rode through Texas and Arkansas and then finally into Missouri. They rolled past farmland and stopped in cities and towns, most with names she didn't recognize. People got off and others got on, and the brakes would squeak and the bus would eventually lurch forward again, toward the next destination. Stopping and starting, all day long and then into the night, the engine rumbling beneath her seat. By the time the first driver was replaced by a new one, she recognized no one from the original bus station, but even then she tried to remember every face she saw. The woman who was crocheting had been replaced by a young man with short hair, carrying an olive-colored duffel bag. Army, maybe, or Marines, and when he pulled a phone from his pocket, Beverly's heart slammed in her chest. She pulled her baseball cap lower and stared out the window, wondering if the young man worked with Gary, wondering if he could have possibly found her already. She wondered again about the hidden powers of the Department of Homeland Security. She had lied to Gary and Tommie and neighbors and friends, and though she hadn't been raised to lie, she'd had no other choice. Across the aisle, the young man with the short hair put his phone back into his pocket and closed his eyes and leaned his head against the window. He hadn't so much as peeked in her direction, and little by little, her heart began to slow again. Though exhausted, she found it impossible to sleep.

In Missouri, the bus stopped again. Another station, another nameless place. Beverly sent Tommie ahead of her, off the bus, then eventually followed him. She led him to the ladies' room in the terminal, ignoring the irritated expression of a heavyset woman in a floral-print blouse. She used water from the faucet and wax to dampen Tommie's cowlick, and though she had little money to spare, Tommie was six and growing fast and she knew he needed to eat. There were two apples and two granola bars in her own backpack, but that wasn't enough. In the convenience store across the street, she bought milk and two hot dogs but nothing for her own growling stomach. She decided she could have one of the apples in an hour, even though she knew she could eat both of them and the granola bars and would likely still be hungry. At the register, because there was a camera, she kept her head tilted down, the brim of the hat shielding her face.

They got on the bus again. Tommie remained quiet, flipping through the pages of his book. She knew he could read it by now; she had read it so often he had probably memorized it, as well. Instinctively, she knew that Tommie was more intelligent than most children his age; he picked things up quickly and always seemed to understand situations and ideas far beyond his years. When she looked at him, she sometimes saw Gary's eyes, but his smile was his own, and his nose resembled hers. She sometimes saw him as a baby and a toddler and on his first day of kindergarten, the images merging in her head, making Tommie perpetually familiar and yet always new and different. Beyond the window, she saw farmland and cows and silos and highway signs advertising fast-food restaurants one or two or three exits ahead. Beverly ate one of the apples, chewing slowly, trying to savor it, to make the flavor last. She'd sewn most of the money she had saved into a hidden pocket in her jacket.

Later, they left that bus for good. They were somewhere in Illinois, but still a long way from Chicago. She sent Tommie ahead of her, watching as he took a seat on the bench in the terminal. After a couple of minutes, she went to the ladies' room, where she hid in a stall. She had told Tommie to wait, so he did. Ten minutes, then fifteen, and then twenty minutes, until she was confident that anyone else who'd been on the bus had already departed the station. Once she was sure it was quiet, she stood in front of the cracked and dingy mirror in the restroom. She quickly removed her wig but kept her hair pinned up and put the baseball hat back on. Now she was a short-haired blonde. The sunglasses went into her backpack, and she applied heavy mascara and black eyeliner. When she emerged, the bus station was devoid of people except Tommie. She told him to stand near the restroom when she went to the ticket window again. She bought tickets for the next bus that was leaving, not caring where it went, only that it would take her in some random direction and make her journey that much harder to follow. Again, she mentioned she was traveling with her sister, and again she sat apart from Tommie; again, they boarded the bus at separate times.

And then, after another day and a half on the bus, she and Tommie stepped off for good. They left the station and walked toward the highway. Near the on-ramp, she put out her thumb and caught a ride with a woman driving a station wagon, who asked them where they were going. Beverly answered that she could drop them anywhere, and the woman gazed over at Beverly and Tommie and saw something in Beverly's face and didn't ask any more questions. In time, the station wagon came to a stop in a small town, and Tommie and Beverly got out. From there, they hitched another ride—this time from a middle-aged man who smelled of Old Spice and sold carpets for a living— and when Beverly made up a story about her car breaking down, Tommie knew enough to stay silent. They eventually arrived at another small town. Beverly and Tommie grabbed their backpacks, and Beverly brought Tommie to get something to eat at a roadside diner. Beverly asked for a cup of hot water and added ketchup to it, making a thin soup, while Tommie had a cheeseburger and fries and a slice of blueberry pie and two glasses of milk.

On the next street over, she spotted an inexpensive motel, though she knew she didn't have enough money to stay more than a couple of nights. Not if she intended to rent a place. But it would have to do for now, and after she got Tommie settled in the dated but functional room, she went back to the diner and asked the waitress if she could borrow her cellphone to make a quick call, along with a pen and a napkin. The woman—who reminded Beverly a little of her mom—seemed to sense the urgency of Beverly's request. Instead of making a call, Beverly pretended to do so and then, with her back turned, she searched local real estate listings. There weren't many, and she jotted down addresses and then cleared the history before returning the cellphone. After that, she asked strangers on the street for basic directions and found the dingy apartments first, but they were no good. Nor was the equally dingy duplex. Nor was the one house she'd been able to find. But there was one listing still to go.

In the morning, after bringing Tommie to the diner for breakfast and then back to the motel, she went out again. Aside from the two apples and granola bars, she hadn't eaten for three days. She walked slowly, but even then she had to stop and rest every few minutes, and it took a long time to find the house. It was on the distant outskirts of town, in farm country, a grand two-story place surrounded by massive live oaks, their limbs stretching in every direction like gnarled, arthritic fingers. Out front, the patchy grass was slightly overgrown with dandelions and goosegrass and prostrate knotweed. A dirt pathway led toward a covered front porch sporting a pair of ancient rocking chairs. The front door was candy-apple red, ridiculous against the dirty and flaking white paint, and the sides of the house were thick with azalea and daylilies, the decaying blooms like splashes of color in a forgotten forest. The house was fifty or a hundred years old and isolated enough to keep prying eyes away.

She cupped her hands to various windows so she could see inside. The colors on the first floor were dizzying—orange paint on the kitchen walls, a burgundy wall in the living room. Mismatched furniture; wide, scuffed pine plank flooring covered with thin rugs in the hallway and living room, linoleum in the kitchen. Sills painted so many times she wondered whether she would be able to open the windows. But she walked back to town and asked the waitress at the diner if she could borrow her phone again. She called the owner of the house and returned later in the afternoon, so she could go inside. She made sure to delete the call, just in case. For that visit, she donned the same disguise she'd used on the night they ran away.

As she'd walked through the house, she knew it would need work. There was a ring of lime in the sink, grease on the stovetop, a refrigerator filled with food that could have been there for weeks or months. Upstairs were two bedrooms, two bathrooms, and a linen closet. On the plus side, there were no water stains in the ceilings, and the toilets and showers worked. On the back porch, there was a washer and dryer, both of them rusting but still functional, as well as a water heater that looked almost new. Next to and above the appliances were shelves stacked with odds and ends, along with cans and cans of latex paint, enough to paint the entire interior, all different colors, at least a dozen. On the floor in the corner was a dirty plastic bucket filled with rollers and paintbrushes, along with a pan, surrounded by rags that looked anything but new. It was nothing like the house she had shared with Gary, with its harsh modern exterior and his clean, straight-lined furniture and organized cupboards, nothing ever out of place. Their home had been like something from the future, as cold and empty of feeling as outer space, while this home radiated a feeling of familiar comfort.

Even better, the owner worked with a regular handyman for any repairs, so all she had to do was call if there were problems. Utilities were included, and the house came furnished, albeit with furniture that was anything but new. The couch was worn but comfortable; there was a newer-model television and an ancient DVD player in a cabinet, end tables, and lamps with shades that didn't quite match. There were beds and chests of drawers in the bedrooms and towels in the bathrooms. In the small pantry off the kitchen, there was a broom and mop, various cleaners— most half used—and other assorted stuff. There were lightbulbs and two extension cords, a toilet-bowl brush and plunger, a fly-swatter, a box containing nails and screws and a small hammer. There was a wrench, as well, and two types of screwdrivers. Next to the tools, there was half a box of AA batteries and two nine-volts. A dehumidifier. Rags and sandpaper and a medium-sized stepladder. There were sheets and pillowcases in the linen closet upstairs, though they would need to be washed. There were plates and glasses and utensils in the kitchen drawers and pots and pans and even some Tupperware in the kitchen. It was as though the people who'd lived here had vanished into the ether one day, stealing away in the middle of the night, carrying only what they could. Knowing they had to get out, knowing it was time to run. From the law, from something dangerous. Taking only what would fit in the trunk of their car and abandoning everything else because they simply had to get away.

Just like her and Tommie.

Beverly had run her finger along the counter, hearing a fly

buzz past her and noting dirty fingerprint smudges on the refrigerator and grease stains high on the kitchen walls. She could live here, she'd thought, and the idea had made her feel almost dizzy with possibility. She could turn it into a real home, and it would be hers and Tommie's, just the two of them. Beyond the windows, she had noted the nearby barn, which she was told was being used for storage and was definitely off-limits. It mattered not at all, since Beverly had brought practically nothing with her, let alone anything she needed to store in a barn. Her eyes drifted to Tommie, who was sitting on a tree stump near the road. She had brought him with her this time but had asked him to wait outside. He was examining the back of his fingers, and she wondered what he was thinking. Sometimes she wished he would speak more, but he was a child who generally kept his thoughts to himself, as though his deepest desire was to move through the world quietly, attracting as little notice as possible. In time, perhaps, he would change, and as she'd stared at him, she knew she loved him more than she'd ever loved anyone.

Now it was morning, and they were in their new place, but other details remained blurry. She remembered that the owner didn't have a lot of questions or ask for references, which had been both a blessing and a surprise; she'd paid cash for the deposit and the first month's rent, but how long ago had that been? Four days? Five? However long it was, she'd been able to enroll Tommie in school and make sure that the bus would pick him up; she'd also been able to go grocery shopping, so he would have milk and cereal for breakfast and sandwiches for his school lunches. At a small store down the road, she'd bought only as much as she could carry and had hunted for bargains. For herself, she bought oatmeal and dry beans and two bags of rice and butter and salt and pepper, but Tommie needed a more-varied diet, so she'd splurged on half a dozen apples. She also bought hamburger and chicken drumsticks, though both packages were almost out of date and had been marked down to less than a third of the normal price. She'd separated the hamburger and chicken into individual portions right away before putting all of it into the freezer; she removed one portion per day for Tommie's dinner, which he ate with either the beans or the rice. At night, after watching television, she read him *Go, Dog. Go!* and made sure he brushed his teeth. With the weather warming, she'd promised they would explore the property behind the house.

She hadn't, however, had the energy to do much more than that. She sat for hours in the rockers out front and slept a lot when Tommie was at school and the house was quiet. Though her exhaustion had remained almost overwhelming since they'd arrived, standing in the orange-walled kitchen reminded her that there was work to do before the house would seem like theirs. After placing the empty glass in the sink, she pulled an old cookie jar from the cupboard. She lifted the lid and found the money roll she'd stashed after moving in. She removed a few bills, knowing she needed to go to the store again, since the groceries were almost gone. After that, she wanted to clean the kitchen from top to bottom, starting with the stove. She also had to empty the refrigerator of all that had been left behind. Getting rid of the god-awful orange walls meant scrubbing them beforehand, as well, to get them ready for painting. She'd always dreamed of a bright-yellow kitchen, something cheerful and welcoming, especially if she added another coat of glossy white paint to the cabinets. After that, she could pick wildflowers, maybe arrange them in one of the jelly jars she'd found in the cupboard. Closing her eyes, she felt a pleasant twinge of anticipation as she imagined how it might look when she was finished.

She counted the remaining money before hiding it again. Though she'd kept a running total in her head, touching and counting the bills made the sum more tangible somehow. It wasn't enough to live on forever, but as long as she was fine with subsisting on rice and beans and oatmeal, she had time, even if she included the next month's rent. It was hard, though. On the previous trip to the grocery store, she'd secretly pulled two grapes from a bunch that she couldn't afford, and the natural, sugary flavor nearly made her moan with pleasure.

Still, the money would run out sooner rather than later, no matter how careful she was or how much she budgeted. She would have to get a job, but that meant paperwork and documents. Social Security number, maybe even a driver's license. Some employers might require a phone number, as well. She couldn't possibly use the first two; Gary, no doubt, had already put out an internet alert, which was why she hadn't bothered to bring her identification with her in the first place. Nor did she have a phone. On her first day, she'd found an abandoned cellphone in the nightstand, but it required a password or fingerprint to access, so it did her no good at all—not to mention the fact that it was someone else's, even if they'd left it behind. All of which meant she was off the grid: exactly what she needed but a solution that brought with it problems. She supposed that she could lie—simply jot down phony identification numbers on the application—but that also carried risks. Wages were reported to the IRS, and the employer would eventually learn the truth. Which further meant that Gary would learn the truth, too. From his lofty perch at the Department of Homeland Security, Gary had access to virtually any information he wanted.

She knew she needed to find a job that paid cash—babysitting or cleaning houses, or maybe cooking meals or reading books for someone who was elderly. She wondered if there was a bulletin board somewhere in town that would list such opportunities, and she reminded herself to look for one.

Today, she thought, *I will find the energy to do all that I need to do.*

From upstairs, she heard Tommie's door squeak open. She watched as he padded down the steps while rubbing the sleep from his eyes, dressed in one of the two shirts she'd thrown into his backpack. She wondered how long it would be before the other kids began to make fun of him for wearing the same clothes over and over. From the refrigerator, she retrieved the milk; from the cupboard, she pulled a box of Cheerios. There was sugar in the cupboard, left by those who'd lived here before, but she didn't trust that it was safe to eat. Who knew what sort of icky critters had decided to breed in there?

She poured the Cheerios into a bowl and brought the bowl and spoon to the table. She kept the small bottle of his hair wax on the counter and added a dab to her palms. She smoothed his cowlick, then kissed him on the cheek.

"How did you sleep, sweetie?"

He merely shrugged, but she'd expected that. He was quiet in general, but in the mornings, getting him to speak was sometimes like pulling teeth. She reached for the peanut butter and jelly on the counter and the last two pieces of bread in the loaf. She made a sandwich, wrapped it in plastic, and placed it into a paper bag, along with the last apple and enough change to allow him to buy milk. She wished she had enough money for Cheetos or granola bars or Nutter Butters, or even sliced turkey or ham, but it just wasn't possible. When the lunch was ready, she squeezed the bag into Tommie's backpack, then took a seat at the table, almost aching with love for him.

"Honey? I asked you a question."

He took a bite, and only after swallowing did he answer. "Okay."

"Just okay?"

When he nodded, she waited. "Did you have a bad dream?" As soon as she asked, she realized she could be speaking about herself.

He shook his head.

"Honey? I'm trying to talk to you. Did something happen last night?"

"It was loud."

"What do you mean?" she asked, trying to keep any concern from her voice. It couldn't have been Gary; there was no way he could have found them yet.

"There were crickets. Like a million of them. I think there were frogs, too."

She smiled. "We're in the country, so you're probably right."

He nodded. Took another bite.

"How do you like the school? And your teacher?"

For the life of her, Beverly couldn't remember the teacher's name, but then again, there wasn't much time left in the school year and she'd only been at the school long enough to sign him up, so she supposed she could be forgiven for her lapse.

"Tommie?"

"She's okay," he said with a sigh.

"Have you made any friends yet?"

He ate another spoonful of cereal, then finally looked up at her. "Can we get a dog?"

He'd asked for a dog before, yet another reminder that there was so much more she wished she could do for him. Gary had never allowed one, but even though that life was behind them now, she knew she couldn't afford to take care of a dog. And who knew when they'd have to run again? "We'll see," she hedged.

He nodded, knowing exactly what her answer meant.

When Tommie was finished with his cereal, Beverly tugged at his shirt, straightening it, then helped him on with his backpack. Still barefoot, she ducked upstairs to her bedroom and put on her shoes before walking with her son toward the stump near the road, where they sat and waited for the school bus. The air was becoming soupy, and she knew it was going to be another hot one.

The bus arrived minutes after they'd taken their seats, and as Beverly watched Tommie silently board the bus, she noticed the heat was already turning the horizon into liquid.

9.

THE SMALL GROCERY STORE nearest the house wouldn't be open for at least an hour, so after the bus vanished in a swirl of gravel dust, Beverly wandered back inside, thinking it was finally time to tackle the oven.

She went to the bathroom and made a quick ponytail, using a rubber band she found in one of the drawers, then searched under the kitchen sink and in the pantry for the cleanser. She sprayed the surface of the stovetop and began to scrub, noting the burns and scratches, but some of the spills seemed welded to the surface. With a strange sense of satisfaction, she wrapped the tip of a butter knife in the dishrag and, bearing down hard, watched the crusty remains slowly curl away.

After the stovetop, she'd nearly sweated through her shirt from exertion. She sprayed cleaner into the oven, knowing it needed to soak for a while, then went upstairs to the bathroom and removed her shirt. She washed it with a bit of shampoo, then hung it to dry over the shower curtain. It was pointless to put a single piece of clothing in the washer. After that, she started to get ready. She slipped into a clean shirt, pinned up her hair, and slid on the wig, becoming a short-haired brunette again, before wrapping her chest in the Ace bandage. She added dark foundation, changing her complexion, and applied dark lipstick. After donning her sunglasses and baseball hat, she barely recognized herself in the mirror. Perfect.

She left the house and marched down the gravel road that led toward town, feeling the crunch beneath her feet. She stopped twice to peek over her shoulder at the house, trying to gauge when it could no longer be seen from the road. Since moving in, she'd automatically turned toward the windows whenever she heard a vehicle approaching, watching to see if it slowed, and she wanted to know how far away a vehicle could pull over and park without being seen.

It took almost an hour to walk the three miles to the store; it would take longer on the way back because she'd be carrying bags, one of which would include a gallon of milk. She knew it was good exercise, just as she knew she was already too thin and that too much exercise was the opposite of what she needed. As she'd glanced in the bathroom mirror while hanging her shirt, she was able to count almost every rib.

The store was family-owned, not part of a chain. It was called Red's and looked as though it had been in business since Kennedy was president. Across the street, there was a gas station that appeared equally dated, next to a small hardware store. After that, there was a bunch of nothing for at least another mile, until the motel and the diner. It might be less expensive to shop if she ventured farther into town to the bigger stores, but that meant a much longer walk.

Unlike in major grocery stores, the selection was limited, but that didn't matter, because her list was limited. Into the cart she piled apples and milk and bread and another box of cereal. She found more hamburger and chicken, but this time nothing was marked down. Despite her worries about money, she splurged on carrots and cauliflower, knowing that Tommie needed vegetables. She could steam the cauliflower, add milk and butter, and serve it like mashed potatoes or simply roast it. With every item added to the cart, she mentally subtracted the cash she knew she had. She didn't want to have to ask the cashier to take something away that had already been rung up. She didn't want any unnecessary attention.

There was one woman in line at the checkout, and Beverly could already tell that the cashier was the chatty sort. Next to the checkout stands was a rack of magazines; Beverly picked one up. When it was her turn, the cashier pulled the cart forward and began unloading items, already beginning to talk. Beverly stood in profile—exposing more of her back than her front to the cashier—her gaze buried in the magazine to keep the woman from speaking with her. From the corner of her eye, she watched the cashier ringing up items. The woman's name tag read PEG. Beverly set the magazine aside as the last item was loaded and reached for the bills she'd stashed in her pocket, suddenly remembering there was something she needed to know.

"Is there a bulletin board with job listings anywhere? Like cleaning or babysitting?"

"There's a board near the exit, but I don't have any idea what's up there," Peg said with a shrug. She loaded the items into plastic bags. "Did you find everything?"

"Yes," Beverly said. She reached for the first of the bags, looping one of the plastic handles around her arm.

Peg glanced up, then seemed to peer even closer.

"Excuse me, but don't I know you? You look sort of familiar."

"I don't think so," Beverly mumbled. She reached for the other bags and began walking toward the exit, feeling Peg's eyes on her, wondering if Peg was in the store the last time she'd shopped, feeling a growing sense of dread. Why else would Peg think she seemed familiar? What else could it be?

Unless . . .

For a moment, she felt almost as though she was about to drop the bags; questions began to tumble and spin through her mind like clothes in the dryer.

What if Peg's husband worked for law enforcement?

What if Peg's husband had seen a bulletin about her and brought it home?

What if Peg's husband had asked Peg to stay on the lookout?

What if . . . ?

She stopped and closed her eyes, trying to remain steady on her feet, trying to slow her mind.

"No," she said aloud, opening her eyes. That couldn't have happened. There was no doubt Gary had already instituted a nation-wide manhunt—*Kidnapper on the loose!*—but would Peg's husband have brought home the report? To have his wife study it, so she could watch for random wanted strangers, in case they wandered into the store? In a town like this? She wasn't even sure if Peg's husband was in law enforcement; in fact, she wasn't even certain that Peg was married at all.

It was just her mind playing tricks again. The very idea bordered on the impossible, and besides, even if the impossible had happened, Beverly reminded herself that she now looked nothing like any of her recent photographs. Peg must have seen her on her previous shopping trip, that's all. For all Beverly knew, Peg said the same thing to every stranger who walked into the store, an opener for a chatty conversation.

Taking a long breath, she decided that Peg hadn't recognized her.

She decided she was just being paranoid.

10.

At the bulletin board near the exit, there weren't any listings for the kinds of work Beverly needed, which meant she'd probably have to venture farther into town. Maybe she should talk to the waitress at the diner again; perhaps she knew of someone personally who might need some cooking or cleaning or babysitting. But that meant walking in the opposite direction—with groceries—so it would have to wait.

Instead, on the walk home, she thought about the clothes Tommie needed, if only because she hoped it would keep her arms from aching. But they ached anyway, and she wished she had a car or even a bicycle with a basket.

Back at the house, Beverly put the groceries away and headed to the bathroom. As she had earlier, she washed the shirt she'd been wearing with shampoo, since it was practically soaked through. The heat of the day was already atrocious, like invisible steam, sticky and thick. She thought about putting on the earlier shirt, but it was still damp, and what was the point? Tommie wasn't home, and knowing she had more cleaning to do, she took off her disguise and unwrapped the Ace bandage. Then—thinking, *Why not?*—she took off her jeans, as well. She might as well be comfortable. In her bra and panties, she returned to the kitchen to finish the oven.

She'd imagined she'd be weary from the trip to the store and back, but she actually felt . . . *good*. Like she had energy to burn. *I escaped,* she told herself. *Tommie is safe, and now we have a home, and there's no way that Peg recognized me.* The realizations made her almost giddy with possibility, and she laughed aloud. On the kitchen counter was an old radio, and she turned it on, adjusting the dial until she found the music she wanted. Beyond the window, people worked in the distant fields, but they were so far away she wasn't worried she'd be seen half naked.

Besides, she reasoned, *it's my house and I have things to do.*

First up was to get rid of all the old food. Cleansers, she could keep. Who would poison cleansers? She remembered seeing trash bags under the sink and, pulling a couple from the box, she shook them open and set them near the refrigerator. There was no reason to check the dates; just toss everything, except for what she'd purchased recently. Into the garbage bag went cheese, condiments, pickles, jelly, olives, salad dressings, and something no doubt disgusting that had been wrapped in foil and forgotten. Even an old pizza box with a couple of pieces that could have been used as a substitute for concrete. She did the same thing with the freezer, which meant trashing everything except the chicken and hamburger. It took all of ten minutes, and she lugged the now-full trash bag to the huge green garbage can she'd spotted behind the house, the one that would be picked up by the road. She should have asked the owner when the garbage truck came by, but she assumed that she'd figure it out eventually.

Next she emptied the cupboards, tossing that garbage bag as well. Afterward, she stood before the refrigerator and cupboards, opening the doors one after the other, seeing their emptiness, except the food she needed for Tommie and herself, and suddenly feeling even better.

I am finally and truly moving forward.

She turned her efforts back to the oven. The cleanser had done its work, and the grime came off easier than she expected. It didn't appear new when she finished—there were still scorch marks on both sides, impossible to remove—but she suspected it was cleaner than it had been in years. Once that was done, she got the beans soaking in water from the tap.

The sight of the beans reminded her that she should probably eat—she hadn't had anything all day—but she didn't want to break her rhythm. Instead, she wiped the counters, paying special attention to the corners, and scrubbed at the lime stain in the sink.

Climbing onto the counter to wipe down the upper cabinets, she again noticed minor grease stains on the wall and ceiling. Dragging out the stepladder, she started in on the ceiling, spraying cleanser with one hand and scrubbing with the other. When her arms got tired—which they did a lot—she shook them, then went back to work. The walls came next. Neither the ceiling nor the walls had to be perfect, of course—just clean enough for the primer and paint to stick—but it still took almost three hours to finish.

Afterward, she put the cleansers and stepladder away, set the rags on top of the washer, and finally made her way to the shower. She luxuriated in the spray of hot water and her own sense of accomplishment.

In front of the mirror, she dressed and, after towel-drying her hair, brushed out the tangles. Tommie would be home from school soon.

II.

SHE WAITED ON THE STUMP out front, idly watching the field-workers in the distance, until she heard the low-throated rumble of the bus resonating in the oppressive heat. As Tommie rose from his seat at the rear of the bus, she stood. Watching him through the bus window, she wished that he'd been in the midst of a conversation with one of the other kids and would linger at the door while saying goodbye. But he didn't; he simply stepped off and trudged toward her as though his backpack, and life, were weighing him down. She reached for the backpack, offering a quick wave to the driver, who waved in return.

"How was school?" she asked as the bus pulled away.

Tommie shrugged, but this time she smiled, knowing it had been a dumb question. Her mom used to ask her the same thing, but school was always just . . . school.

She ran her hand through his hair. "How about an apple when we get inside? I went to the store today."

"Did you buy Oreos?"

"Not this time."

He nodded. "Then I guess an apple will be okay."

She squeezed his shoulder and the two of them walked into the house together.

12.

TOMMIE HAD NO HOMEWORK—THERE was never homework in first grade, thank God—so after she handed him an apple, they did a bit of exploring around the property. Not that there was much to see other than the barn that was *definitely off-limits*, which looked older than the house and would likely fall down as soon as the next storm hit. Still, they eventually found a meandering creek shaded by dogwood trees. She wasn't sure how she knew what kind of trees they were, just as she wasn't sure how she knew they bloomed in the spring. She assumed she must have read it somewhere. When Tommie tossed the apple core into the water, she had an idea, something from her own childhood.

"Let's see if there are any tadpoles, okay? Take off your shoes and socks."

After Tommie's feet were bare, she rolled up his pant legs, then did her own. They walked into the water, not far, but the bank was shallow.

"What's a tadpole?" Tommie asked.

"It's a baby frog," she said. "Before it gets legs."

Bending over, they walked slowly, and Beverly spotted the familiar black wiggling creatures. Tommie wasn't sure how to catch them, so Beverly bent lower, making a cup with her hands. She scooped one out, holding it for her son so he could see. For the first time since they'd been at the house, she saw what seemed to be excitement and wonder in his expression.

"That's a tadpole? And it's going to turn into a frog?"

"Soon," she said. "They grow pretty fast."

"But these aren't the frogs I heard last night, right?"

"No. Those were grown-up frogs. But maybe we should let this guy go, so he can get back to the water, okay?"

She let the tadpole go while Tommie hunted for another one. It didn't take long before he tried to scoop one into his hands, only to have it escape. On his third effort he was finally able to show her. Again, his expression warmed her heart, and she felt a surge of relief at the idea that he would eventually get used to living in a place like this.

"Can I bring some to school for show-and-tell? On field day?"

"Field day?"

"The teacher said that instead of school, kids stay outside all day. And there's a big show-and-tell."

Beverly dimly remembered such days when she'd been in elementary school: There were races and games and prizes, and the fire department brought a truck, and parent volunteers brought cookies and cupcakes and other snacks. She recalled that her mom had shown up for one of them, but for whatever reason she'd been asked to leave, and Beverly could remember how she'd stomped off, shouting at everyone.

"When is field day?"

"I'm not sure exactly. But it's this week for sure."

"You'll have fun. I used to love field day, because it meant I could play with my friends all day long. But as for bringing the tadpoles, I suppose we could put them in a jar, but I don't know how long they can live that way, especially if they're in the sun for hours. I'd hate for something bad to happen to them."

For a long moment, he was quiet. He let the tadpole go and scratched at his cheek with a dirty finger. "I miss my old room."

Whoever had slept in his current bedroom obviously wasn't a child. The closet and chest of drawers were still full of clothing for an adult, and the bed was oversized. There were paintings, not posters, on the walls.

"I know you do," she said. "It's hard moving to a new place."

"Why couldn't I bring more of my toys?"

Because I couldn't carry them. Because people at the bus station would have remembered. Because running meant we had to travel light.

"We just couldn't."

"When can I see Brady and Derek again?"

They were his best friends, also left behind. She smiled at the irony. When she was little, there were kids in her class with exactly the same names.

"We'll see," she said. "Probably not for a while, though."

He nodded, then bent lower, looking for tadpoles again. Barefoot, with his pants rolled, he struck her as a throwback to a different generation. She prayed he wouldn't ask about his father, but he seemed to know that it wouldn't be a good idea. There were, after all, still bruises on his arm from the last time Gary had grabbed him.

"It's different here," he finally said. "I can see the moon through my window at night."

Because it was more than he generally volunteered, she couldn't help but smile again.

"I used to read you *Goodnight Moon*. When you were little."

He knitted his small brow. "Is that the one with the cow jumping over the moon?"

"That's it."

He nodded again, then went back to searching. Caught one, let it go. Caught another and then let it go, as well. Watching him, Beverly was suffused with love, glad she had risked everything in order to keep him safe.

After all, Tommie's father was, on average days, a very angry, dangerous man.

But now, with his wife and child gone, he was likely even worse.

13.

THE REST OF THE AFTERNOON was quiet. Tommie watched cartoons, and Beverly examined the paint cans stacked near the washer and dryer before locating not only a can of primer but at least half a can of yellow paint called Summer Daisy, which might not be the exact tint she would have chosen but was a thousand times better than god-awful orange. There was a beige she might be able to use in the living room, even if it was a bit bland, and an almost full can of glossy white for the kitchen cupboards. Kind of mind-boggling to find so much paint, but in a good way, like the house had been waiting all along for her and Tommie to claim it.

She took a closer look, too, at the paintbrushes and rollers. On closer inspection, they were obviously used but looked clean enough to suffice. And unless she wanted to make a trip to the hardware store and spend money she didn't have, they would have to do.

She brought everything she thought she'd need to the kitchen before starting dinner. Tonight would be chicken, boiled carrots, beans. She added extra carrots to Tommie's plate, but when he didn't finish them, she reached over, eating them one by one. Though Tommie wanted to turn on the television again after dinner, she instead suggested a game. She'd spotted a box of dominoes in the cabinet in the living room, and though it had been a long time since she'd played, she knew the rules were simple enough for Tommie to grasp. He did; he even beat her a couple of times. Once he began to yawn, she sent him upstairs for a quick bath. He was old enough to do it alone—he'd lately started reminding her about that—so she let him be. Since he didn't have pajamas, he slept in his underpants and the shirt he'd worn to school. She thought again about kids at school beginning to tease him and knew she'd have to find him something else to wear, as long as she could find bargains.

Money. She needed more money. Life always came down to money, and she felt her anxiety suddenly rise before forcing the feeling away. Instead, she sat with Tommie on his bed, read *Go, Dog. Go!* before tucking him in, and then retreated to the rockers on the front porch. Residual heat lingered from the day, making the evening pleasant; the air vibrated with the sounds of frogs and crickets. Rural sounds, country sounds. Sounds she remembered from her own childhood. Sounds she never heard in the suburbs.

As she rocked, she thought about the years she'd spent with Gary and how the sweet and charming demeanor that she'd fallen in love with changed within the first month of marriage. She remembered him sneaking up behind her to kiss her neck after she'd just poured a glass of wine. *White* wine, not red, and she'd collided with him when she turned. The wine splashed onto his shirt, one of his new ones, and though she'd apologized immediately, she'd laughed, as well, already planning to rinse the shirt before dropping it off at the dry cleaner's the following morning. She was about to flirt with him—*I guess I'll have to get you out of that shirt, handsome*—but even as the thought was forming, he slapped her across the face, the sound deafening and the sting intense.

And after that?

In retrospect, she knew she should have left then. Should have known that Gary was a chameleon, a man who had learned to hide his true colors. She wasn't naïve; she'd seen the TV specials and skimmed magazine articles about abusive men. But her desire to believe and trust had overridden her common sense. *That's not him,* she told herself. Gary apologized as he wept, and she'd believed him when he said he was sorry. She'd believed him when he said he loved her, that he'd simply reacted. She'd believed him when he said it would never happen again.

But because she'd become a living cliché, her life descended into one. Of course, he eventually slapped her again; in time, those slaps turned to punches. Always in the stomach or in the lower back, where the bruises couldn't be seen, even though the blows would leave her crumpled on the floor, struggling to breathe, her vision fading to a tunnel. In those moments, his face would turn red and the vein in his forehead would bulge as he screamed at her. He would throw plates and cups against the wall of the kitchen, leaving glass shattered around her. That was always the end of the cycle. The out-of-control anger. The shouting. The infliction of pain. But always, instead of ending for good, the cycle would begin anew. With apologies and promises and gifts like flowers or earrings or lingerie, and though she continued to hear the warning bells in her head, the sounds were drowned out by a burgeoning desire to believe that this time he'd changed. And for days and weeks, Gary would again be the man she married. They would go out with friends, and people would comment on their perfect marriage; her single girlfriends would tell her how lucky she was to have walked the aisle with a man like Gary.

Sometimes she even believed them. As time passed, she would remind herself not to do anything to make him angry. She would be the perfect wife and they would live in the perfect home, precisely the way he wanted it. She'd make the bed with the duvet straight and neat, the pillows fluffed just right. She'd fold and stack his clothes in the drawers, organized by color. She'd shine his shoes and line up the items in the cupboards. She'd make sure the television remote was on the coffee table and angled exactly toward the corner of the room. She knew what he liked—he made sure that she understood—and her days were spent doing all that was important to him. But just when she thought that the worst was behind her, something would happen. The chicken she cooked might be too dry, or he'd find towels still in the dryer, or one of the houseplants on the windowsill had begun to wilt, and his face would suddenly tighten. His cheeks would turn red, his pupils would grow smaller, and he'd drink more in the evenings, three or four glasses of wine instead of only one. And then the following days and weeks were akin to walking through a minefield, where a single misstep would lead to the inevitable explosion, followed by pain.

But that was an old story, right? Her story was the same as that of thousands, maybe even millions, of other women. Now she understood that there was something wrong with Gary, something that could never be fixed. And Gary had a sick and intuitive kind of radar, one that seemed to understand how far he could actually go. When she was pregnant, he hadn't laid a hand on her; he'd known she would leave him if he did anything to possibly hurt the baby. Nor had he touched her in the first few months after Tommie was born, when she was sleep-deprived. It was the only time during the marriage when she'd let her responsibilities in the house slide. She still cooked his meals and did his laundry and shined his shoes and kissed him the way he wanted, but sometimes the living room was cluttered when he came home from work, and sometimes Tommie had drool or spills on his clothing. It wasn't until Tommie was five or six months old that he slapped her again. On that night, Gary had bought her a negligé, the box wrapped with a pretty red bow. She'd always known that Gary liked to see her in negligés, just as he was particular when it came to sex. He always wanted her to whisper certain things, he wanted her hair and makeup done, he wanted her to beg for him to take her, he liked her to talk dirty. On that day, though, when he came home with the negligé, she was utterly exhausted. Tommie had cried inconsolably for much of the previous night, and it had continued while Gary was at work. By then she'd lowered her guard; by then she'd convinced herself that the anger and the shouting and the pain were behind her, so she told him that she was too tired. Instead, she promised to wear the negligé the following evening, and they could make it a special night. Which wasn't what Gary wanted. He wanted her that night, not the following night, and all at once she was blinking back tears, her cheek on fire with his handprint.

Again, the apologies. Again, the gifts in the aftermath. Again, the knowledge that she should have left. But where would she have gone? Back home, with her tail between her legs, so others could tell her that she'd made a mistake by getting married too young? That she'd made a mistake by falling in love with the wrong man? Even if she could face the endless judgment of others, he would find her there. *It would be the first place he'd look.* As for going to the police, Gary *was* the police, the most powerful police in the entire world, so who would believe her? More than that, there was also Tommie to think about. For a long time, Gary doted on Tommie. He talked to him and played with him and held Tommie's hands as Tommie began to toddle around the house. She knew how hard it was for children to grow up with only a single parent; she'd made a vow that she'd never do that to Tommie. That Gary wouldn't change diapers didn't seem all that important when he was willing to spend so much time with his son, to the point that Beverly sometimes felt neglected.

Beverly now understood that Gary was doing the same thing with Tommie that he'd done with her. He pretended to be someone other than who he really was. He pretended to be an ideal, loving father. But Tommie grew older and sometimes dropped a sharp toy that Gary would step on, or there would be puddles on the bathroom floor after Tommie took a bath. The anger inside Gary could hibernate, but it couldn't rest forever, and as Tommie aged, Gary saw increasing imperfections in his son. He recognized elements of Beverly in Tommie's personality. He became again the man he truly was. Beverly knew all about the stern voice and occasional shouts; what she hadn't expected were the bruises she began to find on Tommie's thighs and arms. As if Gary had squeezed too hard, or maybe even pinched his son.

She hadn't wanted to believe that Gary could do something like that. When Beverly did something wrong, Gary would tell her that she'd done it on purpose. But Tommie was just a little kid, and Gary had to understand that toddlers made mistakes, right? That nothing Tommie did that angered his father was done on purpose? Beverly went to the library, but the information she found wasn't much help. Oh, she'd read it all. Books, articles, tips from law enforcement, theories of psychologists and psychiatrists, and the reality was mixed. Sometimes an abusive husband also became abusive to his children, and sometimes he didn't.

But the strange bruises . . .

There was also the fact that Tommie had changed from a

laughing, smiling, and outgoing toddler to the quiet, introspective little boy she now knew. Tommie never admitted anything, but Beverly started to see fear in Tommie's expression when Gary's car pulled into the driveway after work. She saw a forced enthusiasm when Gary prodded his son to kick the ball around the yard. She also remembered how Tommie had fallen when he was learning to ride a bike a few months earlier. The training wheels should have kept him upright, but they hadn't, and Tommie cried in her arms with skinned knees and elbows while Gary ranted about how uncoordinated his son was. She remembered how, over time, Gary showed less interest in Tommie; she remembered how he began to treat Tommie more like property than simply a child to love. She remembered how Gary told her that she was spoiling Tommie and that he would grow up to be a mama's boy. She recalled that on Tommie's first day of kindergarten, Gary hadn't seemed to care about anything other than the fact that his eggs were overcooked at breakfast.

And the strange, unexplainable bruises . . .

Gary might be Tommie's father, but Beverly was his mother. She had carried him and delivered him. She'd breastfed him, and she was the one who had held him in her arms night after night until he finally learned to sleep more than a few hours at a stretch. She changed his diapers and cooked his meals and made sure he got his vaccinations and brought him to the doctor when his fever was so high that she'd been worried he might get brain damage. She helped him learn to dress himself and gave him baths and loved every minute of all those things, reveling in Tommie's innocence and continuing development, even as Gary continued his endless cycles of abuse with her, always in the hours after Tommie went to sleep.

In the end, she told herself, she'd had no choice but to do what she had. Law enforcement was out; going back home was out.

Anything associated with her previous life was out. She had to disappear, and leaving Tommie behind was inconceivable. If she wasn't around, on whom would Gary vent his anger?

She knew. In her soul, she knew exactly what would happen to Tommie, so when she made her plan to run, it was always for both of them, even if it meant that Tommie had to leave his friends and toys and pretty much everything else behind, so they could begin an entirely new life.

14.

DESPITE THE LATENESS OF THE HOUR, Beverly wasn't tired. She was bubbling with steady, nervous energy—probably because she'd been thinking about Gary—so she left the rocker and returned to the kitchen. Spying the cans of yellow paint and primer, she felt her spirits lift in spite of her memories. The kitchen would be so cheerful when she was finished. She turned on the radio, keeping the volume low so Tommie wouldn't wake up, but the music began to work its magic, drowning out her previous thoughts.

Now, with the world black beyond the windows, she remembered Tommie's smile while catching tadpoles and let herself believe that everything was going to be okay. Yes, there were challenges, but everyone had those, and people needed to learn to not sweat the small stuff, right? For the present she had food and shelter and safety and anonymity, Tommie was in school, and she'd figure out what to do about the money. She was smart and capable, and there was always someone who needed cleaning or cooking or babysitting or someone to read to them because their eyesight had declined with age. And Tommie would adapt. Even if he hadn't mentioned any new friends yet, he'd meet a boy or a girl in his class soon enough and they'd play at recess, because that's what little kids did. Little kids weren't caught up in who was who or what someone did or even if they wore the same clothes day after day. Kids just wanted to play. And Peg?

She laughed aloud at how silly she'd been as she exited the store, laughed that the idea had taken root at all. Not that she'd let her guard down, of course. Gary would have gotten the word out through government channels by now, distributing a suspect report or most-wanted listing, but it wasn't as though he could personally speak to every police officer or sheriff in the country. For the time being, she was just a name and an unfamiliar photo on a poster hanging on the wall of the post office or in some email inbox, along with images of terrorists or white suprema-cists or bank robbers. In a world where crime was rampant and people did awful things every single day, it simply wasn't possible for anyone in law enforcement to keep up with individual names and faces and descriptions from everywhere in the country. It was hard enough trying to keep up with the bad things that hap-pened locally.

What had she been thinking?

"I'm just making sure we're safe," she whispered.

She wished again that she'd brought more clothes for her and Tommie. In her closet . . . No, she corrected herself. It wasn't her closet, not anymore. In her *old* closet, she had a beautiful pair of Christian Louboutin pumps, with gorgeous red soles, the kind that celebrities wore at fancy galas or movie premieres. Gary had bought them for her birthday, and it was one of the few gifts she'd received without violence precipitating it. She'd never owned another pair like them. She probably could have squeezed them into her backpack, and maybe she should have. It might have been nice to slip them on every now and then, just to stare at them, like Dorothy in *The Wizard of Oz* with those ruby slippers, but then again, not really. It wasn't exactly the same, now that she thought about it, because the last thing she wanted was to return to the life she'd lived before. This was her new home, and she was standing in her new kitchen.

"And tomorrow the walls will be yellow," she whispered.

They needed another cleaning, though, so grabbing the same rag she'd used earlier, she began scrubbing again, taking her time, making sure the primer would stick. Cleaning and scrubbing, while the music sometimes made her feel like dancing. She could already imagine how pretty the kitchen would look when morning sunlight filtered through the windows.

It was late by the time she finished. Really late. For some people, it might even be considered morning, and because Beverly wanted to make sure she heard Tommie when he woke up, she lay down on the couch in the living room. Somehow she dozed off, like her brain simply decided to shut down, but she was awake even before she heard Tommie coming down the steps.

Gone was the relief from the night before. She didn't feel like she had after waking from the dream about the pirate or even when her mind had begun tumbling after Peg mentioned that she looked familiar. Rather, there was a low-level sense of dread, like an unpleasant hum, one that hinted she'd missed something important in her escape.

Gary would have found her identification and phone in the house, signaling her intent to stay off the grid. Without ID, she wouldn't be able to fly anywhere, so Gary's first stops would be the train and bus stations. She'd already known that, though, which were the reasons for her precautions. She'd also known there were a dozen buses headed in different directions that morning, and Gary would learn that, too, but since he had no idea when she'd left, she would be more difficult to trace. What would Gary do next?

He'd speak with the ticket sellers, but what would he learn? No one would remember a mother and son. No one would remember a long-haired blonde. After that, he'd probably start interviewing the bus drivers, but with so many possibilities that weekend, it would take time. He might, however, eventually stumble across her driver, but what would he learn? Again, no mother and son traveling together. He would also learn that the driver had been replaced with another and that no mother and son had either arrived at a destination or departed together. Even if either driver had seen her and Tommie sitting together by glancing in the rearview mirror—doubtful, since Tommie was so small—would the second driver remember exactly where and when they'd gotten off? Who could possibly remember such a thing, especially after the passage of time, with so many stops, with so many people getting on and off every step of the way? It would be akin to remembering a random face in a passing crowd.

She was safe, she decided, because she'd been careful. She was safe because she'd thought of everything, because she'd known exactly how Gary would conduct his search. And yet she could still feel the anxiety, inching upward inside her like bubbles rising through water, and when the realization suddenly came to her, it felt as though Gary himself had punched her in the stomach.

Cameras, she thought.

Oh God.

What if the bus stations had cameras?

PART III

Colby

I5.

In the morning, I went for a run beneath a cloudless Florida sky. The air was thick with humidity, and by the time I hit the beach, I had to strip off my shirt and use it as a makeshift bandanna to keep the sweat from pouring into my eyes.

I ran in the hard-packed sand near the water's edge, passing by Bobby T's and a string of motels and hotels, including the Don, before turning around and making my way back to my place. I wrung out my shirt, shorts, and socks before hopping in the shower to cool off. Afterward, all clothes went into the washer, and only after two cups of coffee did I feel ready to start the day.

Picking up my guitar, I spent the next couple of hours tweaking the song I'd sung for Morgan, thinking again that it was close but not exactly right and feeling that there was something special there, if only I could find it. As I continued to tinker, however, my thoughts kept returning to the question of whether I would ever see Morgan again.

I had lunch, went for a walk on the beach, then continued trying different variations on the song until it was time for me to leave for Bobby T's. Because it was Sunday, I didn't expect much of a crowd, but when I got there, every table was already filled. Scanning the audience, I noted that Morgan and her friends weren't there, and I did my best to ignore a pang of disappointment.

I played the first set—a mix of crowd favorites and my own songs—then rolled into the next set, and then the third, before I started taking requests. By the halfway point in the show, the crowd had grown. It wasn't quite the size of the Friday-night crowd, but there were a number of people standing, and more people continued to wander in from the beach.

With fifteen minutes to go, Morgan and her friends showed up. Somehow, despite the size of the crowd, they were able to find seats. I caught Morgan's eye, and she gave a little wave. When I had a single song left to play, I cleared my throat.

"This one's going out to those here to have a great time at the beach or pool," I called out with a special smile for Morgan, before launching into "Margaritaville." The crowd whooped and began to sing along. Before long I saw Morgan and her friends join in, which ended the show on a high note for me.

16.

By the time I finally set my guitar aside, the sun had gone down, leaving only a sliver of yellow at the horizon. While I began packing up, a few people from the crowd approached the stage, offering the usual compliments and questions, but I kept the conversation brief and made a beeline for Morgan and her friends.

As soon as I was close, I could see the delight in Morgan's expression. She was wearing white shorts and a yellow blouse with a wide scoop neck that showed off her sun-kissed skin.

"Cute," she said. "I assume you were directing that song at me and my friends? Because of what I mentioned they were drinking at the pool?"

"It seemed fitting," I agreed. The dim lighting at the bar cast her fine-boned face in moody shadow. "How was your day? What did you end up doing?"

"Not much. We slept in late, rehearsed for an hour and a half, and hung out by the pool. I think I got too much sun, though. My skin feels hot."

"What did you rehearse?"

"Our new dance routines. There are three songs, which is long for us. We're at the point where we know all our moves, but it takes a lot of repetition to make sure we're perfectly in sync."

"When will you film it?"

"This Saturday at the beach. Right behind the Don."

"You'll have to let me know what time so I can be there."

"We'll see," she chirped. "What are you doing now? Do you have plans?"

"I was thinking of getting something to eat."

"Would you like to come with us? We're going to Shrimpys Blues."

"Would your friends care?"

"It was their idea," she said with a grin. "Why do you think we were waiting for you?"

17.

I LOADED MY TRUCK while they called for an Uber in the parking lot. I figured I'd just follow their car, but Morgan jogged toward me while calling to her friends over her shoulder, "We'll meet you there!

"Assuming you don't mind, of course," she said as she reached me.

"Not at all."

I helped her into the truck, then got in on the other side. The Uber had already arrived, and her friends were squeezing into the back seat of the generic silver midsize sedan. As soon as it edged into traffic, I pulled out behind it.

"I have another question about your farm," she said.

"Seriously?"

"I find it interesting."

"What's your question?"

"If your chickens aren't in cages, why don't they run away? And how do you even find the eggs? Wouldn't they be all over the pasture? Like an Easter egg hunt?"

"We have fencing around the pastures, but chickens are social creatures, so they like staying near one another. Plus, they like the shade, which is also where their food and water is. As for the eggs, they're trained to use nesting boxes, which deposit the eggs in a drawer so we can collect them."

"You train your chickens?"

"You have to. When a new batch of chickens comes in, I stay with them, and whenever a chicken squats to lay an egg, I scoop it up and put it into the nesting box. Chickens generally prefer to lay their eggs in dark and quiet places, so once they're in the box, they think, *Oh, this is nice,* and they begin using it regularly after that."

"That is so cool."

"I guess. It's just part of the job."

"Do you do other farming things? Like . . . do you drive a tractor, too?"

"Of course. And I have to know how to repair them, too. I also have to do a lot of carpentry, plumbing, and even electrical work."

Her expression brightened. "Look at you. You're like a man's man. It must be nice to know that if there's ever a zombie apocalypse, you'll be one of the survivors."

I laughed. "I can't say that I've ever thought about it that way."

"It makes my life seem boring by comparison."

"I don't know about that."

"What's your sister like? I mean, I know she's an artist and you live together, but how would you describe her? In three words?"

I leaned back against the headrest, not sure how much I wanted to tell her, so I went with the basics. "Smart," I began. "Talented. Generous." Though I could have added that she was also a survivor, I didn't. Instead, I went on, explaining how Paige had mostly raised me, which was a big part of the reason we were so close.

"And your aunt?" she pressed.

"Tough. Hardworking. Honest. It wasn't easy for her after my uncle died, but once we started making changes at the farm, she became her old self again. The farm is pretty much her whole life now, but she loves it. Lately she's been trying to talk me into expanding into grass-fed organic beef, even though we've never raised cattle and I don't know a thing about it."

"That might be a good idea. People love having healthy options when they shop."

"Yeah, but there's a lot more to it. Having enough pastureland, for instance, or finding a good processor and arranging transportation, or choosing the right breeding lines, and finding customers, along with a zillion other things. It might be more hassle than it's worth."

Ahead of me, the silver midsize began to slow before pulling into the parking lot of the restaurant. When it came to a stop, I veered around it and found a spot.

Inside, the hostess led us to a booth in the back corner of the restaurant. As soon as we took our seats and after a few gushy compliments on my show, the interrogation began. Like Morgan, her friends couldn't believe I was a farmer, and they expressed the same curiosity that Morgan had about my daily activities. They also grilled me about my childhood, my family, and my years in the band. Between drinks and our meals, I managed to glean a few details about them, as well. Stacy had been raised in Indianapolis, had a boyfriend named Steve, and wanted to be a pediatrician; Holly was from a small town in Kentucky and had grown up playing practically every sport available. Maria hailed from Pittsburgh, had a boyfriend, as well, and nurtured a dream of working on *Dancing with the Stars*. "Realistically, though, I'll probably end up working at a dance studio and maybe open my own one day. Unless my mom lets me choreograph with her."

"Will she?"

"She says I still have a lot to learn." She rolled her eyes. "She's kind of a hard-ass that way."

Unlike Morgan, Maria had no compunction about showing me their TikTok page. She queued up a video of the four of them dancing and handed me her phone. When it concluded, she pulled up a second video, and then another.

"I think he gets it," Morgan interrupted, trying to reach for the phone.

"Just a few more," Maria protested, waving her off. I could see why they were popular; their performances featured K-pop–level choreography and were sexy in a fun but not over-the-top way. I wasn't sure what I'd been expecting, but I was definitely impressed.

The interrogation turned my way again after that; like Morgan, they were mainly interested in the chickens and tomatoes but frowned at the fact that the farm grew tobacco. And, as I'd done for Morgan, I told them about my rebellion and the band years and how I'd actually become a farmer in the first place. Morgan was clearly resigned to her friends' scrutiny of me; from time to time our eyes met and she seemed to be silently apologizing.

They refused to let me pay; instead, we all added money to the center of the table, enough to allow for a generous tip. I found myself thinking that each was as impressive, in her own way, as Morgan. Without exception, they were confident, ambitious, and self-possessed.

When we left the restaurant, Morgan and I trailed behind the others. Studying her in the doorway's muted pools of light, I had the feeling that if I ended up ever seeing her again, I was going to be in trouble.

"I like your friends," I remarked. "Thanks for letting me tag along."

"Thanks for being such a good sport," she said, giving my arm a quick squeeze.

"What's on your agenda tomorrow?"

"Nothing definite. I'm sure we'll rehearse in the morning, and we'll probably spend part of the day at the pool, but Holly also mentioned that she might want to go shopping or visit the Dalí." Then, as if suddenly realizing who she was talking to, she went on. "It's a museum in St. Petersburg devoted to the works of Salvador Dalí. He's a surrealist painter."

"My sister mentioned something about it," I said.

She must have heard something in my tone. "You're not interested?"

"I don't know enough about art to be either interested or uninterested."

She laughed that rumbling, deep laugh again. "At least you cop to it. How about you?"

"I haven't decided. I'll probably go for a run, but after that, who knows?"

"Will you write another song?"

"If something comes to me."

"I wish that happened to me. That songs just came to me. I have to struggle with it."

"I'd love to hear anything you've written. Especially now that I've seen you dance."

"Yeah," she said, "about that. Maria's really proud of our routines."

"She should be. You're all great. Had I known about you, I would have followed you like the other gazillion people."

Just then, a flash of headlights appeared, signaling the arrival of the girls' Uber. I saw Holly glancing at her phone and the car's license plate, confirming the match as they headed toward the car even before it came to a stop.

"If you'd like, I can give you a ride back to the hotel."

"I'm going to ride with my friends, but thanks." Then, after a beat, "I'm glad you had a chance to get to know them."

"For sure."

She stood there for a second more, apparently reluctant to leave. "I should probably go."

"Probably."

"We might come to your next show."

"I'd like that."

"And if you write another song, I want to be the first to hear it."

"I can do that." I had the sense we were both stalling. The next words came almost automatically. "Have you ever been kayaking?"

"Excuse me?"

"My friend Ray told me about this place where you can rent kayaks and paddle through the mangroves. He said it was a pretty cool thing to do."

"And why are you telling me this?"

"I was wondering if you'd like to go with me. Tomorrow, since you don't have anything officially planned, I mean."

It wasn't the smoothest way to ask a girl out, but in that moment it was all I could muster.

She put her hands on her hips. "What time are you thinking?"

"Nine or so? That way you can be back in time for the Dalí or the pool or whatever."

"Can you make it ten? Because of rehearsal?"

"Sure. How about we meet in the lobby?"

She touched my arm again, her gaze meeting mine. "I can't wait."

18.

IF ANYONE HAD TOLD ME before I came here that I'd go on a date when I was in St. Pete Beach, I would have laughed. But as I watched Morgan leave, I couldn't help feeling pleased, even as I wondered what I was getting myself into.

There was something . . . *charismatic* about her. The word popped into my head as they drove away, and the more I thought about it, the more apt the description became. While much of what I'd learned about her amplified the differences between us, it struck me that I was the only one who seemed concerned about it. Somehow the fact that we both loved music was common ground enough for her. For now, anyway. Or at least enough for a first date.

But where was it leading? That was the part I couldn't figure out. Was it a serious first step, or were we moving toward a simple fling? I'm sure a lot of guys would have been happy with the latter, and with anyone else, I might have been.

But I was drawn to Morgan in ways that felt deeper than that.

I liked her, I thought, then suddenly shook my head, knowing that wasn't quite right.

I liked her a lot.

19.

I DON'T THINK IT WAS nerves, but whatever the reason, I woke at dawn and couldn't go back to sleep. Instead, I went for an early-morning run, then tidied up the condo. After my shower, I swung by the grocery store to replenish the snacks and drinks in my cooler.

Assuming I'd get wet, I threw shorts on over a bathing suit, grabbed a spare T-shirt, and wiggled into my flip-flops. By then it was half past nine and I started for the hotel.

The lobby of the hotel was as grand as the rest of the pink palace, bustling in the morning sunlight. Checking my phone, I noted a text from Ray informing me that I'd be starting at four tomorrow instead of five, which meant I'd be playing an extra hour—no big deal; I responded that I'd be there on time. When Morgan finally appeared, she was dressed casually, a turquoise bikini peeking out beneath a white halter and faded denim shorts. She had a Gucci beach tote slung over her shoulder and a pair of expensive sunglasses perched in her hair.

"Hey there," she said. "Sorry I'm a little late, but I wasn't sure what to wear."

"I think you'll be fine," I assured her. "Do you have everything?"

When she nodded, I swept my arm toward the door, and a minute later we were rolling down the long, ramped drive.

"How did rehearsal go?"

"Same as always. Just when I think we're almost there, Maria notices something else we still need to work on."

"Where do you rehearse? I haven't seen you on the beach in the mornings when I'm out for my run."

"We use one of the conference rooms on the main floor. We're probably not supposed to, but no one at the hotel has complained yet."

"So, you're saying you're a rule breaker?"

"Sometimes," she offered. "Isn't everyone?"

"I wouldn't have guessed that about you."

"There's still a lot about me that you don't know."

"Care to share?"

"Only if you ask the right questions."

"All right." I pretended to ponder the possibilities. "Tell me about your previous boyfriend."

"I never told you that I had a boyfriend."

"Then consider me a good guesser."

"What do you want to know?"

"Anything. What was he like? How long did you go out?"

She sighed. "He was pre-law, two years older than me, and we met during my freshman year. But I was very involved with music and dance and my classes, and I wanted to hang with my friends, too. He had trouble understanding that. He'd get upset when I wasn't able to spend as much time with him as he wanted, or he'd suggest that I blow off piano practice or whatever, and it began to irritate me. So after a couple of months I ended it, and that was that. How about you? Tell me about your ex-girlfriend. Or maybe it's just . . . girlfriend?" She gave me a sidelong look.

"Definitely an ex," I assured her, before giving her the brief rundown on Michelle, our incompatible schedules, and her eventual move out of town. While listening, Morgan absently polished the lenses of her sunglasses with her halter, her expression serious.

"Do you regret that it didn't work out?"

"Maybe a little, at first. Not so much anymore."

"I never regretted breaking it off," she said.

"It's good to know you can dump someone without a care in the world."

"He deserved it."

"It was his loss."

She smiled. "By the way, my friends approve of you. They think you're nice, even if they're still not a hundred percent sure it was a good idea for me to join you today."

"They could have tagged along."

"It's not that they're afraid you're going to do anything," she explained. "It's just that I'm the youngest, and sometimes I think they feel they have to watch out for me."

"Like your parents?"

"Exactly. According to them, I've led a sheltered life, which makes me a bit naïve."

"Are they right?"

"Probably a little," she admitted with a laugh. "But I think most people in college are naïve. It sort of goes with the territory, especially if you grew up in a nice neighborhood and had a good family. What do any of us really know about the real world, right?

Of course, if I said that to my friends, they would add that I'm also being defensive."

I glanced over at her. "For what it's worth, you don't strike me as naïve," I said. "You carry Mace, after all."

"I think they're talking about my emotions."

I wasn't sure what to say to that, so instead, I steered the conversation to easier topics. We talked about movies and songs we liked, and after I explained how my uncle had taught me to play the guitar, she told me that she knew the words to practically every song in half a dozen Disney movies even before she started school. She talked to me about her years in dance and the concerts she'd performed and raved about her private vocal coach in Chicago. Even in college, she'd traveled to see him every other week, despite the other time-consuming requirements of her major. When she finally mentioned the names of the managers she would meet in Nashville and the singers they represented—as well as their strengths and weaknesses—along with the vagaries of the music business in general, I thought again that Morgan was a lot more than a pretty face. There was a sophistication to her that I'd never seen in someone so young, and I was struck by the realization that my own attempts at chasing my dream had paled in comparison. While she'd been thoughtfully building her skills one step at a time and laying the groundwork for later success, I'd just been having fun.

Strangely, I wasn't jealous about that, nor was I jealous that she'd had advantages and opportunities that I didn't. Instead, I was happy for her, mainly because I remembered how much the dream had once meant to me. I also simply liked listening to her talk, and I realized the more I learned about her, the more I wanted to know.

When we reached Fort De Soto Park, I followed the signs and parked in a gravel lot near a wooden shack that offered kayaks for rent. Both of us got out of the truck and headed toward the attendant, who took the cash and handed each of us a paddle and a life preserver.

"If you have suits, you might want to leave your clothes in the truck," he suggested as he put the money in the register. "Unless you don't mind being wet when you drive back to wherever you're going."

Back at the truck, I did my best not to stare as Morgan stripped to her bikini. I set her clothes and mine on the front seat and grabbed my sunglasses and a baseball hat out of the glove compartment. I watched as Morgan placed her phone into a waterproof case, something I hadn't even thought to bring.

"Do you need sunscreen?" she asked, reminding me of something else I'd forgotten. "I brought some if you didn't."

"If you wouldn't mind."

She squeezed the tube, dispensing lotion into my hand, which I smeared all over my arms and face.

"Do you want me to get your back?" she asked.

I wasn't about to say no—I liked the thought of her hands on me—so I nodded, and soon enough I felt the lotion being spread on my skin, a sensation more intimate than she probably assumed it was. "Do you need me to get your back, too?" I asked.

"I had Maria do it earlier, but thanks."

When we were done, we put on the life jackets and carried the paddles toward the kayaks, which were already at the water's edge. The attendant gave us a quick lesson about how to hold the paddles, the importance of long, smooth strokes, and how to paddle backward to help change direction. Finally, he issued directions to a channel that led through the mangroves.

"Will we capsize?" Morgan fretted as she stared out at the water.

"These kayaks are pretty wide, so I wouldn't worry," the man said. "Hop in and I'll give you a shove."

We each climbed into our own kayak, feeling it bobble slightly. At the man's instruction, I bent my knees slightly and watched Morgan glide backward toward me after her kayak was launched. We turned and started paddling over the glassy water.

"It hardly wobbles at all," Morgan announced, sounding surprised.

"That's because you weigh fifty pounds."

"I weigh a lot more than that."

"How much more?"

"I'm definitely not going to answer that question."

I chuckled, both of us settling in to enjoy the scenery. There were puffy clouds in the distance, but the sky was electric blue overhead, turning the water into a brilliant mirror. In the foliage we saw terns and ospreys, while turtles sunned themselves on partially submerged logs.

Beside me, Morgan paddled, effortlessly graceful.

"So . . . is this what you do on your dates back in North Carolina? Bring girls out to experience nature?"

"I've never been kayaking, either."

"That didn't answer my question."

"I live in a small town. There's not much to do other than enjoy nature. The river, a trip to the beach, walking trails through the forests. It's not like there are a lot of clubs and bars where I live."

Up ahead, a fish jumped, and Morgan pointed with her paddle.

"What kind of fish is that?"

"I'm guessing it's a tarpon, but I can't be certain. They're supposed to be great fishing because they put up a good fight."

"Do you fish?"

"I've been a few times, but it's not my thing. Believe it or not, Paige enjoys it more than I do, but don't ask me where she learned. It's not something we did a lot when we were kids."

"What's it like living with your sister? I don't think I know any brothers and sisters who live together as adults."

Again, I wondered how much to tell her, before realizing it wasn't the right time. "I know it might seem odd to other people," I admitted. "Sometimes it seems odd to me, too. But then again, I've never lived alone, so I guess I'm just used to it. I don't really think about it that much."

"My sister and I are pretty close, too, but I don't know if I want to live with her in a few years."

"You said before that she's nothing like you, but what does that mean?"

"She couldn't care less about music or singing or dance or piano. She's always been a gifted athlete, ever since she was little. She was a natural at every sport—soccer, softball, junior Olympics in track, and then finally volleyball, which turned out to be her passion. She was recruited by a dozen different colleges and will be starting at Stanford in the fall. It doesn't hurt that she's almost six feet tall and a straight-A student, of course."

"She is tall. . . ."

"I know. She gets it from my mom's side. I've always been the runt of the litter in my family."

"It must be such a challenge for you," I offered, with a mock sad face. "If I had my guitar, I'd play you a mournful song."

"Oh, shut up," she retorted, splashing a little water on me with her paddle, making me duck.

We continued our easy paddling, enjoying the stillness. After a while, remembering the directions, I kept my eyes peeled for the opening that led to the channel through the mangroves. Eventually I spotted it and steered toward it. At the mouth, it was nine or ten feet wide, but it narrowed quickly, making it difficult for us to paddle side by side.

"Do you want to go first or should I?"

She hesitated. "Normally I'd ask you to go first, in case there's a bear or a giant python or whatever. But I might want you in the back in case I tip over. So you don't leave me behind."

"I wouldn't leave you behind," I protested. "Besides, I don't think there are any bears here. And you're probably not heavy enough to tip over the kayak even if you tried."

"Which only leaves me worried about giant pythons."

"I'm pretty sure that won't be an issue, either. But just so you know, it's usually the second or third person in line that gets attacked by a snake. The first one is already past the snake by the time it realizes what's happening and gets ready to strike."

"Then by all means, I'll lead the way."

I smiled, following a few feet behind her. Within a minute, the channel had narrowed even more and the branches above us formed something akin to a tunnel. The water was as smooth as a tabletop, the air cooled by the shade. Watching Morgan paddle, I noted that she moved with the unbroken ease of the dancer she was. In the trees on either side of us, crabs scurried on the branches. I was watching one of them when I heard her calling out to me.

"Are you still there?"

"I'm right behind you."

"Just making sure."

I don't know how long the channel was, but we remained beneath the tunneled canopy of branches for ten or fifteen minutes. Occasionally she would point to something she'd seen—usually a crab or cluster of crabs—and call out to check if I was still behind her, which struck me as silly, because it would have been nearly impossible to turn around even if I wanted to. Mostly, though, we paddled in silence in what seemed to be another world, both eerie and serene.

In time, the channel began to widen, more sunlight broke through the canopy, and, with a few more strokes, we emerged into a large estuary.

"That was awesome," Morgan said, her eyes wide. "For a few minutes there, it felt like I was lost in time."

"I had the same feeling."

"Where are we?"

"I have absolutely no idea."

"Do you know how to get back?"

"Same way we got here, I guess."

The sun had risen in the sky, and the sudden lack of shade made it feel even more intense. Morgan rested her paddle in her lap and continued taking in the scenery while I did my best not to stare at her exposed skin, glistening with a delicate sheen of sweat.

The current was weak but enough to allow our kayaks to drift farther apart. When I dipped my paddle into the water to close the gap, I noticed a shadow in the water maybe six feet behind Morgan. From my angle, it looked like a log or a rock, but strangely it also seemed to be moving.

A few quick strokes and I zipped past her. As soon as I peered over the side of my kayak into the water, I realized what I was seeing.

"What are you doing?" Morgan asked, rotating her kayak.

"It's a manatee," I responded in a hushed voice.

The top of it was maybe a yard below the surface, and I watched its huge, wide flippers paddle almost in slow motion. By then Morgan was approaching, excitement and apprehension in her expression.

"Are they dangerous?"

"No, but it's probably illegal to get too close. I don't know for sure, though."

"I want to see," she said, paddling in my direction. I leaned over and grabbed her kayak, slowing it until it stopped. Morgan stared into the water.

"It's huge!" she whispered.

I had no idea how big manatees generally were, but it seemed to be only a little shorter in length than our kayak, maybe the size of a small hippo. Though they sometimes appeared in North Carolina, sightings were rare, and I'd never been that lucky. As I watched, Morgan found her phone and started to take photos. Examining them, she frowned.

"You can't see it very well. It looks like a big gray blob."

"Should I hop out and see if I could nudge it even closer to the surface?"

"Can you do that?"

"Not a chance."

I watched as she rolled her eyes, then she suddenly got excited. "Oh wow! It's surfacing! Can you push my kayak a bit?"

Using my paddle, I gave her kayak a gentle shove; she closed the distance to the manatee. Even though I was farther away, I realized that it did indeed seem to be rising. The amorphous shape began to clarify, revealing its head and the wide, circular fluke as it rotated first in one direction, then the opposite. My eyes drifted from it to Morgan, who was busy taking pictures as I maneuvered my kayak.

"It keeps moving farther away!" she lamented.

I used my oar to push her again. After a few more photos, she lowered the camera.

"Do you think we're bothering it?"

"I'm sure they see kayaks out here all the time." From the corner of my eye, I noticed another shadow off to the right.

"I think we're about to have company. There's another one."

It was slightly smaller than the first one, and Morgan squinted to make it out.

"Do you think they're related? Like a mama and her baby?" she asked.

"I haven't the slightest idea."

"Will there be more? Like, do they usually swim in pods or whatever they're called?"

"Why do you keep asking me these questions? I'm a farmer from North Carolina. I know nothing about manatees."

Her eyes flickered with mirth. "Would you mind taking off your glasses while I've got my phone out? And lifting the brim of your hat?"

"Why?"

"I want a photo of you in the kayak. You look all sporty."

I complied and she took a photo, though the way her thumb was moving, it was probably closer to a dozen. She immediately scrolled through them. "Okay, perfect. There are some good ones here."

We stayed with the manatees until they started migrating toward deeper water. Taking that as our cue to head back, I led the way to the opening.

"Do you want to go first or should I?"

"You lead this time. But like I told you before, don't leave me behind."

"What kind of guy do you think I am?"

"I'm still processing that question, but I promise to let you know the answer as soon as I do."

I grinned, heading into the mangroves, paddling slowly and peeking over my shoulder regularly to make sure I wasn't going too fast. Meanwhile, Morgan kept up a stream of unanswerable questions about manatees. Did I think the two manatees were going to mate? When was the mating season? Did they spend most of their time in places like this or in the open ocean? In response, I told her that I'd google the answers and get back to her. To which she said, "Stop for a second."

I did, rotating in my kayak. She had her phone out and was tapping, then began to scroll. "Manatees can weigh up to twelve hundred pounds," she read aloud, "and they breed year-round, but most are born in the spring and summer. They generally inhabit marshy, coastal areas like this and can be found as far north as Virginia. They demonstrate abilities similar to dolphins', so they're smart. From the pictures on the Web, it looks like a pudgy dolphin crossed with a miniature whale."

"Look at you, helping the uninformed."

"Glad I could be of service," she said. "Lead on."

We continued to backtrack, and about halfway we encountered two kayakers approaching from the opposite direction. We moved to the right while ducking our heads, the other kayakers veered left and ducked as well, but there were still only inches between us when they floated past.

We finally emerged into the wider channel again, then further retraced our journey, talking easily, both of us recounting some of our favorite childhood antics. As we approached the shore, the attendant spotted us and directed us in, pulling our kayaks onto the hard wet dirt. I felt a bit stiff getting out, but Morgan seemed perfectly limber as we walked back to the truck.

Reaching into the cab, Morgan pulled out her tote.

"Turn around and don't peek," she warned, stepping away and leaving a whiff of coconut oil in the air. "My bottoms are wet, and I want to change into my shorts."

I did as she asked and, at her signal, turned around and saw that she had also pulled her halter over her top.

"My turn," I said, and we traded places; I changed into my dry shorts and tossed my wet suit into the truck bed. Morgan chose to keep her bikini bottoms on the seat beside her, and I noted that they were so small, I could have hung them from the rear-view mirror.

I asked the attendant for directions to a picnic area, which turned out to be only a few minutes away. As I drove, I saw Morgan scrolling through her photos.

"I'm not sure whether I like the photos of the manatees better or the ones of you."

"Hmm," I said, tilting my head. "Is that a compliment or an insult?"

"Neither. I can always get more pictures of you, but I doubt that I'll see another manatee while I'm here."

"Are you hungry?"

"A little," she said. "I had breakfast, so it's not like I'm starving."

"What did you have?"

"A green tea before rehearsal and a green drink afterward."

I nodded, even though I didn't have the slightest idea of what a green drink was.

I slowed the truck when I saw the picnic tables, then pulled into the parking area. None of the tables were occupied, and I zeroed in on one in the shade of a tree I couldn't name but assumed was some sort of oak. Climbing out, I retrieved the cooler from the bed of the truck and started toward it, Morgan beside me. I plunked the cooler on the table and slid open the lid before pulling out grapes, nuts, cheese, and crackers, along with two crisp apples.

"I wasn't sure what you might want, so I picked stuff at random."

She reached for an apple. "This will be perfect," she said. "Did you bring anything to drink?"

"Iced teas and water."

"Did you happen to get a tea that's sugar- and caffeine-free?"

"Actually, I did." I handed the appropriate bottle to her, and she glanced at the label.

"Pomegranate and hibiscus," she read. "Well done."

Taking a seat, I cracked open a bottle of water, then reached for the nuts and the cheese. After a quick debate, I took some of the grapes and the other apple, as well.

"Unlike you, I didn't have breakfast. I'm starved."

"Eat what you want. You brought it all. I just wish you would have brought cookies, too. I'd love a good homemade cookie. Or even a couple of Oreos."

"You eat cookies?"

"Of course I eat cookies. Doesn't everyone?"

"You don't look like you eat cookies."

She rolled her eyes. "Okay, yes, I generally try to eat nutritious food, but I also have a crazy metabolism, so if I want a cookie or two, I'm going to enjoy it. If you ask me, there's way too much pressure on women to be thin instead of strong and healthy. I knew too many girls growing up who had eating disorders."

Once again, I was struck by not only her self-assurance but her thoughtfulness—especially for someone not long out of her teenage years—and I thought about those things while I opened the nuts and peeled the wrapper from the cheese. Morgan sipped her tea and ate her apple while we settled into easy conversation. I asked her about her hobbies and interests outside of music; I also answered a few more questions about the farm. In time, we settled into silence. Other than the sound of birdcall, there was nothing, and I realized that I liked the fact that she didn't feel the need to break the spell.

She took another sip of her tea, then I felt her eyes focus on me with renewed attention. "I have a question, but you don't have to answer."

"Ask whatever you'd like."

"How did your mom die? I'm guessing it was cancer or an accident of some sort? Since she was obviously young?"

I said nothing right away. I'd known the question would come, because it almost always did. Usually I tried to deflect or give a vague answer, but I realized I wanted Morgan to know.

"My mom had always been a sad person, even as a teenager," I began. "According to my aunt, anyway. She thinks it was depression, but from what I've been able to piece together since then, I'm pretty sure my mom was bipolar. I guess it doesn't really matter, though. For whatever reason, when she was feeling particularly low, she slit her wrists in the bathtub. Paige was the one who found her."

Morgan's hand flew to her mouth. "Oh my God. That's awful! I'm so sorry. . . ."

I nodded, momentarily flashing to the past, some memories vivid, other parts hazy to the point of disappearing. "We'd just come from school, and when we called for our mom, there was no answer. I guess Paige went to the bedroom to try to find her—I don't really remember that part. But I do remember Paige grabbing me by the hand and dragging me over to the neighbor's house. After that, I remember the police cars and the ambulance and all the neighbors standing outside. I don't remember my aunt and uncle coming to get us, but I guess they had to have been there to take us to the farm."

"Poor you," she whispered, her face pale. "Poor Paige. I can't imagine finding my mom like that. Or even seeing something like that."

"For sure."

She was quiet before reaching for my hand. "Colby, I'm sorry for asking you about it. We were having such a nice day and I had to blow it."

I shook my head, comforted by the warmth of her hand atop my own. "You didn't blow it. Like I told you, it was a long time ago, and I don't remember much. And besides, no matter what happens, I'm not going to forget that we saw manatees when we were out in the kayaks today."

"So you forgive me?"

"There's nothing to forgive," I insisted.

She studied me from across the table, as though trying to decide whether she believed me. Finally, she let go of my hand and reached for the grapes, pulling off a small bunch. "The manatee *was* pretty cool," she said, obviously attempting to change the subject. "Both of them were. It almost felt like we were on the nature channel."

I smiled. "What would you like to do now? Should I get you back to your friends so you can head to the Dalí or go shopping?"

"You know what I'd really like to do?" She leaned forward, resting her arms on the picnic table.

"No idea."

"I'd like to watch you write a song," she said.

"Just like that? You think I can turn it on and off like a faucet?"

"You're the one who told me that things just come to you."

"What if nothing has come to me since the last one?"

"Then maybe think about how you felt when you saw the manatee."

I squinted, skeptical. "That's not really enough."

"Then how about the two of us having a picnic?"

"I'm not sure that's enough, either."

At last, she rose from the table. She walked to my side and leaned over; before I realized what was happening, her lips pressed lightly against my own. It wasn't a big kiss or even a particularly passionate kiss, but it was tender, and I could taste a hint of apple on lips so soft they seemed almost perfect. She pulled back with a slight smile on her face, knowing she'd caught me off guard.

"How about a song about a glorious morning and first kiss, then?"

I cleared my throat, reeling a bit from what had just happened. "Yeah," I said. "That might work."

20.

On the drive back to the condo, Morgan texted her friends furiously between occasional bouts of small talk.

"Keeping your friends up-to-date?" I asked.

"I told them we saw a manatee. Sent them pics."

"Are they jealous?"

"They're shopping, so I doubt it. After that, they're planning to laze by the pool."

"No Dalí?"

"I guess not. And they also mentioned visiting Busch Gardens in Tampa tomorrow."

"That sounds fun."

"Do you want to join us? We were thinking about heading out right after rehearsal, maybe around ten or so? And spend the day there?"

"My show is at four tomorrow, so I can't."

"Aww . . ." she said, sounding more disappointed than I'd expected.

Though we kept the conversation light on the drive, my mind

kept returning to the kiss and what, if anything, she'd meant by it. Was she really just trying to inspire a song? Had she felt bad about bringing up my mom? Or did she actually want to kiss me because she was attracted to me? As much as I tried, I couldn't figure it out, and Morgan had been no help at all. Right after she'd pulled back from the kiss, she popped a grape into her mouth and returned to her spot across from me, as though nothing had happened. She then asked me my zodiac sign. When I told her I was a Leo, she noted that she was a Taurus, casually mentioning that people from those two signs find it difficult to get along with each other. She said it with a laugh, however, leaving me even more confused.

At the condo, I pulled into my usual parking spot, then grabbed the cooler and started up the wooden steps to the second floor. Morgan trailed behind me with her bag over her shoulder, our flip-flops slapping in unison.

"I don't know why, but I thought you were renting a place right on the beach."

"Not all of us have doctor parents who pay for accommodations."

"That may be true, but you also said it was your first real vacation in years. It might have been worth springing for someplace with a sunset view."

"I didn't need one. I'm singing on the beach, so I get to see amazing sunsets all the time. This place is mainly for sleeping and changing and doing my laundry."

"And writing songs," she added.

"Only when the mood strikes."

As I opened the door, I was thankful I'd tidied it up earlier and equally thankful I'd kept the air-conditioning on. It was hot and growing steadily warmer, the approaching summer already making its presence known.

I set the cooler inside the door, feeling nervous in a way I hadn't expected. "Can I get you a drink? Water or beer? I think there's another tea left in the cooler if you want that instead."

"I'll take a tea," she said.

I pulled another tea out, and grabbed a bottle of water for myself. I watched as she twisted off the cap while checking out the living room.

"It's nice here. I like the decor."

It was standard Florida Beach Vacation Rental, with functional, inexpensive furniture, pastel pillows, and garage-sale-quality paintings of fish and boats and beaches hanging on the walls.

"Thanks," I said. When I booked it, I'd barely perused the photos because I was mainly focused on the price.

She motioned to the music equipment and guitar heaped in the corner near the couch. "So this is where it happens, huh?"

"I usually sit on the couch, but really I can write anywhere as long as I can play the guitar while I do it."

She placed her tea on the coffee table, then gingerly took a seat on the couch. She leaned back, then sat forward, shifting around on the cushions.

"What on earth are you doing?" I asked.

"I'm trying to catch whatever it is you have that makes writing songs so easy."

I shook my head. "You're funny."

"I'm a lot of things," she said. "But I also have a confession to make. I brought some of my work with me today. A song I've been working on, I mean. I have most of the lyrics and some of the music, I think, but I was wondering if you'd listen to what I've done. I'd like to get your impressions."

"Show me what you've got," I said, feeling a bit honored. I grabbed my guitar and took a seat next to her on the couch.

Meanwhile, Morgan set her phone on the coffee table before rummaging through her bag. She pulled out a spiral notebook, the kind high school and college students used. When she saw me staring at it, she shrugged.

"I like to use pen and paper," she said. "Don't judge me."

"I'm not judging." I leaned over to the end table and waved my own notebook at her. "I do the same thing."

She smiled at that before setting the notebook on her lap. "Showing this to you makes me nervous."

"Why?"

"I don't know. Maybe because you're so talented?"

At first, I wasn't sure how to respond. Finally: "You don't need to be nervous. I already think you're amazing."

I wasn't sure where the words had come from; they seemed to have formed without conscious thought. For a moment, noting how she dropped her gaze, I wished I hadn't said it, before realizing that she might actually be blushing. Not wanting to push, I drew a long breath.

"What genre of music are you interested in?" I asked. "And what kind of song are you thinking?"

I watched her shoulders drop a little before answering. "Right now I'm mostly interested in country-pop. Like early Taylor Swift? But probably more pop than country, if that makes any sense."

"What have you got so far?"

"I have the top-line melody and some of the lyrics for the chorus. But I'm struggling with everything else."

"All songs have to start somewhere. Do you have the music written down?"

"I made a recording on my phone. On the piano." She opened the notebook to the appropriate page, then handed it to me and pointed. "Right here," she said, before reaching for her phone.

After a beat, she pulled up the recording. "This is just for the chorus, okay?"

"Got it."

She pressed PLAY, and after a couple of seconds, piano chords in a minor key rang out, making me sit up and lean in. I assumed that I'd hear her singing on the recording, but she'd only recorded the piano accompaniment. Leaning toward me, her finger on the page with the scribbled lyrics, she whisper-sang along with the melody, almost as if she was embarrassed to be heard.

There wasn't much to the song at that point—maybe ten or fifteen seconds—but it was indeed enough to remind me of something Taylor Swift might have written when she was starting out. It mirrored the thoughts of a woman who, after a breakup, realizes that she's better than ever and is flourishing on her own. Not a new idea, but one that would resonate with an audience—particularly females—since it spoke to the universal truth of accepting oneself. It was a theme that never grew old, especially when set to a hooky melody that would make everyone want to sing along.

"What do you think?" she asked.

"It's a fantastic start," I said. "I really like it."

"You're just saying that."

"I'm not," I said. "What were you thinking of after this? Music or lyrics?"

"That's kind of where I'm stuck. I've tried a lot of things, but nothing seems to be working. It's like because I'm not sure of the lyrics, I'm not sure about the music, and vice versa."

"That's common in the early stages."

"What do you do when it happens to you?"

"I start trying things, without editing or judging myself. I think it's important to give every idea that comes to me a shot, no matter how weird," I said. "So let's do that, okay?"

I listened to the recording again, following along with the lyrics. I listened a third, then a fourth time, absently strumming my guitar. When I shut off the recording and played the music on my guitar alone, I let my instincts take over. Morgan stayed quiet as variations began to sprout and overlap in my head. I strung together a few new chords to follow the chorus, but they didn't feel right—too generic. I tried again, but the next attempt felt awkward. I kept noodling and experimenting for a while, forgetting Morgan's presence as I searched for those critical few bars. Eventually I found the chord progression that seemed to work, then tricked out the rhythm to give it more syncopation. I stopped and played it again and was suddenly sure that the song could be very commercial—maybe even a hit. I ran through it again with greater confidence, catching Morgan's eye. Before I could ask what she thought, she clapped her hands, bouncing a little in her seat.

"Wow!" she exclaimed. "That was amazing!"

"You like it?" I grinned.

"I love it, but watching you and your process was the best part. Hearing you experiment until you found what worked."

"I only just started."

"You've been playing for almost twenty minutes."

As usual, time had stopped for me while I lost myself in the music. "But you're sure you liked it?"

"Loved it. And it even gave me some new ideas for the lyrics."

"Like what?" I asked.

She launched into the story she wanted to tell and the feeling she wanted to capture. She improvised a couple of catchy phrases that struck me as defiant yet upbeat with a definite hook, and I found myself wondering why I hadn't gone in that direction. We also played around with the tempo and rhythm, and as we brainstormed I could tell she had far more of a gift than she gave herself credit for. Her instinct for commercial music was well honed, and when she broke down the lyrics and the melody for the first stanza, the floodgates opened and the song took on a momentum of its own. An hour passed, then another. As we worked, I could feel her excitement growing. "Yes!" she'd exclaim. "Just like that!" Or "Can you try something like this?" while humming a bar or two. Or "How about this for the lyrics?" And every now and then, she'd have me sing the song from the beginning. She sat close to me, her leg warm against my own as she scribbled lyrics in the notebook, crossing out rejected words or phrases. Little by little we worked our way to the finish, fading out in the same minor key in which the song opened. By the time we stopped, the sky beyond the sliding glass door had turned from blue to white, shot through with pink highlights. When she turned to me, she couldn't hide her joy.

"I can't believe it."

"It went well," I said, meaning it.

"I still want to hear it one more time from the beginning. I want to record the whole thing in one go, too, so I don't forget."

"You won't forget."

"You might not, but I'm taking no chances." She snapped a photo of the lyrics, then readied the phone for a recording. "Okay," she concluded, "let's hear it from the top."

"How about you sing this time, instead of me? It's your song."

"It's our song," she protested. "I couldn't have done it without you."

I shook my head. "That's where you're wrong. I might have clarified your thoughts, but it was your idea, your story, and, for the most part, your music. That song has been inside you for a while. All I did was help you allow it to come out."

Her expression was skeptical. "I think you're wrong."

"Read the lyrics," I insisted, tapping the page. "Show me one line that was all mine."

She knew there weren't any; I might have added a few words here and there, but that was more about editing than creating, and she'd come up with the hook and the easily remembered phrases.

"Okay, but the music was really yours."

"You had it all, you just needed help breaking the logjam. Every phrase and key change, you led." I pressed on. "Morgan, I've never written a country-pop song before. It's not what I do. Trust me—this song is yours, not ours. We both know it's a song I'd never be able to write, if only because I'm a guy."

"That I do accept," she said, laughing in agreement before growing quiet again. "I still can't believe how fast it all came together," she murmured. "I've been working on that song on and off for weeks. I'd almost given up, until today."

"That happens to me, too," I admitted, nodding. "I've finally accepted the idea that songs come only when they're ready to come, never before that. I'm just glad I could be part of it."

She smiled before placing a hand on my knee. "Thank you," she said, her voice husky with—what? Gratitude? Wonder? "This was . . . the best learning experience I've ever had."

"You're welcome. And now I want to hear you sing it."

"Me?"

"It's your song. You should sing it."

"It's been a long day," she demurred. "My voice will sound tired."

"Stop making excuses."

While she hesitated, her hand remained on my knee, its warmth spreading through me.

"Okay," she relented, clearing her throat. Removing her hand, she reached for the notebook. "Just give me a little bit to get ready."

I watched as she rose from the couch and moved to the center of the room. "Hit the RECORD button when I'm ready, okay?" she directed.

She clasped her hands in front of her, as though steeling herself. When she finally raised the notebook and nodded, I pressed RECORD on her phone, then set it on the coffee table between us.

At the sound of the opening bars, Morgan seemed to come alive. Her limbs suddenly loosened; her face glowed as if incandescent. Before she reached the end of the first stanza, I was electrified.

Adele, Taylor, or Mariah had nothing on the voice emerging from the petite young figure before me. Her range and control were incredible, and her sound was *huge*. I couldn't believe that delicate frame could produce the deep, soulful sound of a diva in her prime. I was stunned. Forcing myself to concentrate on the accompaniment, I struggled to make sure I didn't miss a cue. Morgan's performance, on the other hand, appeared effortless, as though she'd been singing the song for years. She made adjustments on the fly, riffing on the lyrics and rounding out the chorus with trills and vibrato I hadn't anticipated. Her presence filled the room—yet as she stared into my eyes, I felt as if she was singing just for me.

People wonder what it takes to be a star, and every successful musician has their own story. In that moment, however, I knew without a doubt that I was in the presence of a world-class talent.

"You're incredible," I finally said as her voice died away.

"You're sweet," she deflected. "I said the same thing about you, remember?"

"The difference is, I'm being honest. Your voice . . . It's like nothing I've ever heard before."

She set her notebook on the table, then moved toward me. Bending over, she tipped my face toward hers and kissed me softly on the lips. "Thank you. For everything."

"You're going to be a star," I murmured, believing it.

She smiled. "Are you hungry?"

The change in subject brought me back to earth. "I am."

"You wouldn't happen to know where to get a good cheese-burger, would you?"

I watched her saunter around the coffee table, and the day we'd spent together came back in a rush—the kayak excursion, the sun in her hair, the feel of her lips at the picnic table, the sight of her eyes closing as she sang. When I stood from the couch, my legs felt curiously unsteady. *I'm falling for her,* I suddenly realized.

Or maybe, just maybe, I already had.

I cleared my throat, almost in disbelief. "I know just the place."

21.

LEAVING THE CONDO, WE MOSEYED in the direction of the beach, waiting to cross at the ever-busy Gulf Boulevard.

The sky was continually changing colors, and there were still hundreds of people out and about, wading in the surf at the water's edge and slowly gathering up their belongings. I walked beside Morgan, studying the way the rays of the sun brought out red-gold highlights in her dark, lustrous hair. I couldn't help feeling that something in my world had shifted in the short time I'd known her. I'd more or less thought I had my life figured out; spending time with Morgan had changed all of that. I couldn't say why or when it happened, but I felt undeniably different.

"You're thinking about something," Morgan offered.

"It's been known to happen."

She nudged my shoulder, like she had at the hotel the other night.

"Tell me," she urged.

"I'm thinking about the song," I hedged.

"Me, too," she agreed before turning to study me. "Do you

want to work on more songs together? I've worked with other songwriters before, but it's never been like it was today."

I watched her pick her way forward, the breeze flattening her clothes against her willowy figure. "Sure," I said. "I'd like that. But I think I'd like doing almost anything if it meant spending time with you."

My words seemed to catch her off guard. Staring out over the water, she took a few steps in silence and I realized I had no idea what she was thinking. "So," she said brightly, as if to cover her unease. "Where's this place with the cheeseburgers?"

I pointed a little way up the beach where a thatch-covered roof behind the dunes was barely visible. "Right there."

"Do you think we'll be able to find a seat?" She wrinkled her brow. "Since it's sunset hour, I mean? Or will it be too crowded?"

"You do know you tend to ask me questions that I have no idea how to answer, right?"

She threw her head back and laughed, baring the brown expanse of her neck. My mind flashed to the feel of her lips on my own.

"Okay, then let's go with something you *do* know. Do you have any funny farm stories?" she asked.

"Like what?"

"Like . . . there was this chicken once, and his owner chopped off his head because he was going to eat the chicken. But the chicken lived for over a year afterward. I guess the brain stem wasn't affected? But, anyway, the farmer fed it with an eyedropper since it had no head."

"That's not true," I said.

"It is! I saw the video once when I was in New York City. It was at Ripley's Believe It or Not! in Times Square."

"And you believed it, obviously."

"You can google it. The farmer even did a traveling show with the chicken, which was named Mike, by the way. I'll show you when we're eating, okay?"

I shook my head. "I don't have any headless-chicken stories. I could tell you about tobacco worms, but they're not funny."

"Gross."

"They definitely are," I said. "So why don't you tell me something I don't know. Like . . . I know you used to come here with your family, and you went to the lake house in Minnesota, but did you take vacations to other places?"

"Why does that matter?"

"It doesn't. Since this is my first vacation, I'm trying to live vicariously through your childhood. So I know what I missed."

"You didn't miss much," she assured me.

"Humor me."

She kicked up a bit of sand, making whirlwinds in her tracks. "Well," she began, "we traveled a lot when I was a kid. Once every couple of years we'd visit the Philippines, where my paternal grandparents live. When I was little, I hated it. I don't speak Chinese or Tagalog—my dad's family is ethnically Chinese but has lived in the Philippines for generations—and it's so hot there during the summer! But as I got older, I came to appreciate the visits more . . . seeing my cousins, and the food that my grandma cooked. They always spoiled my sister and me, since we saw them so infrequently." She paused, a nostalgic smile on her face. "My parents love to travel, so sometimes we took trips to Hawaii or Costa Rica, but the biggest trip I took was after my freshman year in high school, when my parents took my sister and me to Europe. London, Paris, Amsterdam, and Rome."

"That sounds exciting."

"At the time, I wasn't as excited as you might think. Mainly we toured museums and churches, and in retrospect I can understand the value of seeing works by Da Vinci or Michelangelo, but back then I was bored silly. I remember staring at the *Mona Lisa* and thinking, *This is it? What's so great about it?* But my parents believed such cultural things were important in the molding of young minds."

I smiled as we veered toward Sandbar Bill's. Though every table was filled, we lucked out, catching a couple leaving their seats at the bar, which also happened to offer a view of the sunset.

"Look at that," I said. "It must be our day."

She smiled. "No doubt about it."

22.

WE ORDERED ICED TEAS, making us the only two who weren't drinking beer or cocktails. When the bartender put the menus in front of us, we both ordered cheeseburgers without bothering to examine them.

As we waited, she showed me the video of Mike the headless chicken on YouTube, and at my urging, she told me more about her childhood. She'd attended private school the whole way through—no surprise there, since her parents obviously valued education. She described the familiar cliques and insecurities and students who surprised her in both positive and negative ways, and while our experiences couldn't have been more different, it was clear that—like me—music was the underlying thread in all her experiences. Music was, I thought, a way for both of us to take charge of shaping our identities and to escape our traumas, and when I said as much to her, her brow furrowed slightly.

"Do you think that's why Paige became an artist, too?"

"Maybe." I scratched my chin, remembering. "She used to

sketch the most amazing animals or nature scenes, but then one day she drew my aunt and uncle, and they were so lifelike it could have been a photo. I remember asking her if she would draw our mom, since I didn't really remember what she looked like, but Paige said that she didn't remember her, either." Thinking about Paige, I added, "Maybe that's a good thing."

I felt Morgan's eyes on me as she took a sip of her tea. She leaned a little closer. "I wish you could come with us to Busch Gardens tomorrow. It should be fun."

"I'm sure it will be. But duty calls and all that." Then, glancing over at her: "Maybe we can see each other when you get back? After my show? I can either make us dinner or we could go out."

I saw the flash of her dimples. "I'd like that."

"Good," I said, already knowing I'd count the hours until then. "And I'm definitely going to make it to your dance performance on Saturday—if you're willing to tell me the time, so I don't have to camp out all day, I mean."

"It'll be at noon or maybe a few minutes after."

"I know you have a gazillion followers, but how many videos have you posted?"

"Probably a few hundred," she said.

"You've done that many dance routines?"

"God, no," she said, with a quick shake of her head. "I don't know how many we've done. But basically we create routines to one or two songs, then break up each one into ten or fifteen segments."

"So . . . how are you going to keep it going? Since you're all going your separate ways?"

"We've been talking about that a lot lately, especially this week. They've known for a while that Saturday is my last performance with the group. And until recently, Holly and Stacy also said that they were planning to move on with their lives, too. But now that there's some money in it, I think they're trying to find a way to keep it going, at least through the summer. Maybe figure out a way to rehearse on FaceTime and then get together in person on weekends. They're still trying to figure it out."

"But you're done for sure?"

She was quiet, and I had the sense that she was trying to choose her words carefully. "You already know how I feel about being an influencer, but more than that, I don't want to make a mistake when it comes to launching a music career. Like . . . I don't want people to think that the *only* reason I made it was because I had a social-media following. I've worked too hard for that. I mean, I studied opera, for goodness' sake. Maybe a manager—if I get one—will tell me what to do. For now I'll just post what I've agreed to post, and that'll get me through the next month or so, but after that, who knows? We'll see."

"Will you miss it?"

"Yes and no," she admitted. "I love my friends, and in the beginning the routines were tons of fun, and obviously it was thrilling to watch our accounts blow up. But lately it feels like everything has to be even better—perfect—whenever we film, so it's a lot more stressful. At the same time, I try to remind myself that I learned a lot. I've reached the point where I think I might even be able to choreograph my own music video."

"Really?"

"Maybe. But if not, I'd just call Maria."

I smiled. The bartender brought our cheeseburgers, and we dug in while watching the sunset bloom across the sky. "We've been talking so much about me, but what are you going to do when you go back home?" she asked between bites. Unlike me, she'd removed the bun and was using a fork and knife to eat the burger; she did, however, dig into the fries with gusto.

"Same thing I always do. Work the farm."

"What's the first thing you do in the mornings once you start work?"

"I make sure the eggs are collected, and then I move the prairie schooner."

"What's a prairie schooner?"

I thought about how best to describe it to someone who'd never seen one before. "Remember when I told you that chickens like shade? That's what a prairie schooner does. It's like a big, open-sided tent that's mounted on skids, with nesting boxes along one side. But, anyway, chickens like to eat bugs, and they also poop a lot. So we have to move the prairie schooner every day to make sure they have a clean and fresh environment. It also helps to fertilize the soil."

"Do you move it with a tractor?"

"Of course."

"I want to see you drive a tractor."

"You're welcome at the farm anytime."

"Then what?"

"It depends on the season. I'll check the greenhouse or the crops or see how harvesting is going or work with a new batch of chickens or turn the fields over, and then there's the whole management and personnel side of things, as well as interacting with customers. It goes without saying that something is always breaking or needs repairing. I wake every day with what feels like a thousand things to do. You'd be amazed at what it takes to move an egg or tomato from the farm to a grocery store."

"How do you pull it all off?"

"My aunt does a lot, as does the general manager. I've also learned to prioritize."

"I don't think I'd be cut out for a life like that," she said, shaking her head. "I mean, I'm responsible, just not *that* responsible."

"You don't have to live that life. You're going to be famous."

"From your lips to God's ears."

"Trust me," I said, knowing I'd never been as certain about anything.

23.

ONCE WE FINISHED EATING, we wandered down the beach to the Don. The beachside restaurant was half full; I saw others taking in the evening from loungers at the poolside. Another couple was making their way from the hotel to the beach; lost in their own conversation, they walked past without seeming to notice us. Morgan stopped on the sand just steps from the deck and turned toward me. Staring at her, I thought again that I'd never seen anyone more beautiful.

"I guess this is it," I said.

She seemed to study the hotel before turning back to me. "Thank you for today," she said. "For everything."

"My pleasure," I said. "It was the best day I've had here."

"Me, too," she said, with such tenderness that what happened next seemed inevitable.

I closed the gap between us and tugged her gently toward me. I saw her eyes widen ever so slightly, and for an instant I wondered if I should stop. Though she'd kissed me twice, I think both of us knew this one would be different, that this kiss would carry with it emotions that neither of us had anticipated until this very moment.

But I could no longer help myself, and tilting my head, I closed my eyes as our lips came together, softly at first, and then with even more passion. I felt her body press against mine, and when our tongues met, warmth surged like an underground current through me. Wrapping both arms around her, I heard her give a deep-throated purr, and her hand wound its way up into my hair.

As we kissed, my mind searched for answers, trying to grasp when and how it had happened. It might have been while we were in the kayaks or when I heard her sing or even while we had dinner together—but I suddenly understood that I'd fallen in love with this woman, a woman I'd met only days ago; already, though, I felt as if I'd known her forever.

When we separated, my feelings threatened to overflow, but I forced myself to remain quiet. We simply stared at each other until I finally let out a breath, not realizing that I'd been holding it.

"I'll see you tomorrow night, Morgan," I said, my voice almost hoarse.

"Good night, Colby," she answered, studying my face as if committing it to memory, and minutes later, as I walked down the beach, I found myself reliving the kiss, certain that my life would never be the same.

PART IV

Beverly

24.

BEVERLY COULDN'T STOP THINKING about cameras in the bus stations.

How could she have been so dumb? Hadn't there been a zillion movies and television shows where the government used those cameras to catch spies and criminals? Oh, she knew electronic surveillance wasn't quite as sophisticated as what Hollywood portrayed, but even local television news confirmed that cameras were everywhere these days. They were installed on street corners, in traffic lights, above the cash registers at small businesses. She'd remembered their presence when she took Tommie to the convenience store to get him something to eat, so why hadn't she considered something even more obvious?

With shaking legs and racing mind, Beverly somehow made it to the table, and she was still sitting there when Tommie wandered into the kitchen. He plopped into his seat, wiping the sleep from his eyes. To steady her fraying nerves, she forced herself to rise. She poured him a bowl of cereal, added milk, and brought his breakfast to the table along with a spoon.

She flashed a quick smile, hoping he wouldn't notice she was barely holding it together, then went to make his lunch. Peanut butter and jelly sandwich and an apple, along with change for milk from the cafeteria. No Doritos or Fritos or Oreos or Nutter Butters, sadly, but right now it was all she could do to keep from glancing out the window, expecting to find Gary standing in the yard.

"I heard someone last night," Tommie eventually said.

His words nearly made her jump. She tried to remember the last time he'd spoken first in the morning, without her having to coax it out of him. When his words finally registered, she felt another surge of anxiety.

"That was probably me," she said. "I was up late cleaning the kitchen."

"I heard someone *outside.*"

Water was dripping from the faucet, the *plink-plink-plink* steady and rhythmic, clashing with morning birdsong. An old truck puttered along the gravel road, and she saw an arm wave from the window before it vanished from sight. Mist rose from the fields as though a cloud had dropped from the sky.

"There was no one outside," she said. "I would have heard them."

"He was on the roof."

A year ago, Tommie had begun having nightmares. She thought it had something to do with the television he watched, or maybe the book *Where the Wild Things Are.* In his early nightmares, he would awaken with cries, claiming that he was being chased by a monster. Sometimes the monster was like a dinosaur; other times it was a wild animal or a hooded figure of some sort. And always, always, Tommie swore that the monster was calling his name.

"Are you sure you weren't dreaming?"

"I was awake. I could hear the music from the kitchen."

Had it been Gary, she told herself, he would have already been in the kitchen. Had it been Gary's associates, they would have already loaded Tommie and her into the black SUV with tinted windows. Trying to keep her own worries in check, she found the hair wax and smoothed down Tommie's cowlick, even though her hands were trembling ever so slightly.

"I'll check after you go to school, but it was probably squirrels."

"It called my name."

Beverly closed her eyes, feeling a sigh of relief. It was definitely a dream, thank God. But the relief was short-lived, washed away by her earlier dread like a sandcastle in a rising tide.

"I was singing in the kitchen along with the radio. That's probably what you heard." Her voice sounded strangely tinny and distant to her ears.

Tommie glanced up at her, looking suddenly older than his years and younger at the same time. "Maybe," he finally said, and she decided to change the subject.

"If you want, you can bring a friend over after school."

"I don't have any friends here."

"You will," she said. "I'm sure there are lots of nice kids in your class. Maybe you'll get to know them better on field day. You said that's coming up, right?"

He shrugged, and with that, he grew silent as he finished his cereal. Afterward, he tipped the bowl up, drinking the milk. Beverly thought again that she should eat as soon as she got him off to school, since she hadn't had much the day before. She felt like she could write a book for people who wanted to lose weight; she'd call it *The Too-Broke-to-Eat Diet*.

She loaded Tommie's lunch into his backpack, then walked with him out to the stump by the road. They took a seat, waiting.

"If you want to catch more tadpoles later, I'll try to find an old jar we could use," she offered. "You might not be able to bring them for show-and-tell, but you could bring them back to the house for a while if you want."

Tommie studied the ground. "I don't want to die, Mom," he said.

Beverly blinked. "What did you say?"

He turned toward her, his forehead wrinkled. "I said I don't want them to die, Mom."

"Oh," she said, suddenly thinking about cameras and nightmares and too little sleep and not enough food, and in the rising heat of the morning, it was hard to keep all her thoughts straight. She needed to do better. She needed to make sure that Tommie felt safe.

The yellow bus, squeaking and groaning, came to a stop; the door squealed as it opened. Tommie rose and climbed into the bus without looking back, without even saying goodbye.

25.

CAMERAS.

The word kept ricocheting around her mind like a pachinko ball. She needed a distraction—anything to settle her nerves—but her hands weren't steady enough to start painting just yet. Instead, she went upstairs to Tommie's room. Though he'd had a nightmare, she'd told her son that she would check to make sure, and that's what good mothers did. His window was set into an alcove, making it impossible to see if anyone could even reach the roof. She examined the ceiling and lay down in Tommie's bed. Tried to imagine where the sounds might have been, if there were any sounds, but pretending to be Tommie didn't help.

She went outside, backing away from the house to get adequate perspective. Tommie's room was on the side, and a single glance confirmed that the steep pitch of the roof made it even more unlikely that anyone could have been walking around up there. But one of the oak trees had a branch that stretched over part of the roof, making it essentially a squirrel highway. If there was wind, the branch might even scrape the shingles, and she tried to remember whether there'd been any wind last night.

The only thing that was certain was that no one had been on the roof; no one had whispered Tommie's name. She'd known that already; nonetheless, she was glad she'd made herself sure of it. Just as she was now sure that there'd been cameras in the bus stations. They'd probably been required since 9/11, now that she thought about it, and Gary, she knew, had the power to access all of them.

Though her mind felt even more swimmy than it had over the last couple of days, she forced herself to think. Back inside, she took a seat at the table and rubbed her temples, pressing hard with her fingers.

Gary would no doubt demand to see footage from the local bus station for Friday night, Saturday, Sunday, and maybe even Monday morning. He would sit with his face close to the computer screen, fast-forwarding at times, watching carefully, *searching*. Even if he didn't recognize her right away, he would undoubtedly recognize his son. It might take him hours or days, but she knew with certainty that Gary would eventually figure out exactly which bus they'd taken on their escape from town.

And then? Unless there were cameras on the buses—which she doubted—he would have no idea where she'd gotten off. At that point he'd probably try to speak to the drivers, but would the second driver remember where they'd disembarked? Unlikely, which meant that Gary's next step would be to check the cameras at other bus stations along the route. And again, in time he would probably recognize Tommie. Then he'd keep repeating the process, like a wolf with his nose to the ground while hunting prey, getting closer and closer, zeroing in. He might even find a video of her at the convenience store.

But after that?

The trail would come to an end, because she and Tommie had hitched a ride with a woman in a station wagon. The woman who knew enough not to ask questions.

Could he find the woman? And the carpet salesman who smelled of Old Spice?

Doubtful.

But could there have been other cameras on the highway? Like traffic cameras? Cameras that recorded license plates?

Possibly.

Even if she assumed the absolute worst, the *impossible* worst—that Gary, somehow, had tracked her to this town—what then? He might check the motel, might go to the diner, might even speak with the waitress, but the trail would grow even colder after that. The waitress hadn't known she wanted to find a place to live, and aside from the owner of the house, no one knew they were in town at all. For all Gary knew, she had caught yet another ride with someone else, heading in an entirely different direction.

Gary might be dogged and intelligent and able to leverage the power of federal and state governments to a point that would scare even the bravest ordinary citizen, but he wasn't God.

"I am safe," she said in her most convincing voice. "There is no way he can find me."

26.

STILL, THE ANXIETY WAS SLOW to pass, even when she went over everything again, just to make sure. She was on edge, no doubt about it, or maybe it was more like a super-high tightrope with no safety net, but either way, she knew she wasn't thinking right. She was dwelling too much on certain ideas and forgetting other things completely, and she had to think normally again, if not for her, then for Tommie. He needed her and they were starting over and the orange walls of the kitchen seemed to be pressing in, giving her the beginnings of a headache.

"I need to paint the kitchen," she whispered. "That will make me feel better."

Rising from the table, she retrieved one of the paintbrushes, along with a roller and pan. As she had the day before, she stripped off her shirt and jeans, unwilling to ruin them with paint spatters. She used a butter knife to pry open the can of primer. Paint stores had a machine that shook the cans, but since that wasn't an option, she found a wooden spatula in one of the drawers and used that to stir. The primer was thicker at the bottom, like the goo in a swamp bed, but she stirred and stirred, trying to coax it back to life so she could make the orange on the walls of the kitchen disappear for good.

Who in their right mind would have chosen that god-awful color in the first place? How was it possible to examine all the paint samples the stores had to offer—all the pretty neutrals or pastels or spring colors—and think, *I want my kitchen walls to look like a Halloween jack-o'-lantern?*

The primer seemed as ready as it ever would be, so she poured some into the pan, then pushed the roller back and forth, absorbing the liquid. She rolled the primer onto the walls, striping the jack-o'-lantern and getting as close to the cupboards as she could. After that she used the brush, pleased to discover how easy it was to cut right to the cupboards without leaving so much as the tiniest of smudges.

"I should get a job painting ugly kitchens," she said with a giggle.

Leaving the primer to dry, she rinsed the brush and roller and set them near the water heater on the back porch to dry. She poured the rest of the primer back into the can, rinsed the pan and dried it with a paper towel, then added glossy white paint to it. She retrieved another brush and roller and turned her attention to the cupboards, immersed in her task. When she was finished, she stood in the middle of the kitchen, taking it all in.

The cupboards looked great, almost like new. But the ugly orange color had seeped through the primer, making the walls gray and dirty. She felt the stirrings of a headache.

I should get Tommie some clothes, she reminded herself.

Not only because she didn't want the other kids to tease him, but because she didn't want the teacher to notice. That might lead to a meeting, and the last thing either she or Tommie needed right now was to be noticed by anyone.

Checking the clock, she calculated how much time she would need to get to town, find a place to shop, and get back. If she left soon, there was still time, so after quickly rinsing the paintbrush and roller, she went upstairs and put on the wig and baseball hat and wrapped her breasts in the Ace bandage. She retrieved some money from her stash and left the house, her feet kicking up dust on the gravel road as she walked. And walked. And *walked*. As she passed the store where she'd bought the groceries and neared the diner and motel, she wondered if those two businesses had cameras. And if they did, how long would the recordings generally be kept? A couple of days? A week? A month? They wouldn't be kept forever, would they?

In any case, she needed to keep the lowest profile possible. With that in mind, she crossed the street, keeping her baseball hat pulled low as she passed the diner, then crossed the street again when she passed the motel. Out of an abundance of caution, she stopped and pretended to tie her shoe. She peeked toward the diner and then the motel to see if anyone had stepped out the door to watch her. But there was nothing out of the ordinary, and she reminded herself to be equally careful on the return trip.

She began to walk again, eventually reaching the outer limits of the commercial district. Little by little, businesses crowded either side of the road, and she wished she still had a phone, so she could find the address of the thrift store. Instead, she asked strangers for help. Both were women. The first had been filling up her tank with gas; the second one had been leaving a Hardee's restaurant. Even outside, Beverly could smell the aroma of fried food, and she regretted that she hadn't eaten breakfast. The woman outside of Hardee's told her the thrift store was two blocks farther, in a strip mall set back from the road.

Beverly found the strip mall, then spotted the thrift store, located at one end. It was called Second Chances, and Beverly pushed her way inside. She kept her head bowed when she walked past the cashier, a woman in her sixties with dull gray hair that reminded Beverly of the walls of her kitchen.

Most of the items in the children's clothing section were for babies and toddlers, but she finally found the sizes she needed. The items, though used, were clean, without tears or stains, and just as she'd hoped, the cost was minimal. In the end she picked out four T-shirts, two pairs of shorts, jeans, and a pair of sneakers. She thought that she should have brought her backpack with her, since it would have made carrying everything home easier, but she had to content herself with a plastic bag.

She started the long walk back to the house. The sun was high and bright, and the day was sticky hot. Dizzy because she hadn't eaten, she had to stop every so often to catch her breath. She wished she had a car, but she knew that Gary had placed a tracker on the one she used to drive. She'd seen it beneath the rear bumper months before she'd left for good, the little red light flashing on and off, taunting her to go ahead and remove it and see what good it would do.

The wig and hat made her head hot and itchy, and she felt her makeup melting. When she reached home, she disrobed and hopped in the shower to cool off, then dressed again. She walked outside and took a seat on the stump, just in time. The bus appeared less than a minute later, and she couldn't help feeling a bit of pride that she'd made it. As she had the day before, she exchanged a friendly wave with the driver, thinking maybe, just maybe, things were going to turn out all right.

27.

"I bought you some more clothes today," she said, "so you won't have to keep wearing the same things."

They were at the table, and Tommie nodded as he ate the sandwich she'd made him. She'd also poured him a glass of milk, amazed at how much such a small human being could eat and drink.

"As you can probably tell, I also started painting the kitchen," she added.

Tommie looked up, as though he hadn't noticed the change. "Why did you paint it gray?"

"That's the primer," she said. "I'm going to paint the walls yellow."

"Oh," Tommie said. He didn't seem all that interested, but she figured that most kids Tommie's age didn't care about wall paint.

"Do you want to catch tadpoles again after you finish?"

He nodded again, chewing.

"I also checked the roof," she said. "It's too steep for anyone to walk around on, but there's a branch that squirrels could have used, or the branch might have scratched the shingles. That's probably what you heard, or, like I said, you might have been dreaming."

"I was awake, Mom."

She smiled, knowing he always said the same thing after every nightmare. "Do you want more milk?"

When he shook his head, she saw the resemblance to Gary in the way his hair fell over his eyes, and she wondered when Tommie would ask about him.

"When is Dad coming?"

She knew him so well it sometimes seemed as though she was psychic.

"He's still working," she said. "Do you remember when I told you that? When we left the house?"

"I remember," he said, stuffing the last of his food into his cheeks, but she knew it didn't fully answer his question. Beverly brought his plate to the sink and rinsed it, then did the same with his glass when he finished his milk. In the cupboards—not wet but still sticky, so she was careful when opening them—she found an old mason jar with a lid on one of the upper shelves. She held it out to show him.

"How about we go catch some tadpoles?"

28.

THEY WANDERED DOWN TO the creek, but this time, Beverly didn't join Tommie in the water. Instead, after rolling up his pants and taking his shoes and socks, she took a seat in the low weeds near the bank. Tommie held the mason jar as he slowly waded in the gentle current.

"Before you catch any, make sure there's creek water in the jar."

Tommie scooped water, filling it to the brim.

"Let a little bit of the water out. If it's too full, the tadpoles won't fit."

He did what she suggested, then went back to tadpole hunting. He tried and failed to catch the first one but then caught two.

"How many can I put in?"

She thought about it. "I'm not sure, but they're kind of small, so maybe seven or eight? If you can catch that many, I mean."

"I can catch that many," he answered, and she felt a warm rush at his confidence. Tommie was her mission, her world, and had been since the day he was born. She tried to imagine what he'd look like when he grew older. He'd be handsome, she was certain about that, but other details were beyond her.

"How was school? Did you do anything fun today?"

"We had art today. I got to draw pictures."

"What did you draw?"

"They told us to draw our house."

She wondered which one he'd drawn, their old one or their new one, the one where they lived on their own and were finally safe.

"Is it in your backpack?"

He nodded, his head bowed, uninterested. He bent lower, catching another tadpole.

"I want to see it when we get back to the house, okay? Will you show me?"

He nodded again, lost in his own little adventure, and Beverly flashed on the hours she'd spent coloring with him in the months before she decided to leave. She'd never been one of those parents who thought that everything their child did showed how gifted they were, but Tommie got pretty good at staying between the lines, which she couldn't help but find impressive. She also taught him the basics of printing so that by the time he'd begun kindergarten, he was able to write his own name—and other words—without her help.

She should have bought coloring books and crayons when she went to town earlier. It would help with his adjustment to their new life, and she knew he needed that. His dream last night revealed that in his own childlike way, he was as stressed as she was. She hated that he missed his father, hated that he probably didn't understand why they'd needed to escape in the first place. She wondered how many weeks or months would pass before he realized that from now on it was just the two of them.

They stayed at the small creek for another half hour. In that time, Tommie caught eight tadpoles. All of them were in the jar, alien-like with their odd wiggling bodies. Beverly put the lid on, watching as Tommie put on his socks and shoes. She'd taught him to tie his shoes the year before, though the loops were far from straight.

Tommie carried the jar as they wandered back, his eyes on the tadpoles as he walked beside her. They were rounding the ramshackle barn when Beverly absently glanced toward the house and saw a dirty old pickup truck parked in the driveway.

She blinked, making sure that her mind wasn't playing tricks on her, her heart suddenly slamming in her chest when she understood that what she was seeing was real. Taking Tommie's hand, she backed up, keeping the barn between her and the house, her heart continuing to pound.

"What's wrong?" Tommie asked. "Why are we stopping?"

"I think I lost my bracelet," she improvised, knowing she hadn't even brought a bracelet with her when she and Tommie escaped. "I must have left it at the creek, so let's go check, okay?"

Her legs were wobbly as she led Tommie back to where they'd started. In her mind's eye, she could still see the pickup truck in the driveway. Who had come to the house, and why? She tried to slow her racing thoughts, aware that Tommie was watching her.

It wasn't the police or the sheriff, not in a pickup truck like that.

It wasn't a black SUV with tinted windows.

Nor had she seen a group of men swarming over the property. If they were Gary's men, they would be wearing suits and sunglasses and have short-cropped hair, so who else could it be? She kept trying to think, but ideas became jumbled until she took a long deep breath, which seemed to help. "Think," she muttered. "Think."

"Mom?"

She heard Tommie but didn't respond. Instead, she tried to but couldn't remember if the owner of the house had been driving a truck—she hadn't paid enough attention. But why would the owner come to the house? To check on how she was settling in? Because there was paperwork she'd forgotten? Or maybe she'd sent a handyman over to fix something—hadn't the woman told her she worked with a handyman, or had Beverly imagined that?

Was that who it had been? The handyman? Would he come over even if she hadn't contacted the owner to have something repaired? Or was it someone equally innocuous, like a salesman or a person who needed directions?

Questions, questions circling her mind, without answers.

At the creek, she let go of Tommie's hand. Her palms were sweating. She felt almost faint, like she was about to pass out.

"I wonder if I left it where I was sitting," she said to Tommie. "Can you check? I'll look over here."

She bent low, trying to stay out of sight, and realized she could still see the rear bumper of the old dirty pickup truck in the distant driveway, beyond the thick foliage of the dogwood trees. But she had to fake it, had to pretend to search for her bracelet, so that Tommie wouldn't become frightened. She had to act the part like a performer onstage, even as the word *truck* began to flash in her mind like a strobe light, along with the obvious questions. *The truck, the truck, the old dirty truck! Who was it? Why had he come?*

If it *was* one of Gary's henchmen, he wouldn't be content to simply knock at the door. He would go inside and search. He'd see a small backpack slung over the kitchen chair. He'd see the plate with sandwich crumbs and a glass with milk residue in the sink, but what would that tell him other than that someone had been there? He'd have to venture upstairs, to their rooms, but since they'd brought almost nothing with them and the closets were filled with other people's clothes, there was nothing he would be able to trace back to either Beverly or Tommie . . .

Except . . .

She froze at the thought of *Go, Dog. Go!*, Tommie's favorite book, along with the Iron Man action figure.

Both were on the nightstand. If the man so much as peeked in the room—and it had to be a man, Beverly decided—he would no doubt find them, but the question was whether Gary would have noticed she'd taken them.

She wondered if the man was in the house now. Wondered if there was more than one man opening drawers and checking the refrigerator and hunting for books like *Go, Dog. Go!* and Iron Man action figures. She wondered if he wore black leather gloves and if he had a gun beneath his jacket while another equally dangerous man kept a lookout. She wondered whether he would wait for her or decide to search for her, and as she scanned the pasturelands beyond the creek, she knew there was nowhere to hide.

"Maybe it fell off while I was walking," she said to Tommie. "You keep checking around here, okay? I'll be right back."

The words sounded shaky to her ears, but she forced herself to retrace her steps toward the ancient barn. She crept to the corner and peered around the side, at the house.

The truck was still in place, but a moment later she saw some-one step down from the porch and walk toward the truck. It was definitely a man—she could tell by the way he moved; he was wearing jeans and a long-sleeved shirt and work boots along with a baseball hat. He was also alone. She was certain he would suddenly stop and turn in her direction, but instead, he simply pulled open the door and climbed into the truck. Soon she heard the engine start, and then the truck was backing out. When it reached the gravel road, it headed in the direction opposite the town, toward God knew where.

She waited, then waited some more. But other than the sound of birdsong, there was nothing. In time, she crept toward the house. She wanted to make sure that no one was still inside, that it wasn't a trap. She stepped up onto the porch and saw dusty footprints leading to the door, imprinted on the mat, and then heading back toward the porch steps.

When she opened the door, no footprints were visible; there were none on the linoleum floor in the kitchen or on the stairs, either. Upstairs, she saw *Go, Dog. Go!* and Iron Man on the stand next to Tommie's bed. In the bathroom, her clothes hung from the shower-curtain rod, and her wig was near the sink, just where she'd left it. Nothing seemed to have been disturbed.

Still, she remained shaky as she hurried back to the creek. Tommie continued to kick through the grass and the dirt before noticing that she'd approached.

"Did you find it?" he asked.

"No. I guess it's just lost."

He nodded before picking up the jar. "How long can I keep them?" he asked.

The sound of his voice was soothing, even if she still felt far from normal.

"We'll bring them back after dinner, okay?"

29.

BACK AT THE HOUSE, she opened Tommie's backpack and studied the drawing that he'd made, hoping it would stop her from thinking about the truck and the man who'd shown up out of the blue. When she saw the image of their old house, with its flat roof and large windows, she felt sad but smiled anyway.

"This is great. You're quite the artist."

"Can I watch cartoons?"

"For a little while. While I make dinner, all right? Do you want me to bring your tadpoles to sit with you?"

"Uh-huh," he mumbled as they went to the living room. She turned on the television; luckily, cartoons were on.

"Don't sit too close to the screen. It's not good for your eyes."

He nodded, lost in the show in just a few seconds.

She put the jar on the coffee table and retreated to the kitchen. She realized that she'd forgotten to defrost the chicken—or was it supposed to be hamburger tonight? Because she kept picturing the man with the truck, it was all but impossible to remember.

"Is it chicken or hamburger tonight?" she called out.

"Hamburger," Tommie called back.

Oh, that's right, she thought. They'd had chicken the night before, with beans and carrots, and she'd nibbled on the carrots that Tommie hadn't finished. . . .

From the freezer, she pulled out two servings of hamburger, hesitated, then put one of them back. With her stomach clenched like a fist, there was no way she'd be able to eat a full meal. Nor, she realized, was she even hungry.

She found a ziplock bag, slid in the serving of hamburger, then placed it in warm water to thaw. She sliced carrots and cut a few florets from a stalk of the cauliflower. All went onto the baking sheet. She turned on the oven, knowing it would take a few minutes to reach the desired temperature, and saw that her hands were trembling.

She couldn't stop looking out the window to scan the gravel road out front. Were they safe here? And if they weren't, where could they go? She didn't have enough money for another escape, for bus tickets and rent and food, and as she put the baking sheet in the oven, she wondered how much time she had if Gary really had sent the man with the pickup truck.

Minutes? Hours?

Or was she allowing her thoughts to run away from her again, just as she'd done with Peg?

She went to the front door and, after opening it, stared again at the dusty footprints on the mat and on the steps. This wasn't like Tommie and his dream that someone was on the roof, not in the slightest. And it wasn't like Peg, who'd said something she probably said to every single stranger who showed up at the store.

This was real, no doubt about it.

From the living room, she could hear the cartoons; every now and then, Tommie laughed. She cooked the hamburger in a frying pan, conscious of the knot in her stomach. When the vegetables were soft, just the way Tommie liked them, she put most of the food onto Tommie's plate and called him to the table. They ate their meal largely in silence, Beverly picking listlessly at some of the cauliflower. She felt jumpy, poised for sirens and flashing lights and a sudden angry pounding on the door.

But no one came.

As she put the dishes in the sink, she reflected that if Gary had sent the man, he wouldn't waste any time coming for them. He wouldn't risk the chance that she'd run again; he wouldn't risk losing Tommie. Last year, after he'd punched her, he warned her that if she ever tried to leave or take Tommie from him, he would track them to the ends of the earth and, after he found them, she would never see Tommie again.

But all remained quiet.

"How about we let the tadpoles go?" she said to Tommie, and the two of them made the walk back to the creek. As she watched her son open the jar and release them, she was certain that their house would be surrounded upon their return.

Still, other than the sound of frogs and crickets, there was nothing. Back at the house and too wearied from her day to play a game, she allowed Tommie to watch cartoons again, until he began to yawn. She sent him upstairs to take a bath and brush his teeth, and she set out the shirt and pants and sneakers she'd bought earlier in the day. She tried to figure out how many hours had passed since she'd first seen the man with the truck at their house. If Gary couldn't get here promptly, he would order the local police or sheriff to do his bidding, so where were they?

She read Tommie *Go, Dog. Go!* and kissed him on his cheek and told him that she loved him. Then, downstairs, she sat on the couch, waiting. She watched for flickers of headlights to flash on the walls, waited for the sound of approaching car engines.

More time passed. Then even more hours, until it was long

past midnight, and the world outside remained dark and still. But sleep was out of the question, and when she finally went to the kitchen to get a glass of water, the walls still struck her as depressing. And if, God forbid, it was their last day in the house, then there was no way she was going to be stuck with gray and gloomy walls.

Opening the can, she stirred until the yellow paint resembled summer daisies, then poured it into the pan. She used the roller and brush she'd allowed to dry near the water heater, coating the grayish gloom on the walls, taking her time, and even before she finished, she knew she wanted to add a second coat, which she started right after finishing the first. While she was at it, she decided, the cupboards could use another coat, as well, and she was still painting after the sun came up and Tommie wandered down the stairs for breakfast.

30.

DESPITE THE LACK OF SLEEP, Beverly felt surprisingly good, mainly because no one had so much as driven on the gravel road past her house all night long and she'd somehow been able to finish the kitchen. Nor had Tommie had a nightmare; when asked how he'd slept, he shrugged and told her it was fine and ate his cereal, just like he did most days.

She saw him off to the bus and waved at him after he took his seat. To her delight, he raised his hand as well, which made her think he was getting used to his new life.

Inside, the kitchen walls were a bright and cheery yellow, and the cupboards seemed as though they belonged in a showroom. It was amazing how much a single color could change the entire atmosphere, and Beverly suddenly remembered her idea about collecting wildflowers for the jelly jar. She went outside again, plucking whatever blooms she could, put them in the jar, and brought the arrangement to the table. Stepping back, she took in the kitchen as a whole, feeling pleased. It was beautiful, the kind of kitchen she'd always wanted, and she wondered again who had been crazy enough to think that orange walls could look half as good.

But the burgundy wall in the living room had to go, even though a nap was probably what she needed more than anything. She knew she was running on nervous energy stemming from yesterday's scare—just as she knew she'd likely collapse later—but the burgundy felt intolerable, like something from a creepy funeral home.

She turned on the radio before getting started. First, she disconnected all sorts of cables attached to the television. The cabinet against the wall was heavy and she had to empty it of its contents, including the television and DVD player, leaving the items scattered around the living room. Even then she could barely move the darn thing. By the time she'd made enough room to squeeze behind it, her arms and back were aching. She returned to the kitchen and rinsed the roller and the paintbrush, shaking out the water on the front porch, replacing them with dry ones. There was hardly any primer left, but it would have to do. Bringing everything to the living room, she poured the remainder into the pan. She rolled it onto the hideous burgundy wall in long, wide swoops, like she was directing a marching band, and with every stroke, the room looked better and better.

Now and then, the deejay came on between songs, telling jokes or announcing concerts or highlighting the latest news, always from somewhere else, places she'd never been. This town, as far as Beverly could tell, was the kind of place where nothing exciting ever happened at all, and she felt her mind filtering back to her worries about Tommie's nightmare and Peg and cameras in the bus stations and the man with the truck who'd come to her house. She scolded herself for allowing her paranoia to run unchecked and wondered if she was going to be looking over her shoulder for the rest of her life, but she assumed she probably would.

"We're safe because I worry," she whispered. "And I worry to keep us safe."

The primer ran out when the wall was halfway finished, and she wondered whether there was more on the back porch. She glanced around at the living room, which looked as though a tornado had swept through it—Tommie would probably think she'd gone crazy—but unless she was willing to move everything back into place, then move it all again tomorrow and one more time after the wall was finished, the living room would have to remain in this state for a day or two. Besides, she couldn't exactly leave the wall half-primed.

On the way to the porch, she grabbed the can of yellow paint, thinking she might as well put that away while she tried to find more primer. But as she was placing it on the shelf, she accidentally knocked over another can. It toppled to the concrete floor, sounding strangely empty. She noticed that the lid had partially opened, and mildly curious as to why someone would store an empty paint can, she lifted off the rest of it. Inside was a large baggie filled with marijuana, along with a pipe and a lighter.

She wasn't a prude—she'd smoked weed in the past—but she hadn't liked the way it made her feel, so it wasn't her thing. There wasn't a whole lot—not like the bricks she'd seen in movies—but to her, it seemed too much for a casual user. Raising her eyes, she also noted the number of other paint cans on the shelves and couldn't help wondering if any of those contained marijuana, as well. In the corner was a low step stool. After putting it in place, she checked the other cans one by one, feeling the liquid slosh when she shook them. She breathed a sigh of relief; the last thing she needed was to be found in a house filled with drugs. If kid-

napping didn't put her away for life, then the drug charges definitely would. She brought the baggie to the kitchen, wondering
whether the people who'd lived here before—no doubt the same
ones who'd painted the kitchen the god-awful orange—had either forgotten about the drugs or left them behind on purpose
because they hadn't wanted to be caught with them. Either way,
it explained why the house had been in move-in condition; just
as she'd assumed, the former residents were likely on the run. It
also explained why the owner hadn't asked too many questions
and was more than happy to take cash. She was used to tenants
with issues she'd rather know nothing about.

But Tommie shouldn't be living in a home with drugs, that
much Beverly knew for sure. She pulled a coffee mug down from
the cupboard, mashed the buds into tiny grains, then filled the
baggie with water and washed all of it down the sink drain. She
turned on the garbage disposal for good measure. As for the pipe
and lighter, she simply threw them into the weeds as far from the
house as possible, knowing that even if Tommie did eventually
find the pipe, he wouldn't have the slightest idea of what he was
seeing. She also decided that it would be a good idea to check the
rest of the house, just to make sure Tommie didn't find anything
he shouldn't.

It was only when she returned to the kitchen to start her search
that she realized there was a paper bag sitting on the counter. She
gasped.

Tommie's lunch.

She must have forgotten to put it in his backpack. The clock
on the wall showed it was already approaching half past ten. She
didn't know what time he usually ate at school, but she knew she
didn't have much time, and she raced upstairs. She quickly
donned the wig and the hat and grabbed her sunglasses but didn't

bother with either foundation or the Ace bandage, since all she was going to do was drop it off with the secretary. She'd be in and out of the school within a minute.

But how to get there?

The school was miles and miles away, too far to walk, which meant that her only hope was to catch a ride with a Good Samaritan. Like the old lady in the station wagon, or the carpet salesman who smelled like Old Spice. There was never much traffic on the gravel road out front, but maybe she would get lucky.

Seizing the lunch bag, she trotted out the door and toward the road, turning in the direction of town.

She walked for six or seven minutes, glancing over her shoulder periodically, until she finally spotted a car coming up behind her. If she simply held her thumb out, she feared, the driver would ignore her; instead, she began waving her arms, the universal cry for roadside assistance. As expected, the car slowed, coming to a stop a short distance from her. The woman behind the wheel of the compact silver SUV was in her thirties, with her blond hair pulled back into a messy ponytail. Beverly walked toward the driver's side, watching as the window lowered.

"Thank you for stopping," Beverly started. "I know this might sound crazy, but I forgot to give my son his lunch and my car won't start," she babbled, holding up the bag. "I really need to get to the school and was hoping you could give me a ride. Please. It's an emergency."

The woman hesitated, momentarily confused, and Beverly couldn't help feeling that she seemed familiar, like someone Beverly had seen on television. It was evident that the woman had probably never picked up a stranger before, and Beverly could almost see her mind clicking through the options.

"Oh, ummm . . . Yeah, I guess I can do that," the woman finally offered. "I'm sort of headed in that direction anyway. You're talking about John Small Elementary, right?"

"That's it." Beverly nodded, feeling a surge of relief. "Thank you so much. I can't tell you how much this means to me."

Before the woman could change her mind, Beverly rounded the car and climbed in. The woman seemed to study Beverly in a way that made Beverly want to make sure her wig and hat were on straight.

"What did you say your name was?"

"Beverly."

"I'm Leslie Watkins," the woman said. "I think I've seen you at the school. My daughter Amelia goes there, too. Fourth grade. What grade is your son in?"

"He's in first grade," Beverly said, knowing she'd only been to the school once, when she'd enrolled Tommie.

"With Mrs. Morris or Mrs. Campbell?" She gave Beverly a tentative smile. "I volunteer at the school a couple of times a week. I know pretty much everyone there."

Which explained how the woman had recognized her, Beverly realized. "I'm not sure exactly," she said. "I *should* know, but we just moved here, and with all the chaos . . ."

"I get it," the woman said easily. "Moving is always stressful. Where are you from?"

"Pennsylvania," Beverly lied. "Pittsburgh."

"And what brought you to this part of the world?"

As though I can answer that question, Beverly thought. "I just wanted a fresh start," she responded after a beat. She wished the woman would be more like the elderly woman in the station wagon or the owner of the house, who'd known enough not to ask so many questions. From behind her, Beverly heard a small voice.

"Mama . . ."

The woman's eyes flashed to the rearview mirror. "Almost there, Camille. You doing okay, sweetie?"

Beverly stole a quick peek over her shoulder, amazed she hadn't realized there was a child strapped into the car seat behind her. How could she have missed that?

"How old is she?"

"Almost two," the woman replied, her eyes still on the rearview mirror. "And today she's my errand buddy. Right, sweetie?"

"Bud . . . dy," Camille repeated, her voice small and high-pitched.

Beverly gave a quick wave, remembering Tommie when he was that age, when every day he'd learned something new. He'd been such a pleasant toddler; she'd barely noticed the supposed terrible twos, even as they were happening.

"She's beautiful," Beverly commented.

"Thank you. I think so, too. Mama's pretty lucky, isn't she, Camille?"

"Lu . . . cky," Camille echoed.

Beverly turned back around, still recalling images of Tommie when he was little, and soon enough they left the gravel road, turning onto an asphalt ribbon that stretched between farms on either side of her. In her lap she held the bagged lunch, wondering again how she'd forgotten to put it in Tommie's backpack and hoping she would get there in time.

"Do you know when the kids eat lunch?"

"The younger grades eat at eleven-fifteen," she said. "Don't worry. I'll have you there in plenty of time. How do you like our little town so far?"

"It's quiet."

"That it is. It took me a while to get used to it, too. We moved here five years ago to be closer to my husband's parents. They love spending time with the grandkids. . . ."

From there, Leslie prattled on, asking only the occasional question and speaking like a local tour guide. She told Beverly about her favorite restaurants in town, some of the shops worth visiting near the waterfront, and the rec center, where Beverly could sign Tommie up for T-ball or youth soccer or practically anything else her son might be interested in. Beverly listened with half an ear; she knew she didn't have the money to sign Tommie up for anything.

A few minutes later they turned onto the school property, and Beverly felt a sense of déjà vu as they drew near the building. She caught a glimpse of the fields off to one side; on the other were the jungle gym and the swings. She wondered if Tommie had played on them yet; as a little girl, she loved to swing. She could remember begging her friends to push her higher and higher, so it almost felt as though she were falling.

Like in the dream, the one with the pirate, the one from a couple of nights ago . . .

Beverly jerked and Leslie flinched at the movement, concern in her eyes. To head off questions, Beverly quickly thanked Leslie again as the car came to a stop. She turned in the seat, throwing a wave to Camille before opening the door and jumping out. She waved one last time as Leslie drove off.

When she entered the building, the familiarity she'd previously experienced gave way to a slight feeling of disorientation. Where she thought she'd find a secretary at a desk, there was nothing but empty space; where she thought she'd find the door to the principal's office, there was a long hallway, and the whole place struck her as more cramped and claustrophobic than she remembered. It was only after shaking her head that she realized she was picturing Tommie's old school.

"The one he left behind," she whispered. Hearing footsteps, she turned as a woman approached.

"Hi," the woman called out. "Were you speaking to me?"

"No, I'm sorry. I just got a little turned around."

"What can I do for you?"

"My son is in first grade," she started, before explaining what had happened and finally proffering the lunch bag.

"I'd be happy to bring it to him," the woman said with a smile. "Which teacher does he have?"

She knew she'd be asked, but why couldn't she remember? She really needed to have Tommie remind her again. "I'm sorry, but I'm not sure. He's new here."

"It's not a problem," the woman said with a wave. "The first-grade classrooms are right next to each other. What's his name again?"

Beverly told her as she handed over the bag.

The woman seemed to study her before coming to a decision. "No worries. I'll take care of it."

"Thank you," Beverly said, and after watching the woman re-treat down the hallway, Beverly left the school, relieved. She re-traced her path to the road and started walking at a steady pace, feeling the weight of the sun on her back. Vehicles sped past her in either direction, some of them slowing but none of them stop-ping. She didn't mind; instead, she found herself thinking about the woman she'd just seen at the school. It was clear that the woman didn't recognize Tommie's name, and while he hadn't been there long, it would be nice to believe that Tommie was in a school where the staff knew every child, especially the ones who were new, since they were the ones who might need a little extra attention. And Tommie was so quiet, he could easily vanish into the background. No wonder he was having trouble making friends.

Maybe, she thought, she should redo his room to help him settle in and be more comfortable. Get rid of all the clothes and paintings and other grown-up stuff, so it felt like a kid's room. Not today, but maybe this weekend. They could make a fun project of it. It would be great if she could get him some posters for the walls, but she realized she wasn't sure what Tommie would want. Would he like skateboarding or surfing posters, football or baseball? She supposed she could ask him, but the truth was, she couldn't afford any.

The idea of redoing his room made her remember the room she'd prepared for him in the months before he was born. She'd known he was going to be a boy—she told the ultrasound technician, *Yes, absolutely!* when asked if she wanted to know the sex of the baby—and the following weekend she'd found a classic wallpaper border to go with the light-blue walls she could already imagine. On the wallpaper were scenes of a boy doing country things—fishing from a dock, walking alongside a scruffy but happy dog, dozing beneath a tree—and Gary had made jokes about it, even though he agreed to purchase it. She'd spent days painting, hanging wallpaper, and assembling the rest of the furniture. They got a crib and changing table and chest of drawers and a glider-rocker she could use when breastfeeding, and when Gary had given her money for baby clothes, she browsed in stores, wanting to buy everything she touched. The outfits were precious, the cutest clothes she'd ever seen, and she could imagine Tommie in all of them.

Those were happy times, some of the best. Gary wasn't drinking or hitting her, and she was able to drive a car instead of having to walk everywhere. Never in a million years would she have expected her life to turn out the way it had, and she thought about all that had happened since the moment she woke Tommie in his bed and told him they were going on an adventure.

Lost in her thoughts, she barely noticed the walk or the passage of time. It was only when she reached the gravel road that she realized how weary she actually was. She felt as though she were running a marathon where the finish line kept receding into the distance, but she continued to put one foot in front of the other. On either side of her were crops, green and leafy in the late-spring sun; beyond the crops, there was a pasture dotted with barns, odd-looking outbuildings, and a massive greenhouse. Near one of the barns were a tractor and two pickup trucks, tiny from her vantage point, and as always there was a cluster of people in the fields, doing whatever it was farmworkers did. Eyeing the greenhouse, she thought about the marijuana she'd found in the house.

Couldn't marijuana be grown in a greenhouse?

Sure, but at once she laughed at the absurdity of trying to link the two. For all she knew, the greenhouse wasn't even being used, but the idea was sticky enough to make her wonder again if there were more drugs in the house. She reminded herself to make sure there weren't, sooner rather than later.

By then she could see the house in the distance, and she passed a second cluster of fieldworkers, this one closer to the road than the other group, maybe fifty yards away. They were bent over and examining the leafy plants, their faces shadowed by the hats they were wearing. From the corner of her eye, however, she noticed one of them slowly stand upright and stare in her direction; three others in his proximity did the same—like meerkats, or as though they'd been choreographed. Pulling her baseball cap lower, she picked up her pace, but she could almost feel their eyes lingering on her, as though they'd been waiting for her to return.

31.

BY THE TIME SHE REACHED the porch, her heart was pounding, and Beverly tried to calm her nerves. She thought again that she was simply being paranoid—of course there were farmworkers at farms, and the sight of anyone walking in the middle of nowhere was an oddity. Besides, it wasn't as though any of them had followed her to the house; when she glanced over her shoulder, they were back to work. She reminded herself that unless she learned to keep her thoughts from bouncing around like marbles tossed onto a granite table, she wasn't going to be any good for either herself or Tommie.

Removing her wig and hat, she climbed the stairs to the bathroom. A shower would help clear her head, but as she started to strip off her sweat-soaked clothes, she suddenly remembered the marijuana. On impulse, after readjusting her shirt, she opened the mirror of the medicine cabinet. To her, it appeared to house a small pharmacy. There were all sorts of prescription medicines, most with names she didn't recognize, but one she did: Ambien, for sleep. She vaguely remembered seeing the commercials. Assuming that all of them could be dangerous for Tommie, she tossed the bottles into a small wicker basket near the door. She searched the drawers and cabinet beneath the sink next, and then, grabbing the wicker basket, she carried it to the kitchen, where she dumped the contents into a plastic garbage bag.

"Where else would I hide drugs?" she muttered aloud, realizing she had absolutely no idea, which meant she had to look almost everywhere. She didn't want to think that Tommie was the type of child who'd find pills or powders and ingest them, but who knew for certain? Children sometimes did dumb things simply because they didn't know better. And anyway, who knew what other dangers there might be? Like faulty wiring or lead paint or rat poison or switchblades? Or what if there were other terrible things, like dirty magazines or Polaroids with the kinds of images children should never see? Even worse, what if there were guns? Weren't all little boys interested in guns?

She thought again that she should have done this the moment they'd moved in, but better late than never. She started with the kitchen drawers, checking them one by one, digging through clutter and cooking utensils and half-used candles and pens and sticky notes and all the other kinds of junk that accumulated in drawers. Because her thoughts still seemed swimmy—she really should have showered to help with that—she kept each drawer open after searching it, so she didn't lose her place. After that, she checked the cupboards loaded with pots and pans and another set of cupboards filled with bowls and baking items and Tupperware, leaving those doors open, as well, to confirm that she'd checked everything.

She pulled out everything from beneath the sink, finding all sorts of cleansers, including the ones she'd previously used. Some of them were poisonous, which meant they should be stored somewhere else, maybe on the high shelves in the pantry, where

Tommie couldn't reach them. For now, though, she left them on the floor.

In the pantry, she cleared the shelves, intending to reorganize them all later, but thankfully there were no more drugs or other terrible things. As for the living room, she'd already removed everything from the cabinet, so there weren't too many other places to search, and it took only a few minutes. The next step was the hall closet, which was crammed with jackets, along with a small vacuum cleaner, a backpack, and other assorted odds and ends. On the top shelf, she found hats and gloves and some umbrellas, and as she pulled it all from the closet and examined the items one by one, she thought it would probably be a good idea to box most of it up to store somewhere else—no reason to put any of it back. Besides, she was on a roll, and not wanting to disrupt her rhythm or slow down, she moved next to the back porch.

A quick survey revealed that the shelves needed to be completely reorganized. On one of the lower shelves was a can of paint thinner; a small rusted hatchet and equally rusted saw sat right next to it. There was a power drill on the same shelf. Staring at them, she marveled that Tommie hadn't already hurt himself. As in the pantry and the closet, she pulled everything from the shelves, piling it at her feet. She checked the paint cans a second time before reaching for a half-opened bag clearly marked with a skull and crossbones. The label showed that it was for use on rodents, and though she could practically guarantee there were mice in the house, there was no way on God's green earth that she'd ever spread poison around, so into the garbage it went. She used a small step stool to put the paint thinner, hatchet, saw, and drill on the top shelf for now, but everything else could wait. She wanted to get through the house before Tommie got home, so she dragged the bag inside with her and went up the stairs.

In the hallway, she went through the linen closet, thinking all of it should probably be washed, so she left it piled on the floor; in her bedroom, she checked the closet along with the chest of drawers and the nightstand, her garbage bag at the ready. Tommie's bathroom was next, until finally she turned to his bedroom.

It was there, under his bed, in the first place she probably should have looked, where she found the guns.

32.

THERE WERE TWO OF THEM, neither of them a handgun, one longer than the other, and both with barrels that were as black and terrifying as death itself. Beside them were two open boxes of ammunition.

Beverly choked out a sob, praying that her eyes were playing tricks on her, but when she focused on the guns again, she was swamped with self-loathing and burst into tears. Curling into a ball on the floor, she knew she'd failed her son. What kind of mother was she? How could it not have even occurred to her to make sure Tommie's room was safe? In her mind's eye, she kept seeing Tommie peek under the bed, his eyes bright with excitement as he reached for the guns. He'd pull them out and sit on the floor, feeling the weight and the cold, slick metal of the barrel. He would recognize the trigger and know exactly what it was for. He might even trace it with his finger, just to see what it felt like, and then . . .

"That didn't happen," she croaked, trying to convince herself, but the vision continued to unfold like a nightmare, drowning her words. She broke down completely then, giving in to the images and weeping until she was too exhausted to continue. She had no idea how long she cried, but when she regained a measure of equilibrium, she realized she had to take care of this right now, before Tommie came home.

Resolutely, she reached for the first of the rifles, tamping down her fear that it might go off. She pulled it gently by the stock, sliding it across the wooden floor, making sure the barrel was pointed in the opposite direction. While she still had her courage, she carefully reached for the other one, feeling like she was attempting to defuse a bomb. This one was a shotgun. She had no idea whether either of them was loaded—she wasn't even sure how to check for something like that—and once they were on the floor beside her, she reached for the boxes of ammunition.

Now, though, as she stared at the weapons that could have killed her son, she wasn't quite sure what to do. She had to hide all of it or, better yet, get rid of it. But that was easier said than done. You don't just toss a gun into the bushes, after all, but she couldn't imagine keeping them anywhere in the house, either.

I have to bury them, she thought.

She tried to remember if she'd seen a shovel. She hadn't, but she assumed there might be one in the barn. The idea of going there frightened her, though. Not only had the owner told her the barn was definitely off-limits, but if there were guns and drugs in the house, who knew what else might be stored out there? Just what kind of place was this?

She didn't know; all she knew for sure was that the guns had to go before Tommie got home. Rising to her feet, Beverly stumbled down the stairs. Once out the door, she veered in the direction of the barn. As she continued to collect herself, sunlight hammered down, thickening the air to the point that it seemed to absorb all sound. She heard no crickets or birdsong; even the leaves in the trees were still. The barn stood in shadow, as though daring her to proceed, daring her to learn the truth of why it was off-limits.

As she approached, she wondered whether she'd even be able to get inside. For all she knew, the door might be chained shut with one of those indestructible locks, or, despite its appearance, it might have some sort of security system that included . . .

Cameras.

The word brought with it a sudden need for caution, and she halted while scenes from the last few days tumbled through her mind.

An owner taking cash for rent without asking too many questions . . . Drugs and guns in a house where the previous tenant had left in a hurry . . . A man with a truck appearing at her door . . . Men in the fields surrounding her house who seemed to take a more-than-casual interest in watching her . . .

All she knew for sure was that she didn't want to learn what the owner might be up to and that it was time for her and Tommie to move on. There was something terribly wrong with this situation, and she should have recognized it earlier. She should have known the whole thing was too good to be true. Though she didn't have enough money to leave, she'd somehow figure it out, even if she had to hold up one of those cardboard signs begging for money on the side of the road. It wasn't safe here, not any longer, and at the very least going somewhere new would make it more difficult for Gary to find her.

She turned, backtracking to the house, relieved by her decision. Nonetheless, she didn't want the guns in her house for a single minute longer. Knowing she still had to bury them, she went to the kitchen, eyeing the chaos. In the open drawer near the stove, she'd seen a large metal spoon—the kind used for stirring a pot of stew—and she retrieved it. It might take a while, but as long as she could find soft earth, it should work.

Outside near the house, she began to search for a spot where the ground wasn't too hard or dry. She couldn't dig near the big trees, because the roots probably sucked up all the water, but as she was thinking about it, she suddenly remembered the creek. The ground there should be softer, right?

She quickly headed in that direction, but on the off chance that Tommie would want to hunt for tadpoles again, she ventured a ways beyond the spot they frequented. Dropping to her knees, she tested the earth, relieved to find that it yielded easily, in small but regular scoops. She worked methodically, making sure the hole was long and deep enough to bury both of the guns and the ammunition. She didn't know how deep they needed to be, because she didn't know anything about the creek. Did it widen after big rainstorms? Did the whole area become a pond during a hurricane?

She supposed it didn't matter. She and Tommie would be long gone before anything like that happened.

But she was running out of time. Tommie would be home soon, and she needed to get this done. She hurried back toward the house, only to freeze mid-stride. For a long moment, she couldn't even breathe.

The pickup truck from the day before was in her driveway again.

PART V

Colby

33.

THAT NIGHT I DIDN'T FALL asleep for hours. I told myself that I couldn't have fallen in love, that real love required time and a multitude of shared experiences. Yet my feelings for Morgan grew stronger by the minute, even as I struggled to understand how something like that could even be possible.

Paige, I thought, could probably help me make sense of it. Even though it was late, I called her cellphone, but again there was no answer. I suspected she would tell me that I was suffering from a wild infatuation, not love. Maybe there was some truth in that, but when I thought about my previous relationship with Michelle, I realized that I'd never experienced the overwhelming emotions I'd felt with Morgan, even at the beginning of our relationship. With Michelle, there'd never been a time when I felt the need to make sense of what was happening between us. Nor had the world ever faded away when we'd kissed.

Assuming what I was feeling was real, I also wondered where our relationship might lead and whether anything would come of it. My logical side reminded me that we'd be going our separate ways in just a few days, and what was going to happen after that? I didn't know; all I knew for sure was that I wanted more than anything to spend as much time with her as possible.

After finally drifting off in the early hours of the morning, I slept in for the first time since I'd arrived in Florida, waking to a morning sky that seemed almost ominous. Already, the heat and humidity were oppressive—the kind that promised thunderstorms later—and sure enough, a check of the weather on my phone confirmed it, right when I was supposed to be performing. A quick text exchange with Ray let me know that I should plan to come in anyway. They'd be monitoring the weather, he assured me, and would call the show when they needed to.

I went through my normal morning routine, even though nothing else was normal at all. My thoughts were dominated by Morgan; when I ran past the Don, I couldn't help but look for her; when I stopped to do pull-ups on some scaffolding near the beach, I conjured the smoothness of her skin. After my shower, I swung by the grocery store and pictured Morgan rehearsing in the conference room or screaming with delight as she rode the roller coasters at Busch Gardens. Putting some chicken breasts in my shopping basket, I wondered what she had told her friends about the day we'd spent together, or if she'd said anything about it at all. Mainly, though, I tried to figure out whether she felt the same about me as I did about her.

That's the part I couldn't work out. I knew there was mutual attraction, but did her feelings for me run as deep as mine for her? Or was I simply a way to pass the time, a fling to add spice to her vacation before her real life began? Morgan was, in many ways, still a mystery to me, and the more I tried to figure her out, the more elusive understanding seemed. Uncertain what the evening would bring, I bought two candles, matches, a bottle of wine, and chocolate-covered strawberries, even though I knew she might want to go out instead.

Back at the condo, I put everything away and took a few minutes to straighten up the rooms. With nothing left to do and Morgan on my mind, I reached for my guitar.

I plucked out the melody of the song that I'd played for Morgan on the beach the other night, still nagged by the knowledge that it wasn't quite right. The lyrics needed more dimension, a specificity that I hadn't quite nailed.

Crossing out bits and pieces of what I'd already written, I thought about the way Morgan made me feel—not only the emotions she inspired but also how differently I saw myself through her eyes. There had only been a handful of times in the past when a song almost seemed to write itself, but that's what I started to experience. New lyrics felt effortlessly resonant, anchored now with details plucked from our day together. Meanwhile, I ramped up the driving energy of the chorus, already envisioning a multilayered recording that would give it the sound of a gospel choir.

A glance at the clock warned me that I was almost running late. I didn't have time to scribble the new lyrics into my notebook, but I already knew it wasn't necessary. I tossed on a clean T-shirt, hurriedly collected what I needed for Bobby T's, and scrambled down the steps. Overhead, clouds were rolling and twisting as though gathering energy before exploding. I made it with only five minutes to spare, noting that the crowd was less than half the size of my previous show, though every seat was still taken. I didn't expect to see Morgan in the crowd but nonetheless felt a jolt of disappointment at her absence.

I played my show, filling the extra hour mostly with requests, while the clouds continued to grow even darker. Halfway through, the breeze picked up and started to blow steadily. For the first time since I'd been performing at Bobby T's, some people began to rise from their seats and head for the exits. I didn't blame them—in the distance I could see dark thunderheads forming on the horizon, and as they approached, I expected Ray to cut the show short at any moment.

Shafts of sunlight occasionally broke through the roiling clouds, creating prisms of color and a glorious sunset. Beyond the audience, the beach had emptied, and as more people continued to leave, I wondered whether Morgan would even show up. Nonetheless, just as the last rays of sun were vanishing, Morgan finally arrived. She'd come in from the beach and was dressed in a flattering yellow sundress; over her shoulder was the Gucci tote I recognized from the day before. Backlit by the shifting light, she appeared like an otherworldly vision. She offered a small wave, and I instinctively found myself launching into the song that I'd been working on, the one I suddenly knew I never would have finished without meeting her.

Even from a distance, I could see delighted recognition on her face as the first notes filled the room. Though I typically sang to the audience as a whole, I couldn't help focusing most of my attention on her, especially as I sang the new lyrics. When the song ended, the audience was quiet before suddenly exploding into a longer-than-usual wave of applause, interrupted only by a bright long streak of lightning that split the sky over the water. Seconds later, a deep growl of thunder rolled down the beach like a slow-moving tumbleweed.

The applause died out as most of the remaining crowd rose from their seats. I could already see Ray walking toward me and making a slashing gesture below his chin. I immediately set my guitar aside as Ray stepped up to the microphone, announcing that the show was finished. By then I was wending my way toward Morgan.

"You made it," I said, unable to hide my delight. People streamed past us onto the beach with an eye on the sky; others hustled in the opposite direction, toward the parking lot. "I wasn't sure you would."

"You played the song," she said softly. She placed a hand on my arm, her eyes glittering. "But it was different this time."

Standing before her, I was about to explain why, but I was struck by the thought that she already knew. Over the water, lightning cut the sky again, followed by thunder, which came more quickly than it had only a few minutes earlier. The wind had a cooler edge now, but all I could think about was the warmth of her hand on my skin.

Searching for something to say, I asked, "How was Busch Gardens?"

She nodded toward the sky, an amused smile on her face. "Do you really want to talk about that now? Don't you think we should leave along with everyone else?"

I reluctantly withdrew my arm. "Let me load up, okay?"

Morgan followed me past the now-empty tables. Ray and other employees had already cleared away most of the equipment, and as I reached for my guitar case, I felt the first drop of rain. I moved quickly, but even before we started for the parking area, that first drop turned into a sprinkle, followed by an almost immediate downpour. I opened the door for Morgan as the clouds unleashed the deluge that had been building all day.

I rounded the truck at a run and hopped up into the cab, my shirt and pants already drenched. Even with the windshield wipers on high, I might as well have been in a car wash. I navigated almost blindly through the parking lot. On Gulf Boulevard, a number of cars had pulled over with their hazard lights blinking, while others simply inched along. Lightning flickered overhead like strobe lights.

"I think I need some dry clothes if we're going out."

"We're not going out in this," she said. "Let's just go to your place, okay?"

Figuring that I was already wet and having driven through hurricanes in North Carolina, I rolled down my window and leaned my head out, trying to spot the upcoming turn. Rain pelted my face and blew into the truck, but eventually I was able to turn off Gulf Boulevard onto a quiet side street.

My face stung in the driving gusts of rain; lightning flashed again, this time almost directly overhead, thunder cracking like a gunshot. All at once, power went off on one side of the street as far as I could see, knocking out the lights. I guessed that my condo, directly ahead, must have been affected, too.

The road was already beginning to flood when we finally reached the condo. I was soaked, with water from the lowered window pooling in my lap. Shrouded in darkness, the entire complex appeared strangely deserted.

Knowing it was pointless to try to avoid the rain, Morgan scrambled and ran to the stairs. I jumped out, as well, key in hand.

Inside, the only light visible was the steady flicker of lightning beyond the sliding glass door. Despite the storm, the air was already becoming stuffy. Morgan came to a stop in the living room, and I stepped around her, leaving small puddles as I walked. In the kitchen cabinet, I found the candles and matches I'd purchased earlier, thankful to have them on hand.

Once the candles were lit, the living room was cast in shadows. I placed both of them on the coffee table, then pulled open the sliding glass door to let in some air. The wind was blowing hard across the small porch, the rain moving almost horizontally.

In the dim yellow light, I noted a smudge of mascara on Morgan's cheek, the slightest hint of imperfection on someone who seemed almost flawless in every way. Her wet sundress clung to her skin, outlining her curves, and the dampness was causing her long hair to return to its natural riot of waves. I tried not to stare, wondering again how she could have come to preoccupy me so fully in such a short period of time. I had barely thought about the farm or my aunt or Paige, and even the music that I loved was focused entirely on her. I was suddenly sure that I would never love another in this way again.

Morgan was frozen in place. The candlelight pooled in her eyes, calm and knowing, as though she understood exactly what I was feeling and thinking. But she remained cloaked in mystery, even as I approached her.

I leaned in and kissed her then, wanting to believe that she could feel the crackling intensity passing through me. When I gently moved to pull her closer, I felt her hand touch my chest.

"Colby . . ." she whispered.

I slowed then and simply wrapped my arms around her. I held her for a long time, reveling in the feel of her body against my own, until she finally began to relax. When I felt her arms twine around my neck, I closed my eyes, wanting the moment to last forever.

In time, she loosened her embrace and took a small step backward.

"I'm going to change into something dry," she murmured. "I brought extra clothes, just in case."

I swallowed, barely able to speak. "Okay," I managed.

Picking up one of the candles, she retreated to the bathroom off the hallway. When I heard the door click shut, I realized I was alone in the living room, unable to imagine what might happen next.

34.

FROM THE LINEN CLOSET, I grabbed a towel and headed to the bedroom, candle in hand. As I stripped off my wet clothes, I tried not to dwell on the fact that a few feet away, out of sight, Morgan had slipped out of her own clothes, as well. I dried off, then pulled on a pair of jeans and my other button-up shirt. I rolled the sleeves up to my elbows and, peeking in the mirror over the dresser, did what I could with my hair. Picking up the candle, I made my way back to the kitchen.

With the power out, the stove was useless, but the chocolate-covered strawberries and wine would still be cool in the refrigerator, along with some of the cheese left over from the picnic. After retrieving it, I sliced the cheese and arranged it on a plate, along with crackers and the strawberries. I had to fish through the drawers to find a wine opener but finally found one and opened the bottle, as well. Taking a pair of glasses from the cupboard, I brought everything to the coffee table. Nervous, I poured myself a glass of wine and took a sip. I wondered whether Morgan would want any.

Beyond the windows, the rain resembled diamond slivers in the unending flashes of lightning. Shadowy palm fronds danced in the wind like puppet figures while I settled onto the couch. Absently rotating the wineglass in my lap, I thought of how Morgan had sounded when she'd whispered my name and wondered what was going through her mind right now. She knew now how I felt about her, but had she known when she arrived at the show? Had she known last night? I didn't know, and though part of me was nervous at the thought that my feelings might not be reciprocated, I also understood there was nothing I could do to change the way I felt about her.

I wondered, too, if I could have fallen in love had I not come here, to this small town in Florida. Not only with Morgan but with anyone. I hadn't fallen in love with Michelle, but deep down I knew that our conflicting schedules were only part of the reason. It had more to do with the farm and the all-encompassing nature of the work. Because there was always something to do, I'd somehow lost the ability to simply relax and enjoy life or to make time for someone special. As an excuse it had been a good one, so subtle as to render me unaware it was happening, but as I took another sip of wine, I understood that I had to make changes unless I wanted to end up like my uncle. I needed to allow myself a break now and then—to write songs or go on walks or simply sit and do nothing at all. I needed to catch up with old friends and open myself to new possibilities and people, and the time I'd spent here only underscored that importance.

There was, after all, more to life than work, and I realized I no longer wanted to be the person I'd recently become. I wanted to embrace those things that were important to me and worry less about the things that were beyond my control. Not sometime in the future but starting as soon as I got back home. No matter what happened with Morgan and me, I knew I would reinvent myself as the person I wanted to be. I'd done it before, I reminded myself, and there was no reason I couldn't do it again.

Rising from the couch, I walked toward the sliding glass doors. Back home, I knew, a storm like this would make me worry about the crops or the chickens or the roof of the greenhouse, but here and now I found the spectacle inspiring in an almost foreign way.

Fate, it seemed, had conspired to make this evening unlike any other I'd spent here, and while there was something perhaps romantic about that notion, I suspected I was reading too much into it. Paige, I knew, would agree with that, but as I continued to take in the thunderstorm, I knew it was something I nonetheless wanted to believe.

Still, I wished that I could have spoken with Paige, if only to ask if what was happening to me was normal. Did love carry with it the power to make a person question everything? Did love make a person want to become someone new? When I thought about Paige and her experience, I wasn't quite sure. She'd been in love once, but she seldom spoke about it, other than to tell me that love and pain were two sides of the same coin. I understood why she'd said it, but I sometimes caught her reading romance novels, so I doubted she was that jaded. I suspected she would understand what I was going through now. I remembered that once she'd met her husband-to-be, she suddenly wasn't around much in the evenings, and in the rare times she was, she seemed buzzy and lighthearted. At the time, I was so wrapped up in my own world, I didn't think much about it, other than to be happy that she and my aunt were getting along. It wasn't until she announced over dinner that she was leaving the farm that I realized how serious things had become with her boyfriend. A phone call followed not long after she moved away, announcing that she'd been married by a justice of the peace. The whole thing struck me as dizzyingly fast—I'd met the guy just once, and only for a few minutes, when he picked up Paige for a date. One day she was the Paige I'd always known, and the next I questioned whether I'd been living with a stranger my entire life. Now, however, I had an inkling of what she was feeling back then; I was starting to grasp that love followed its own timeline and made even radical changes almost inevitable.

I wished I'd brought in my guitar from the truck. Playing something—anything—would have helped me sort through it all, but given the storm, I decided to leave it where it was. Instead, I found my phone and pulled up a playlist of the songs I had written, the ones I thought were my best. I set the phone on the coffee table and had another drink of wine, then returned to the glass doors, reliving the memories that had inspired each of the songs and wondering what would have happened had my uncle not passed away. I wasn't sure that I would have stayed on the farm, but would I have attempted to make music a career, in the same way Morgan was trying to do? At the time it didn't seem possible—and maybe it wasn't—but I couldn't shake a newfound sense of disappointment that I'd never given it a try. Morgan's ambition had ignited something long dormant in me—even as I accepted the idea that she was far more talented than I.

I heard a noise behind me and stole a look over my shoulder. Morgan had returned to the living room with the candle cupped in her hands. She wore a different sundress, with a low scooped neck, and I couldn't help but stare at her. Her hair, like mine, was still slightly damp, the thick waves glinting in the candlelight. The smudge of mascara on her cheek had vanished, but I saw that she'd applied a little makeup that accented her dark eyes and gave her lips a deep, glossy sheen; her arms and legs glowed like satin. I felt my breath catch in my throat.

She paused a few feet from me, as if basking in my gaze.

"You're . . . beautiful," I said, my voice almost hoarse.

Her lips parted as she exhaled, and I suddenly saw in her unguarded expression that her feelings mirrored my own. Open and hungry, her expression told me everything I needed to know: Like me, she had fallen in love with a stranger, upending both of our lives. Moving to the coffee table, she wordlessly set her candle next to mine. She surveyed what I'd set out, then took a moment to focus on the music drifting from my phone.

"You?" she asked.

"Me," I said.

"I don't think I've heard this one."

I swallowed. "It's not one I usually play at my shows."

My voice sounded strangely distant, and I watched as she sat on the couch. As I moved to take a seat next to her, her sundress lifted slightly, revealing a flash of her smooth thigh, a sight that struck me as intensely erotic. I motioned toward the wine. "Would you like a glass?"

"I'm fine," she answered. "But thank you."

"I wasn't sure if you'd be hungry."

"I had something to eat right after we got back. But I might have a strawberry in a minute. They look delicious."

"I bought them. I didn't make them."

"I'm still impressed."

I knew I was talking around the edges of things, but it seemed to be all I could do. With my throat going dry again, I took another sip of wine. In the silence, I had the sudden sense that she was just as nervous as I was, which I found oddly comforting.

"The changes you made to the song were beautiful," she offered.

So are you, I wanted to say, but didn't. "You were my inspiration," I said, trying to sound casual but knowing that I failed.

"I wondered. . . ." she whispered, allowing her hair to fall over her face. Then: "I thought about you all day. Missing you."

I reached out to take her hand and felt Morgan's fingers interlock with mine. "I'm glad you're here now."

I sensed the expectant tension in her hand as she held mine, and I thought again about kissing her. Her eyes were half closed, her mouth partly open, but just as I leaned toward her, a phone began to ring, faint but insistent. When she realized it wasn't my phone, she let go of my hand and rose from the couch. After disappearing into the hallway, she peeked out, ringing phone in hand. She seemed uncharacteristically flustered.

"It's my mom," she explained, her tone sheepish. "She's called a couple of times and I haven't gotten back to her."

"You should probably answer, then."

She reluctantly hit the appropriate button and put the phone to her ear.

"Hey, Mom," Morgan said. "What's up? . . . Yeah, sorry. I know I haven't called, but we've been having a fantastic time. . . . Nothing much. What's that? . . . Is he okay?"

Turning to me, she mouthed something like *Our dog got sick.*

"What did the vet say? . . . Okay . . . Yeah . . . That's good to know. How's Heidi doing with it? . . . Uh-huh . . . Uh-huh . . ."

She said nothing for a while, then: "Well, let's see. We rehearse in the mornings, then usually hang out at the beach or the pool. We've been going to hear some live music and checking out downtown St. Pete. . . . Yeah, they're having a great time. It's Holly and Stacy's first trip to Florida, so it's been fun showing them around. . . ."

I remained silent on the couch, not wanting to distract her.

"Uh-huh . . . No, we haven't been there yet. Maybe in a day or two. We went to Busch Gardens, though. Over in Tampa? . . .

Yeah, it was fun. The lines were short, so we were able to ride just about everything. . . . No, not tonight. We're going to order room service and watch a movie. It was a superlong day," she said, making a guilty face at me.

I stifled a smile.

"Yeah, they're here. We got some photos from the beach right after we arrived. Oh, and I also saw two manatees. . . . At one of the parks, but I can't remember the name. . . . We rented kayaks and went through the mangroves, and they were right there when we turned around. . . . No, actually, they didn't go. I went with someone I met here. . . ."

My ears couldn't help but perk up.

"Yes, Mom. He's nice. . . . He's a farmer from North Carolina. . . . No, I'm not kidding. . . . Colby. . . . Twenty-five. . . . We heard him singing at Bobby T's. He's here on sort of a working vacation. . . ."

She turned her back to me, lowering her voice. "No, he didn't go to college, but why does that matter? . . . Mom . . . Mom . . . It was just kayaking. Don't make a big deal about it. You seem to forget that I'm an adult now. . . ."

I could hear a hint of frustration creeping into her tone. On my playlist, one song ended and another began. I watched as she ran a hand through her hair, tugging at the roots.

"I haven't had time to check that yet. I'll call the apartment manager as soon as I get home, okay? I'm sure it's not a big deal getting utilities turned on. I can figure it out. . . . I haven't had time for that, either. . . . How many times have I told you that I'm not interested in a job teaching music? . . . Yeah . . . Uh-huh . . . I know . . . Sorry, I'm tired and I should probably go. They're motioning to me that they want to start the movie. . . . Tell Daddy and Heidi that I love them. . . . Love you, too."

She hit disconnect and simply stared at the phone. Rising

from the couch, I walked over to her and placed a hand on the small of her back, caressing the smooth skin beneath the fabric.

"Are you all right?"

"Yeah, I'm fine. But sometimes she interrogates me—it's not always a conversation, you know?"

"I'm sure she was just checking to see if you were having a good time."

"And making sure I'm not getting into trouble." She sighed. "But I don't know why her mind even goes there. Especially when compared to other college kids. It's like she can't accept the fact that I'm an adult and am old enough to make my own decisions."

"Parents worry." I shrugged. "It's in their DNA."

A brief but uncertain smile flashed across her lips. "It's so much easier speaking with Dad sometimes. I mean, he's nervous about me going to Nashville, and I'm sure he'd prefer that I get a job teaching, too, but at least he understands why I want to go, and he's always been my biggest fan. My mom, though—she always reminds me about how tough the music business is, how thousands of people have the same dream I do but never make it. . . ."

When she trailed off, I used a finger to brush the hair from her eyes. "They want to protect you from disappointment."

"I know, and I'm sorry. I probably shouldn't have answered. It's why I didn't answer the first two times she called. She keeps talking about this opening at one of the private schools in Chicago, and it doesn't matter how many times I tell her that I'm not interested. It's just . . . hard sometimes."

She turned to face me, leaning in. I wrapped both arms around her.

"Of course it is."

On my playlist, another song began. Morgan put her arms

around my neck and I held her close, thinking how naturally her body seemed to fit with mine. Unconsciously, I shifted my weight from one foot to the other, our bodies swaying in time.

"I remember you singing this song," she murmured, "the first night I heard you play. I was spellbound."

Outside, the wind continued to howl, and the rain continued to blow. The candles bathed the room in a golden glow. I caught the scent of Morgan's perfume, something musky and alluring.

Morgan pressed into me, and when she lifted her gaze to meet mine, I traced the outline of her cheekbone with a finger. Our faces drew closer, our breathing slightly ragged but in nearly perfect harmony.

I kissed her then, hungry and nervous, and when our tongues came together, I felt a jolt run through me, electrifying every nerve. One of her hands trailed down my back and around my side, her touch so light it almost seemed as though it wasn't happening. Her fingers eventually found the bottom of my shirt, and after a quick tug on it, her fingernails skimmed across my skin, the sensation making it almost impossible to breathe. Slowly, she traced the muscles of my abdomen and chest, even as her tongue continued to flicker against my own. Her breaths became shallow; her eyes were half closed, and I could only stare, in thrall to her sensuality. One by one she undid the buttons of my shirt, until it fell open. Pulling the shirt over my shoulders, she locked my arms in place, holding them there for a moment, as though teasing me, before finally allowing my shirt to fall free to the floor. She leaned in and kissed my chest, her mouth trailing upward to my neck. Her heated breath on my skin set my body to trembling, and I reached for the strap on her dress. She bit my neck softly before raising her mouth to mine again. I slid one strap down, followed by the other, then reached for the hem of her dress. Lifting the hem with my finger, I traced the inside of her thigh. I heard her gasp and felt her hand grip the back of my head. She began kissing me with even more passion then, and I found myself slipping away to the place I suddenly knew I was always meant to go. Slowly lowering the top of her dress, I slid it down her body and separated from her then, reveling in her beauty. When the dress hit the floor, I cupped my hands around her small waist, helping her step out of it, knowing I wanted her more than I'd ever wanted anything. Without another word, I picked up a single candle and led her to the bedroom.

35.

AFTERWARD, WE LAY BESIDE each other without speaking for a long time, her body warm against my own, until finally she rolled to her side and we fell asleep spooning in the tangle of sheets.

Waking in the gray twilight of dawn, I kissed her tenderly, unable to hold the words inside any longer.

"I love you, Morgan," I murmured into her ear.

Morgan merely smiled before opening her eyes and staring into my own.

"Oh, Colby," she said, reaching up to touch my mouth. "I love you, too."

PART VI

Beverly

36.

THE MAN IN THE TRUCK had returned.

She tried to slow her breathing as she ducked behind the barn. What would have happened had he arrived ten minutes earlier, while she was in the house? Would he have seen her through the windows? Would he have opened her door? And what if she'd actually entered the barn and been discovered in the place she shouldn't have been?

The burst of adrenaline made her stomach flip. She leaned against the plank siding and closed her eyes, thanking God she hadn't been that stupid, that she'd decided to avoid the barn before it was too late.

I need to calm down so I can think, she told herself, closing her eyes. She hoped he hadn't seen her, hoped he would believe she wasn't home, so he would leave like he had the last time. She hoped he would leave before the school bus arrived. . . .

Oh God . . .

Tommie . . .

Peering around the corner again, she saw the man standing on the porch, looking first one way and then the other. A moment later, he descended the steps and started toward the barn. Beverly flattened herself against the planking, staying perfectly still. She fought the urge to watch his approach.

She heard the barn doors squeak open. In her mind's eye, she imagined him scanning the interior, making sure that nothing had been disturbed. She wondered if he'd done the same thing the day before, when she and Tommie were down at the creek, or whether he was in communication with the farmworkers, monitoring her routines.

Tommie . . .

Please let the bus be late today. She clenched her fists, waiting, until she heard the barn door squeak again, followed by the sound of it banging shut. She remained in place, hoping he wouldn't circle the barn, wondering what he would do if he found her. She considered making a dash for the creek, but just as she psyched herself up to do so, she heard the truck door slam, followed by the engine cranking to life. Finally, she heard the crunch of the gravel as the truck backed out and vanished down the road.

Beverly stood there for what felt like eons, her breaths eventually beginning to slow, before gathering the courage to peek around the barn again. The truck was gone, and as far as she could tell, no one was lying in wait. There was no movement, but she lingered, just to be sure, and then she started running toward the house. She burst through the door, leaving it open, then tore up the stairs.

In Tommie's room, the guns were right where she'd left them. It wasn't possible to carry both the guns and the boxes of ammunition in just her hands, so, thinking quickly, she reached for Tommie's pillow. Removing the pillowcase, she shoved the boxes of ammunition inside, then carefully lifted both guns from the floor by their stocks, keeping the barrels pointed toward the ground as she scooped up the pillowcase.

Now wasn't the time to rush, even if the bus was right out front. She left the room, walking slowly. She gingerly descended the steps, thankful that she hadn't bothered to shut the front door on her way in. Careful not to stumble, she backtracked to the creek, to the hole that she'd already dug.

She put one gun in, then the other, then dumped the ammunition from the pillowcase. Using her hands to speed things up, she refilled the hole. Once that was done, she patted it down, then stomped on it, but there was only so much she could do. It would be obvious to anyone who came this way that something had been buried, but she realized she didn't care.

She was going to get the hell out of here before anyone found out.

37

BACK INSIDE, BEVERLY SCRUBBED her hands at the sink until her skin felt raw, but the soil had left a brownish tint on her palms, like wood stain. Eyeing the chaos on the main floor, she figured she'd have to clean it all before they escaped, not because she cared about the owner but because the man in the truck could come back, and an orderly house might make it appear that they were still living there, which would buy them some time. . . .

And for now? She'd have to thaw and cook the hamburger and chicken and rice, and she'd have to soak the beans and cook them, too, but without a cooler she doubted the food would last more than a day on the road. After that, it would be sandwiches and apples and carrot slices for God knew how long. She had to pack clothes, too, before sneaking away at night. No one would see them, but that also meant there might be no one to give them a ride, and the realization of all she had to do made something collapse inside, fear giving way to another flood of tears.

How was it possible for something like this to happen? To leave one dangerous situation only to end up in another equally dangerous situation? If she lived a hundred lifetimes—a thousand—the odds were almost inconceivable.

She couldn't understand it and recognized that she didn't have the energy to try. Instead, swiping at her tears, she took a deep breath and left the house, descending the porch steps and heading toward the road. She took a seat on the stump, adrenaline fading fast. How long had it been since she slept more than a few hours at a stretch? Too long, that much was certain, and now she was paying the price. With every exhale, like a deflating balloon, the frantic energy of moments earlier was replaced by a blanket of almost overwhelming exhaustion. In the silence, her limbs seemed to be falling asleep, and though she tried to concentrate on the weed and the guns and the secrets in the barn and the man in the truck, she felt strangely disconnected from those things, as though she were watching herself from a distance. From somewhere deep inside, she understood that she had to leave, but the urgency had become a receding tide. It was flowing out and away from her, growing ever-more distant while the rest of world blurred at the edges. She could feel herself beginning to sway as she tried to stay balanced, her body already rebelling. She needed to rest, to sleep. More than anything, she wanted to close her eyes and drift away, if only for a few minutes. What would be the harm? Even if the man in the truck suddenly reappeared, she didn't have the energy to hide. . . .

"No," she said aloud. Knowing she needed to focus, she forced herself to stand. She tried to summon the fear she'd just experienced, but it remained dull and listless, a phantom more than reality.

"Stay awake," she told herself, shaking her head.

She began to pace then, back and forth, like a tiger in a cage at the zoo. Within minutes she heard the bus, a low growl in the distance. The image started as a shimmery liquid mirage, gradually solidifying as it drew near. The brakes squeaked, and then the bus slowed and came to a halt. There was a soft hiss when the doors swung open.

Through the windows, she saw Tommie seated near the rear of the bus and watched as he rose and made his way forward with his backpack slung over his shoulder. Her love for him provided a single moment of clarity, like the sun's rays passing through a cloud. All at once, she felt like herself again, and just before her son jumped down to the road, he turned and waved to someone behind him. Despite her exhaustion, Beverly broke into a wide smile.

He finally made a friend, she thought. When he was close, she reached for his backpack, and they started toward the house. He was home and he was safe and he'd made a friend, but with every step, the clarity faded. She wanted to ask how school was, wanted to ask who he'd been talking to just then, but the words wouldn't seem to come. She reminded herself that they should leave before the man in the truck returned, reminded herself that they had to escape before it was too late, but the fear associated with it had fogged over again like breath on a mirror. She fought to keep her eyes open. Tommie kicked at a small rock on the path, sending it skittering.

"Are you going to come to the school tomorrow?"

The sound of his voice startled her, and it was difficult to process what he'd asked. Finally: "Why would I come to the school?"

"It's field day, remember? Amelia said it's really fun and some of the moms bring cupcakes and cookies. You could come, too."

She couldn't place the name and wondered where she'd heard it.

"We'll see," she said, hearing the words emerge as a mumble. When she opened the door, Tommie came to a stop, taking in the utter disarray. She should have warned him, but it felt like too much effort.

"It's nothing."

She shuffled to the kitchen and grabbed an apple, then led Tommie to the living room. Using the last of her energy, she plugged in the television and reattached the cable, watching as the screen blinked before cartoons came on. It was *Scooby-Doo*, something she used to watch as a child, and Tommie settled on the floor, already transfixed. She vaguely heard him take his first bite as she lay on the couch, her eyes already beginning to close. Absently, she used her foot to push a stack of DVDs to the floor, so she could stretch out further. They hit the rug with a plastic clatter. On the television, Scooby and the gang were being chased in a supposedly haunted amusement park. Even as her mind slowly shut down, she realized she had seen this episode.

"Mommy's really tired, so I'm going to take a quick nap, okay?"

There was so much to do before she left, she thought again, but in the next instant, she felt as though she were falling, and that was the very last thing she remembered before everything shut down and she was fast asleep.

38.

IT WAS DARK WHEN SHE began to stir, the flickers of the television making her squint and then blink before finally opening her eyes. The world beyond the windows was black, the room illuminated by moving light.

"Cartoons," she muttered.

"Mom?"

The sound of Tommie's voice roused her, and more of the room came into focus. The cabinet stood at a cockeyed angle, and there were books and knickknacks piled throughout the room. When Tommie turned toward her, she could see the whites of his eyes, even though the rest of him remained shadowy, like a ghost.

"How long have I been sleeping?" she croaked.

"A long time," he said. "I tried to wake you, but it didn't work."

"Sorry." She pressed her eyelids, then pulled her hair away from her face, trying to summon enough blood flow to actually sit up. All she wanted to do was close her eyes, but when she did, she heard Tommie again.

"I'm hungry."

His voice prompted her to focus, and taking a deep breath, she was able to shift her legs off the couch and sit up. Fighting the urge to lie back down, she clasped her hands, her mind and body still resisting her command to rise. On the television, SpongeBob was talking to a starfish; there was an apple core on the rug already turning brown, along with a second one. She thought to pick them up—or at least tell Tommie to run them to the garbage—but realized she didn't care. She felt like she could sleep for a thousand years, but her son needed to eat. Using the armrest, she pushed herself upward but had to stand in place when she was struck by a wave of dizziness. When it finally passed, she shuffled to the kitchen.

Shunning the overhead light, she turned on the one above the stove. Even that hurt her eyes, and as she made her way to the sink, she nearly stumbled into the pile in front of it before catching herself. She squinted at the clock, trying to calculate how long she'd been asleep. With her mind still swimmy, she couldn't remember what time the bus had dropped Tommie off. It was either a quarter until four or a quarter past four, but either way, it must now be coming up on Tommie's bedtime.

He needs to eat. She felt disconnected from her body as she pulled out a pot and filled it with warm water to thaw a couple of chicken drumsticks. Somehow, she maintained enough muscle control to chop cauliflower and carrots, then tossed them on a baking sheet, which went into the oven. Closing her eyes, she leaned against the refrigerator, her body shutting down until she suddenly remembered what had happened earlier. Though the images of the drugs and guns and the man in the truck were dreamlike, they were enough to make her flinch.

"Tommie?" she called out, trying to keep her voice steady.

"Huh?"

"Did anyone come by while I was sleeping?"

"No."

"Did you see a truck pull up in the driveway?"

"No."

She glanced out the window, trying to understand why the man hadn't come back, but her thoughts remained gummy, everything sort of tangling together. Continuing to lean against the refrigerator, she shut her eyes again. The warning signals she'd perceived earlier felt far away, like they related to someone else, but she had enough sense to remove the rest of the chicken and hamburger from the freezer so it would thaw, as well.

After that, she forced herself to be the mother she knew she was. Though her movements were slow and robotic, she cooked the drumsticks in the cast-iron frying pan, her mind blank while she struggled to keep her eyes open. After loading the food onto two plates, she called for Tommie and heard the television go off before he joined her at the table. Exhaustion smothered her appetite, so she moved most of the contents of her plate onto Tommie's. She yawned once and then repeatedly, and when Tommie finished, she sent him upstairs to take a bath. She didn't bother to clear the dishes. Instead, she stepped out onto the front porch.

In the silver moonlight, she could see the barn, dark and ominous, but the fear felt hallucinatory. From upstairs, she could hear Tommie talking to himself as he splashed in the tub. She reminded herself that they had to escape, but there was so much to do beforehand to make that possible and she couldn't summon the energy necessary to start. Dragging her feet, she left the porch and went upstairs. Her legs were heavy and felt uncoordinated, almost as though she was sleepwalking.

In the bathroom, Tommie had already gotten out and wrapped himself in a towel. His wet hair sprouted in all directions, and when he turned, she saw the infant and toddler he once had been, and something ached inside.

"Did you remember to shampoo your hair?"

"I'm not a baby anymore."

Her thoughts continued to drift of their own volition, slowing further as she followed him to his room. For an instant, the walls were light blue with wallpaper borders that showed old-fashioned scenes from the country, then the room changed back to reality. She found him a clean shirt and underwear, thinking how much she loved him as he crawled into bed. She used her fingers to straighten his hair before kissing him on the cheek.

Zombie-like, she returned to the darkened main floor. Only the light above the stove continued to provide enough of a glow to keep her from stumbling on the clutter.

I have to get ready, she thought, eyeing the chicken and hamburger. But she was operating on autopilot now, no longer in conscious control of her body, and she left the kitchen, heading to the living room. As she lay down on the couch, her mind blank, her eyes were already closing again.

For an instant, she imagined a pirate falling from the Empire State Building, and then all at once, she was asleep.

39.

SHE DIDN'T WAKE UNTIL she heard Tommie coming downstairs, her eyes blinking open. Grayish light was streaming through the windows. As Beverly began to stretch, all that had happened in the last few days came rushing back, the weight of it so oppressive she felt like crying.

She recalled that her mom used to cry a lot in the mornings, memories of her red eyes and the way she'd wrap her arms around her own waist as though trying to hold herself together still vivid. Beverly never knew what to do at times like that, never knew how to make her mom feel better. Instead, she would keep her distance. She'd make her own breakfast and get herself off to school and then, while the teacher droned on, spend the rest of the day at her desk wondering what she'd done to make her mom so upset.

I am not my mother, Beverly reminded herself. Instead, focusing on Tommie, she sat up, struggling to keep the tears at bay and somehow succeeding. By then Tommie had reached the kitchen. Beverly went to join him, recognizing that they'd somehow made it safely through another night. That should have made her feel better, but it didn't; in the back of her mind, she felt a newfound sense of dread, as though the worst was yet to come.

"Did I miss the bus?" Tommie asked, obviously unaware of how she was feeling. "I don't want to be late."

That's right, she remembered. *It's field day.* Beverly eyed the clock. "You'll be fine. Let's get you some breakfast, though."

Her muscles were stiff as she moved to the cupboards. She made Tommie a bowl of cereal and brought it to the table, then flattened his cowlick using the wax on the counter. She plopped into the chair across from him, watching as he started to eat, her mind trying to shrug off the effects of sleep but wandering from the past to the future. Staring at her son, she couldn't help feeling that Tommie deserved so much better. She should have provided him with a normal home and a normal life, but now she was about to uproot him again, because she'd made mistakes that a good mother wouldn't have made. She wondered whether to warn him now or simply wake him in the middle of the night, as she had the last time. She wondered where they would eventually end up and whether she'd find work and how long it would be until their lives felt remotely normal again. She'd tried to do everything right, but somehow it had all gone wrong.

It wasn't fair. No one deserved a life like she was giving her son, and her eyes welled with tears. She turned away, not wanting Tommie to see them.

"Do you like it here?" she asked, her mind continuing to wander. "Sometimes I think it would be nice to live near the beach. Do you remember when we went to the beach? When you were little?"

He'd been young then, still a toddler, and she'd put so much sunscreen on him that the sand stuck to him like glue. They built sandcastles and splashed at the water's edge and tossed grapes for the seagulls, which made Tommie scream with laughter as the birds flocked from one spot to the next. Gary had decided to go golfing instead, and she recalled thinking even then that Tommie was all she'd ever need.

"That was a wonderful day," she reminisced, knowing she was talking to herself more than to him. "We had so much fun— maybe we should try to do that again. Find a place close to the beach, where we could play in the sand or watch the sun go down over the water. Sometimes I think I could just sit and listen to the waves for hours. Wouldn't that be perfect?"

Tommie looked at her. "Amelia said that I could sit next to her on the bus today."

At his comment, Beverly knew her son had missed the hint, and her melancholy deepened as she rose from the table. After swiping at her tears, she made him a sandwich, adding an apple to his lunch, making sure to put it in his backpack. Yesterday felt almost like a lifetime ago.

By then, Tommie was just about finished. He drank the re- maining milk from the bowl, leaving a milk mustache. She wiped his lips. "You know I love you, right?"

When Tommie nodded, she thought again that she should tell him the truth, but the words wouldn't come. Instead, she dropped to one knee, feeling wobbly and hating herself for all she was about to put him through.

"Let me double-knot your shoes so they don't come untied when you're running around."

When she finished, she looped the backpack over his shoul- ders and they left the house, their timing perfect. By the time they reached the road, the bus was already slowing to a stop. She kissed Tommie on the cheek, then walked with him toward the doors of the bus just as they swung open. She watched him ascend the steps and offered a quick final wave, but with his back to her, Tommie didn't seem to notice.

As she turned and headed back toward the house, she saw it as she had the first time, when she thought that she could make it a home. She remembered walking through and thinking that painting the kitchen walls yellow would be perfect. She'd allowed herself to believe that everything was going to turn out okay, but as she continued to stare, she saw it now for the trap that it was, its sole purpose to dangle a dream in front of her, only to crush it.

Dwelling on the unfairness of it all and the mistakes she'd made, she enumerated her failures as a mother. And this time, when the tears started anew, she barely made it to the couch, knowing she couldn't stop them.

40.

By the time she finished weeping, she was wearied and spent. Wiping her face with the bottom of her shirt, she noticed numerous brown smudges on the fabric and realized that she was looking at dirt.

From the digging when I hid the guns. Her face must have been filthy—no surprise since she hadn't showered—and she wondered why Tommie hadn't said anything about it. He had to have noticed, and she suspected that he was reacting just as she had as a child, when she didn't understand what was going on with her mom. In those moments, it was better to pretend that everything was fine, even when frightened. It was no wonder that Tommie hadn't spoken at dinner and barely glanced at her over breakfast. He'd been afraid for her and of her, and the realization made her throat tighten again. It was another mistake, one in a long line of mistakes she'd made recently.

The crying had sapped her energy, and rising from the couch was strangely difficult. She lurched to the kitchen and turned on the faucet. Cupping her hands to wash her face, she could feel flecks of dirt at her hairline and in her ears, even in her eyelashes. A mirror would help, but going upstairs to the bathroom to check would take too much effort.

She eyed the food she'd taken from the freezer the night before, then removed the plastic wrap and set it all on a plate, thinking it would be one less thing she had to do later. She found a large pot in one of the open drawers. Adding water, she began soaking the beans. None of it would be ready to cook for a couple of hours. She considered starting the sandwiches, but as she reached for the loaf of bread, she flashed to an image of Tommie as he sat between her and the old woman in the station wagon, when he'd stared at her with nothing but love and trust in his eyes, and it broke her heart.

The knowledge made her ache, and her thoughts began to scatter again. She remembered Tommie as an infant, when she rocked him late at night; she reflected on the quiet way he now seemed to move through the world. She decided to make the sandwiches later, and though she didn't understand her reason, she didn't bother to question it. She wondered again who in their right mind would ever choose orange walls for a kitchen.

Her thoughts continued to pinball, lighting up one memory after the other, and she knew the only way to shut them down was to go back to sleep. Instead, she pulled the carrots from the fridge and set them on the counter before rummaging through the drawers, trying to find the peeler. She couldn't find it, so she settled for a butcher knife, her hands trembling. She longed for sleep again and understood that it had been the only time in the last few days when she felt safe and hadn't been burdened by worries.

Her movements grew more uncoordinated until her hand

suddenly slipped and the blade cut deep into her forefinger, bringing her back to the present. She yelped—screamed, really— watching as a bead of blood appeared, and then the long gash turned completely red. Blood splattered to the counter and onto her shirt. She pinched the gash with her free hand, momentarily mesmerized, before the sting rose in full fury, morphing into searing pain. When she let her finger go, blood flowed onto the counter. With her uninjured hand, she turned on the faucet, watched the faded-pink water flow down the drain, then shut it off. She used the bottom of the shirt to wrap her finger, thinking that if she were someone else who lived a different life, she'd hop in the car and drive to the urgent care to get stitches.

But that wasn't her life, not anymore, and her eyes filled with tears. *One step at a time,* she told herself. She needed gauze and tape but doubted there was any in the house. There might be Band-Aids in one of the bathrooms, she reasoned, heading up the stairs to the bathroom Tommie used. In the second drawer down, she got lucky.

She pulled out a Band-Aid, but she needed both hands to open it, and blood splattered onto the counter. The wrapping, sticky and wet with blood, made the adhesive worthless. She tried again with another Band-Aid and got the same result. She tried again and again, failing each time, bloody wrappers and Band-Aids dropping to the floor. Finally, she got two of the Band-Aids ready, rinsed the blood from her hand and finger, and dried it using her shirt, squeezing tightly. She applied the first one, followed quickly by the second one. That gave her the time she needed to apply more, and it seemed to do the trick. Her finger throbbed with its own heartbeat as she went downstairs.

The living room and the hallway and the kitchen were wrecks, and the thought of having to clean it all and make the food and pack and escape and somehow find a way to start a new life was simply too much. Her mind shut down like an overloaded circuit, leaving nothing but sadness in its wake.

Exhausted, she went to the couch and made herself comfortable. Closing her eyes, her worries and fears faded away completely the instant she fell asleep.

41.

DESPITE SLEEPING FOR HOURS, she woke feeling as though she'd been drugged. She forced herself upright, her mind working in slow motion, the room gradually settling into focus.

"What a mess," she remarked to no one in particular, amazed again by the clutter spread throughout the room, the cabinet at a cockeyed angle, the wall half primed. She rose from the couch and shuffled to the kitchen to get a glass of water. As she drank, she felt the throbbing in her finger, the deep bruising ache. When she looked at her hand, she saw that the blood had soaked through the Band-Aids, staining them brown. It was gross, but she wasn't about to undertake an attempt to replace them, any more than she wanted to clean the living room or the kitchen or the rest of the house. Or make sandwiches or slice carrots, for that matter. She had no desire to do any of it, at least until she felt a bit more like herself.

Instead, she went to the front porch. She turned from side to side, noting the ever-present farmworkers in the fields, but they were farther from the house than they had been the day before, working on another section of the crop under a grayish cloudy sky. There was a breeze, too, fairly steady, and she wondered if that meant it was going to rain.

Even though rain would complicate their escape, she couldn't really summon the energy to care all that much; instead, she found herself lost in a memory of her mom. Her mom would get super tired, too, sometimes to the point where she'd spend two or three days in bed. Beverly could remember going to the side of her mom's bed and shaking her, asking her to wake up because Beverly hadn't eaten. Sometimes her mom would rouse and drag herself to the kitchen to warm up chicken noodle soup before retreating; other times, there was nothing Beverly could do to wake her.

As hard as those days were, though, they were nothing compared to the days that her mom cried and cried, no matter what Beverly tried to do to help. Beverly remembered being scared whenever that happened. Moms weren't supposed to cry. But it wasn't just the tears or the sobbing, choking sounds that bothered her. It was the way her mom looked, with her dirty clothes and hair poking out in all directions and the haunted expression on her face. She even moved differently, like every step she took was painful somehow.

Nor could her mom ever explain what made her so sad in the first place. It didn't matter if Beverly cleaned her room or didn't, or whether she played quietly or made noise; the blue days always came. That's what her mom always called them. *Blue days.* When she got older and understood what feeling blue meant, Beverly assumed that she meant that figuratively; later, she began to think that her mom also meant it literally. Because that's how Beverly was feeling right now, she realized—she felt as though she were slowly being enveloped in a dense blue fog. It wasn't a pretty blue, either, like the sky or the color she'd painted Tommie's baby room. This was a midnight blue, so dark and deep it seemed to be turning black at the edges, unwelcoming and cold and heavy enough to render caring about anything almost impossible.

"I am not my mother," she repeated, but even then, she wondered whether it was true.

42.

SHE WANDERED INSIDE, TRYING TO shake the idea that no matter what she did to get ready, she'd somehow make a mistake that would catch up to her sooner rather than later.

From the cupboard in the kitchen, she pulled down the cookie jar and reached for the small wad of bills. Thumbing through it, she counted, then double-checked the total, and again she felt the pressure build behind her eyes, knowing it wasn't enough. Not even close to enough, and she conjured the image of her holding up a cardboard sign and begging for money, simply to feed her son.

What was the point in even trying any longer? And why couldn't the owner of the house—*this house*—have been normal? Just an older woman who needed extra money, instead of a woman who wanted to use Beverly for whatever unlawful thing she was doing? In the silence, it was easy to imagine the man in the truck and the owner sitting around a battered kitchen table, with cash and guns and drugs spread in front of them.

The thought made her stomach turn and deepened the dark-blue fog. She zoned out for a while before finally zeroing in on the counter. She saw the knife and the carrots marked with splashes of blood, which made her think about her finger, throbbing with its own heartbeat. Strange how it did that, like it had its own little ecosystem, unconnected to the rest of her. Reluctantly reaching for the knife, she washed the blood from the carrot she'd been working on, then decided there was no way she'd let Tommie eat it, even if she peeled it until it was no larger than a pencil. She tossed it in the sink and reached for another carrot, trying to concentrate, making sure she didn't slip. When she was finished, she reached for the next carrot but decided it would be better to get the chicken going at the same time.

The meat was on the plate where she'd left it, thawed and ready to go. She searched for the cast-iron frying pan in the drawer, not finding it, then realizing that it was still on the stove from last night. Turning on the burner, she tossed in the drumsticks, crowding the pan, and returned to the carrots. But as she reached for the knife, she imagined Tommie soaked to the skin in the pouring rain, in the dark, while passing cars sent more water splashing in their direction. How long would Tommie last before he began to shiver or got sick? The image was heartbreaking. Consumed by it, she wandered aimlessly from the kitchen. She didn't think about what she was doing or where she was going; it was as though she were being pulled by an invisible string, her thoughts fading away to nothing.

She went up the steps and stood at the threshold of Tommie's room. There had been guns under the bed, and she understood that Tommie must have found them but hadn't bothered to tell her. The realization made her mind go blank again; it was too horrible to contemplate. Instead, when the room came into focus, she saw *Go, Dog. Go!* and Iron Man on the nightstand, and she reminded herself not to forget them, but even that registered only dimly. She wondered why she had come to his room in the first place, and it was only when she smelled something burning that she suddenly remembered the chicken.

The kitchen was filled with smoke, fueled by even more smoke rising from the pan. The odor of burned and charred food made Beverly rush toward the stove, instinctively reaching for the handle. It was white-hot agony as her skin audibly sizzled. Beverly screamed and dropped it, the pan crashing back to the stovetop. Tearing through one of the open drawers, she sent dishrags flying while reaching for an oven mitt. Slipping it onto the hand with the cut finger and trying to ignore the pain, she removed the pan from the heat. In another life—one where she didn't have to account for every morsel of food—she would have simply run the pan under the faucet to stop the smoke and then dumped the remains into the garbage, but instead she set the pan back on an unused burner. From the cupboards, she reached for a plate, hoping she could somehow salvage the chicken. She tried to find a set of tongs to grab the drumsticks, but it was tangled with other utensils, and when she tugged it from the drawer, spatulas joined the dishrags on the floor. With smoke still pouring from the pan, she had to peel away the drumsticks, each with one side black and the other raw, and place all of it on a plate. Only when she'd removed all the food did she bring the pan to the faucet to douse the smoke, the surface sizzling as water hit it.

It was then that she felt again the agony of her burned hand, the pain coming in sudden, relentless waves. Blisters were already forming on her palm and fingers. She moved her hand under the faucet, but the cold water hitting her skin amplified the pain, and she jerked it away. Despite the smoke, she could still smell the stench of the burned chicken, the odor almost sickening. There was no way that Tommie could eat any of it, which meant they had even less food to sustain them while they escaped. With one burned hand and the other with a gash in her finger, how would it even be possible to get anything done? It was yet another failure in a long line of failures that made her wonder how she'd ever allowed herself to believe she was fit to be a mother.

43.

BEVERLY SPENT THE NEXT HOURS doing nothing. She barely remembered drifting to the front porch, numb to everything but the dense blue fog that seemed to poison every thought. Her hand and finger throbbed, but, lost in a growing sense of melancholy, she barely felt either of those things.

I need to see Tommie was all she could think.

Only then would things be different; only then would the blue fog go away. Dimly, she was aware that he'd become her lifeline, and she needed to see his serious little face as he stepped off the bus. She wanted to smooth his cowlick and tell him that she loved him. Rising, she peeked through the window toward the clock on the wall and knew the bus had to be coming soon. She left the porch and walked toward the road, uninterested in black SUVs or men in pickup trucks or farmworkers who might be watching her. There was only one important thing.

She took a seat on the stump, pain from the burn forcing its way to the forefront of her consciousness. It occurred to her that she should perhaps wrap her hand or try to find some medicinal cream, but the thought of missing Tommie's arrival filled her with anxiety.

The clouds had continued to thicken, gray thunderheads forming. Leaves in the trees murmured with the changing weather. On a fencepost across the road, a cardinal seemed to be watching her.

Beverly stared up the road, waiting. The pain rose and sank and rose again, making her wince. She opened her hand, allowing the breeze to caress it, but that made it feel even worse, so she closed it again. The cardinal flew away, growing smaller in the distance. Beverly could feel the dark-blue fog all around her, wrapping her in its tendrils.

The bus didn't appear, and she continued to wait, then waited some more. Eventually, farmworkers loaded into the beds of pickup trucks, and the trucks left the fields and turned onto the road, vanishing from sight. The sound of distant thunder rolled across the fields. But there was still no bus.

She returned to the porch to check the time through the front windows. The bus was either half an hour or an hour late, but she couldn't remember which. She walked back to the stump, curiosity slowly giving way to irritation and then to concern as more time passed. When fear finally took root, the blue fog began to clear, though it revealed no answers, only more questions.

Where was the bus?

Where was her *son*?

Beverly felt short of breath as she realized the obvious. She walked, then ran, toward the house and burst through the door. She tried not to think the worst but couldn't help herself; she needed to figure out what to do. Did the bus break down, or did Tommie miss the bus? Was he still at the school? She'd have to walk or hopefully catch a ride. She suddenly wished there was a neighbor nearby, a sweet old lady who brought over a pie to welcome them when they first arrived, but no one had come. . . .

If the bus had broken down, she had to know. If Tommie was still at the school, she had to go get him. She tripped on a pile of detritus from the cupboards and went sprawling, her knee coming down hard on the linoleum floor, but she barely felt it as she scrambled upright again. She thought about the disguise she needed to wear, even though putting it on would take time she didn't have.

She limped up the steps to her room and froze in the doorway. Her room was trashed, clothes strewn all over the floor, closet doors open, even the bed linens on the floor. She blinked, trying to make sense of it.

Had she done this? Yesterday? When she was searching the house? She could remember cleaning out under the sink and the pantry and the closet and the back porch, but by the time she went upstairs, she'd been in such a frenzy that her memories were fuzzy. She'd cleared out the linen closet, but had she done this, as well? She supposed it was possible, but she didn't recall, and if she hadn't . . .

Her throat constricted as she remembered the man with the truck.

Had he come into the house while she was digging at the creek?

She reached for the doorjamb to hold herself steady. She didn't want to believe it, didn't want to think it had taken her that long to dig, didn't want to imagine that someone had torn through the house in her absence and done this, didn't want to consider what might have happened had she been inside when the man burst through the door . . .

No, she thought, fear sharpening her focus. She couldn't go

there, couldn't allow herself to go down the rabbit hole. Right now, Tommie was the only thing that mattered.

Steeling herself, she moved into her bedroom, taking in the destruction. Her wig was just where she'd left it in the bathroom, along with her baseball hat. In the mirror, she noticed the blood on her shirt and she slipped out of it, exchanging it for the one that hung over the shower-curtain rod. When she looked more closely at her reflection, she barely recognized the gaunt, haunted woman staring back at her. But there was no time for makeup. The pain in her hand and finger made pinning up her hair almost impossible, and she winced as she did it anyway. After donning the wig, she put on the hat and looked for her shoes near the bed, which was where she usually left them, but she couldn't see them anywhere. With so many clothes on the floor she had to kick through the piles, without any luck. She looked under the bed, but they weren't there, either, and she suddenly remembered she'd slept on the couch. She must have taken them off downstairs.

She had begun to move toward the door when she happened to glance back at the now-emptied closet, the image slowly coming into focus. A moment later, she felt her legs buckle. Almost faint, she dropped to her knees, staring with a rising sense of horror at the Christian Louboutin red-soled pumps that Gary had once given her for her birthday, the ones she'd left behind.

44.

THEY WERE HER SHOES, no question; she recognized the box they sat in and the tiny scuff mark on one of the toes from the first night she'd worn the shoes to dinner. Nor did she wonder how or why they were in the house.

Gary brought them.

He'd known that she and Tommie would run again; he must have known everything all along. It didn't matter that there were cameras in the bus station; he probably hadn't plastered her image all over wanted posters and distributed them to law enforcement around the country. He didn't need to; he knew she would travel light, so he sewed GPS trackers into their backpacks. And wherever he'd been, maybe even their old house, he simply sat back and watched their progress on his phone or computer for the next few days. He knew she'd hitched rides in strangers' cars, knew she'd stayed at the motel and gone to the diner, maybe even tracked her as she'd visited the house the very first time. He probably pulled it up on some sort of satellite or street map and then used his connections to identify the owner.

Removing her wig and leaving it in the bathroom, she staggered down the stairs, dizzy with her own stupidity. Beyond the windows, lightning flashed, and a boom of thunder followed. Rain began to fall, making the house vibrate as though a train were running past it, but in the grip of her thoughts, Beverly noticed none of it.

Gary had contacted the owner of the house, of course. More than likely, he'd done so on the phone even before the owner agreed to show the house to Beverly. He likely offered some bogus story about the opportunity to help the government with an investigation, perhaps even offered her money and told her what he needed her to do. Which explained why the woman hadn't asked Beverly the ordinary questions or asked for identification or even references. It explained why the woman had been so willing to take cash.

The rest was easy. He'd sent men to check on her, driving beat-up pickup trucks to blend in. And after that? The introduction of a bit of psychological warfare: The first time the man in the truck came, he left the guns and drugs in the house. He'd been careful to remove his boots, though, which explained why there were no footprints inside. Gary knew her and had anticipated exactly how she would react; he knew she would panic if she found prints. The second time the man came, he'd trashed her room in a further attempt to keep her off-balance and terrorize her. At the same time, Gary stationed men in the fields to watch her, so they knew exactly when she intended to run.

Beverly staggered to the couch, her mind beginning to slow as the pieces continued to come together. While she'd picked up groceries or painted the kitchen, Gary had obviously gone to John Small Elementary School and made his arrangements there. He'd explained to the principal and the teacher and the bus driver that Beverly had kidnapped their son. No doubt, he further stressed the fact that Beverly was dangerous and that both guns and drugs were suspected to be in the house; he might even have shown them photographs as proof. He would underscore his concern for Tommie's safety. In a way that sounded both official and reasonable, he would tell them that it was best to simply rescue Tommie when he was at school, when there would be no risk of Tommie being hurt.

And now? Soon the police or sheriff would be summoned, and she'd be arrested. They were, in fact, probably on their way to the house as she sat on the couch, but the thought of spending the rest of her life in prison was nothing compared to the idea that she'd never see her son again.

Tommie is gone, a voice chanted in her head as the blue fog overwhelmed her. *Tommie is gone.* There was no way to fix it, no way out. There was no future for her, no matter what, and as her mind grew blank and fuzzy, she was left only with emotions that were as dark as the fog, and further pieces fell into place. Tommie was gone and she would go to prison and Gary would take his anger out on his son, and her sweet young boy would eventually grow up and become a violent, dangerous man.

Outside, flashes of lightning continued to split the sky, and thunder boomed above the sound of pouring rain. The house grew dim, more oppressive, but it meant absolutely nothing. Life meant nothing, and the future was blacker than the world outside, no matter what she did. Every road she'd imagined had come to a dead end, and there was nothing but oblivion.

Tommie.

She realized that she'd never watch him play soccer or football or hit a home run while she clapped in the stands; she'd never see him dressed up before homecomings or proms. She'd never watch him develop a crush for the first time or bask in excitement early on Christmas morning. She'd never see him drive a car or become a young man or graduate from high school and college, and she'd never hear his laughter again.

All those chances had turned to dust and ashes, but even crying seemed pointless. Doing anything was pointless, and for a long time she couldn't summon the will to move. Her breath slowed while the blue fog thickened, bringing anguish and loss and unlimited sorrow, as though her soul was being inked with poison. The past was a horror show and the future promised nothing but pain, but the present was even worse, suffocating in its intensity.

Deliberately, she rose from the couch. As if in a trance, she slowly climbed the stairs, her hand and knee and finger throbbing in pain, but she deserved all of it, because she'd failed her son.

On the floor in Tommie's room was the plastic garbage bag, the one she'd dragged around the house while searching for drugs. Beverly turned on the lamp and sat on the edge of the bed. Buried in it were the pill bottles she'd found in the bathroom, and she began digging through the sandy rodent killer, searching for what she needed.

She pulled the pill bottles out one by one and read the labels, dropping to the floor the ones she didn't recognize. In time she found the Ambien, the vial more than half full. Dropping the bag, she left the room and went downstairs.

In the kitchen, she ignored the smell of burned chicken and the hamburger that was now spoiling. She ignored the mess and looked past the blood on the counter. Instead, she filled a glass of water from the faucet. Glancing out the window, she knew that Gary would be here soon, along with a host of law enforcement. But she didn't care anymore about being arrested; she didn't care about anything, for there was nothing left to care about and there was no way out.

Wandering back upstairs, she went to Tommie's room and sat on the side of his bed. She dumped the pills from the bottle into her hand, then tossed them into her mouth, washing all of them down with water. She lay back, thinking that Tommie's scent already seemed to have vanished completely. But it would be over soon, the sensation of finality ringing so loud that it muted everything she'd been feeling over the last few hours.

Closing her eyes, Beverly felt momentary relief.

Then she felt nothing at all.

PART VII

Colby

45.

I'd hoped Morgan and I could linger over breakfast, but she told me that she couldn't because of rehearsal. Instead, she kissed me, then hopped into the shower, and after she threw on her sundress, I drove her back to the Don.

A family with children was standing in the hotel lobby, and I saw Morgan's gaze flicker to them before she gave me a chaste kiss that left me longing for more. She'd invited me to come by the pool later to hang out with her and her friends, and though I wanted her all to myself, I accepted that it was their last week together, as well.

I did a shorter run than usual, stopping to pick up breakfast tacos from a stand. I ate them in the parking lot while still sweating, my mind on Morgan. She'd been quiet on the drive to the hotel, seemingly dazed, which I appreciated because I felt the same way. It wasn't possible to fall in love so quickly, but somehow we had, and I think she needed some time to sort through it. I also suspected she wasn't looking forward to the discussion that would inevitably arise with her friends. If she barely understood what had happened, then she probably assumed that her friends wouldn't understand it, either.

As for me, I was also thinking about the fact that Morgan and I had only a few more days together, and I couldn't help but wonder if she'd spend the next couple of hours coming to her senses and realize that she'd been mistaken about her feelings all along.

Sometime after we'd fallen asleep, the power had come on, so after I got back and showered, I took some time to clean up the condo. At the appointed hour, I drove to the Don and made my way to the pool deck. Morgan and her friends were already there, clad in colorful bikinis and soaking up the sun. The small table between the chairs was littered with tubes of sunscreen and a large bottle of water, along with leftover cups of green drinks. Thoughtfully, there was an empty chaise longue saved beside Morgan, topped with a couple of folded towels.

Holly was the first to see me, and she offered a quick hello; the others—even Morgan—waved nonchalantly, as though unaware that Morgan hadn't returned to the hotel the night before. I thought about kissing Morgan but opted not to, in case it embarrassed her, and did my best to play it cool, even though the sight of Morgan in her bikini triggered tantalizing flashbacks. For a few minutes, no one said anything; for all intents and purposes, we could have been strangers who happened to be seated beside one another. Maybe I was wrong, I thought; perhaps Morgan and her friends hadn't discussed the situation at all. Then Maria cleared her throat.

"So, Colby . . . how did *your* night go?" she asked.

As soon as she asked, they all started cackling. With the ice finally broken, I turned toward Morgan.

"Any regrets?" I said under my breath.

Morgan gave me a sunny smile. "None at all."

46.

Thankfully, none of them pressed either Morgan or me about the night before, though by their avoidance of the subject, I was reasonably sure that Morgan had spilled the beans about pretty much everything. Instead, the five of us spent the day chatting and occasionally jumping into the pool to cool off. We ordered snacks from the pool bar, and afterward Morgan and I went for a walk on the beach. I held her hand, thinking how it seemed to fit perfectly in my own.

By late afternoon, everyone was ready to call it quits. Morgan announced she needed a nap, and after hauling our used towels to the bin, I slipped back into my shirt and flip-flops. By then, Morgan had already put on her cover-up.

"Would you like to have dinner later?" I asked.

"What are you thinking?"

"How about a picnic on the beach?"

She took my face in her hands and kissed me gently. "That sounds perfect."

47.

WE ARRANGED TO MEET BEHIND the hotel at half past seven, but like Morgan, I also needed a nap. I fell asleep as soon as my head hit the pillow. Surprisingly refreshed when the alarm went off, I showered and dressed before ordering two Greek salads from a restaurant down the block, one with added salmon and the other with grilled shrimp. On the way back to the Don, I also bought a bag of ice, along with more iced teas and bottled water.

Staking out a spot next to the dune to the side of the hotel, I spread out a sheet that I'd snagged from the condo. I had just opened a bottle of water when I caught sight of Morgan approaching. Rising, I met her with a hug and got her settled on a collapsible beach chair I'd brought along.

"What did you bring?" she asked. "I'm starved."

I pulled the salads from the cooler, and after we finished, we used the dune as a backrest, snuggling in its shade. I put my arm around Morgan, and she curled into me as the sky began its slow and miraculous transformation. Blue faded to yellow; pink highlights cut long swaths toward the water as the sky turned orange and then finally red. As if on cue, the moon started to rise just as the sun was setting.

"I want you to do something for me tomorrow," I finally said.

She rotated toward me. "Anything."

I told her what I wanted, and though she didn't answer, she didn't reject my idea, either, which I took as a positive sign.

Afterward, we went back to my condo, already kissing and undressing on our way to the bedroom. We made love with tenderness and renewed urgency, and afterward, Morgan twined her limbs around me, her head resting on my chest. When she finally drifted off to sleep, I gently untangled myself and rose from the bed. Wrapped in a towel, I went to the living room, which was bathed in silvery moonlight streaming through the sliding glass doors.

As I stared at the moon rising above the trees, I thought about how much I loved Morgan and marveled at how different my own life seemed when viewed through the lens of these new feelings. Naturally, my thoughts turned to the fact that yet another day had passed and that Morgan would be leaving soon, and I wondered again what was going to become of us, dreading the idea that a decision was coming, one that might break my heart.

Back in the bedroom, I pressed my body against Morgan's. Even in sleep, she sensed my presence and responded, her body curling into mine. I breathed in her scent, feeling complete, and though it took a while to fall asleep, I knew that after I finally drifted off, I would no doubt dream of her.

48.

When we woke, Morgan persuaded me to join her and her friends on a visit to the Dalí Museum, an hour after they finished rehearsal.

We held hands as we toured the exhibits, which I'll admit I found more interesting than I expected. Maria seemed quite knowledgeable about the artist and took time to explain why one painting or another was particularly important, and while most of what I saw wasn't exactly my style, there were four or five that I kept returning to to study. They were strange but definitely thought-provoking.

Afterward we went to Clearwater Beach, sinking our bare feet into the powdery white sand and floating in the warm gulf waters. I had to leave early in order to get to my show on time, and I reminded her again of my request, but as usual she deflected. Lingering over a long kiss, I whispered that I loved her, not caring in the slightest what her friends might say after I was gone.

The Thursday-evening crowd dwarfed Tuesday's—no surprise since the weather was idyllic—and more people continued to stream in as I rolled through my first and second sets. Soon there was barely enough room to stand. Again, I was surprised by the number of requests for my original songs—clearly people were familiarizing themselves with my recordings online—and only too happy to mix things up on the evening's playlist. Overall, it was the booziest crowd since the previous weekend, and Ray and the staff struggled to keep up with the drink orders.

When Morgan and her friends showed up with about twenty minutes left in the final set, heads turned at the posse of stunning young women. I immediately launched into the song that had been inspired by her, followed by some sing-along standards to juice the crowd. Though I was still uncertain about how she would react, I cleared my throat and tapped the microphone, getting everyone's attention, before turning my gaze to Morgan.

"I heard an extraordinary singer the other day and asked if she'd be willing to perform a song for you tonight. She has yet to give me an answer, but if you'd like to hear what I heard, let Morgan Lee know how much you want her to come up and join me right now."

The crowd whooped and hollered, just as I'd expected; after registering her embarrassment, I held out my hand to her, urging her forward, while Holly, Stacy, and Maria cheered and excitably nudged her in my direction. Despite her hesitation, it seemed she was less bothered than simply nervous. As she eventually began making her way toward me, the crowd's enthusiasm built to a roar. Her friends followed, already grabbing for their phones and moving closer to the low stage, no doubt so they could film. I helped Morgan onto the platform, stepping back as she finally reached for the microphone. I moved my stool to the side, then retrieved a music stand from the back corner. Morgan pulled up her photos, zeroing in on the one with the lyrics that she'd taken while at the condo.

"Give me a minute to make sure I know all the words, okay?" she whispered, her hand over the mike.

"Of course," I said. "Take your time."

I watched as she went through the words, and it was immediately clear to me that a long review wouldn't be necessary. "For now, why don't I play through the opening stanza and the chorus, and I'll just repeat it until you signal that you're ready, okay?"

She nodded, her eyes still on the screen as she continued to mouth the words. Somehow, her nervousness only seemed to heighten the audience's anticipation.

I started the song's opening stanza, watching for my cue. As I came to the end of the chorus, I saw her nod at me, her body swaying ever so slightly as she raised her eyes toward the crowd. I circled back, repeating the opening, and as soon as she hit the very first notes, I wasn't the only one who was mesmerized. Silence reigned as her throaty voice filled the bar, people paralyzed by its clarity and power. But as she began to dance, her steps taking her from one end of the stage to the other, they erupted, cheering and clapping in time. This was a Morgan I'd never seen before—no trace of the self-conscious girl standing in my living room. Her friends were filming with intense concentration, but I could tell that it was all they could do to keep from jumping up and down.

The song was infectious, inspiring shouts and whistles by the second refrain, and the more the crowd got into it, the more Morgan responded.

There was an operatic quality to her voice, and as she launched into a powerful vibrato toward the end of the song, the audience rose to their feet as one. When she landed the final high note with total confidence, the applause was explosive. She was a sensation, and everyone there knew it.

People immediately called for an encore, but Morgan declined with a shake of her head as she placed the microphone back into the stand. She stepped off the platform, only to be swarmed by her friends, who were almost giddy with excitement.

Because I still had a few minutes left to play—and knowing it would be foolish to follow Morgan with anything I'd written—I picked a perennial crowd favorite, "American Pie." As soon as I embarked on the opening chords, the attention of the crowd swung back to me, and soon everyone was singing along, just as I knew they would. Meanwhile, the girls retreated to their original spot in the back, flushed and buzzing.

When I finished, I spotted the next act waiting in the wings. I set my guitar off to the side to make room for them to set up, then pushed through the crowd to reach Morgan and her friends. By the time I reached them and took Morgan's hand, she seemed strangely subdued.

"You're incredible," I said. "Everyone loved you."

She kissed me softly.

"I still think you're better."

49.

AFTER A CELEBRATORY DINNER, we all went dancing at a club in St. Petersburg. It wasn't the size of a weekend crowd but not bad for a Thursday night, and the five of us danced in a circle to the high-energy techno beats. Or, rather, they danced while I mainly shifted my weight from one foot to the other and did my best not to call attention to myself.

It ended up being a late night, with Morgan riding back to the condo with me while the others hopped in an Uber. On the way, she confessed that Holly and Stacy were already pressing her to post the videos they'd made of her singing.

"What do you think?" she asked, uncertain. "Do you think it would be a mistake?"

"How could it be a mistake?"

"I don't know. . . . Do you think it's good enough? What if, like, some A&R exec comes across the video? It's not exactly studio quality, and my throat has been kinda scratchy lately. I didn't have a chance to warm up and I didn't even know all the words perfectly—"

"Morgan." I took one hand off the steering wheel and laid it firmly over hers. "Stop."

When she turned toward me, I went on. "You were *fantastic*," I said. "If anyone sees that video, they'll see that you have *superstar* written all over you."

Morgan covered her face with her hands in embarrassment, but I could see the smile peeking out between her fingers.

The following morning, I drove her back to the Don. The conversation in the truck was muted, and though we made plans to meet by the pool in a few hours, she was quieter than usual, her expression preoccupied.

I didn't ask the reason, if only because I already knew.

Our time together was quickly coming to an end.

50.

Because I'd be working the following evening, I wanted our Friday night to be memorable. Doing some quick research on the internet, I was able to arrange for a private catamaran ride at sunset. I winced at the cost but tried to remind myself I only lived once.

I also planned to make her dinner afterward, which required yet another trip to the grocery store, as I wasn't sure I trusted that the chicken I'd bought before the power outage would still be safe to eat. I also had to figure out a recipe that sounded good but was also supremely easy. In the end, I didn't make it to the Don until half past eleven.

This time the group of friends was on the beach, and again, a chair for me had thoughtfully been placed beside Morgan's. Though part of me considered inviting only Morgan on the catamaran, by then I'd come to like her friends and figured they'd enjoy it, too. Their excitement at the prospect was even greater than I expected, however—they kept mentioning how much they were looking forward to it, which earned some grateful expressions from Morgan, as well.

She and I wandered off for lunch together alone. Afterward, we walked the beach and waded in the surf to cool off, and it was easy to imagine a life with her in the future, if only I had the courage to make it possible.

In late afternoon, they regrouped in their rooms to get ready; I did the same at the condo, then met them at the Don for the drive to the docks. Though I should have expected it, Morgan's friends had their phones out and were taking selfies as soon as we stepped on board, prompting the occasional eye roll from Morgan. It wasn't a huge vessel—I figured that it was comfortable for up to seven or eight guests—but the girls swooned over the fruit and cheese and complimentary champagne. Surprising me, even Morgan had some, and we all clinked glasses in celebration.

We left the dock and cruised along the waterfront; twice, we spotted dolphins trailing alongside the catamaran. The spectacular sunset somehow seemed closer when out on the water, as though we were actually sailing into it. With the wind in our faces, Morgan leaned into me, and I held her as we skimmed over the gentle waters. Her friends kept trying to get us to pose for photographs, too, but after a couple, Morgan shooed them away, trying her best to preserve the moment for just the two of us.

Once we were back onshore, the girls suggested that we head into downtown St. Pete. Though I offered to go with Morgan in case she wanted to join them, she shook her head and said she'd rather return to the condo with me.

In the small kitchen, Morgan watched while I preheated the oven and popped a couple of baking potatoes in; later I retrieved the marinating chicken breasts from the refrigerator, placing them on a baking sheet. I put them in the oven along with another foiled baking sheet bearing asparagus coated with olive oil and salt.

"I'm impressed," she said, raising an eyebrow.

"Don't be. I googled it this morning."

When I reached for the tomato to start slicing it for the salad, Morgan wrapped her arms around my waist from behind and kissed me behind my ear. "Is there anything I can do to help?"

"You can slice the cucumbers," I said, reluctant to have her move away.

She went hunting in the drawers for a knife, then rinsed the cucumber under the faucet before returning to my side. She was smiling slightly, as though pondering an inside joke.

"What's so funny?"

"This," she said. "Cooking a meal with you. It feels so domestic, but I kind of like it."

"Better than room service?"

"I wouldn't go *that* far."

I laughed. "Did you help your mom in the kitchen when you were growing up?"

"Not really. The kitchen was my mom's place to relax. She'd have a glass of wine and turn on the radio and do her thing. My job—and my sister's—was to clean up afterward. My mom hated the cleanup. I didn't like it, either, but what could I do?"

The timer on my phone dinged, and I removed the potatoes and baking sheets from the oven. Surprising no one more than me, the chicken came out like the recipe said it should. After loading our plates, I brought them to the table along with the salad and a bottle of store-bought dressing. As soon as Morgan sat, she surveyed the table.

"This isn't quite right," she said.

She rose and did a quick circuit of the bedroom and living

room, returning with the candles and the matches. After lighting the candles, she turned out the kitchen lights.

"Better, don't you think?" she said as she resumed her seat.

The sight of her face in the candlelight triggered a memory of how she looked the night we'd first made love, and all I could do was nod.

Morgan genuinely seemed to love the chicken, eating two helpings in addition to half a baked potato and generous servings of salad and asparagus. After clearing the plates, Morgan surprised me by asking if there was any wine left over from the other night. Morgan brought the candles to the coffee table, and I took a seat beside her on the couch, glasses in hand. She was scrolling through the photos from the catamaran. I leaned over to study them, as well.

As pretty as Morgan was in person, I guess I shouldn't have been surprised by how photogenic she was.

"Can you text me those?"

"How about I AirDrop them?"

"What's that?"

She rolled her eyes. "Turn on your phone and hit ACCEPT when it comes up."

I did what she said, and almost instantaneously, the photos were on my phone.

"Do you really not know what AirDrop is?" Morgan laughed.

"If you really understood my regular life, you wouldn't have bothered to ask that question."

She smiled before growing quiet. Staring into her glass, she took a deep breath. I knew what was coming. It was a conversation I wasn't sure I was ready for, the one that had no answers.

"What's going to happen to us?" she asked, her voice subdued.

"I don't know," I answered.

"What do you want?" she asked, her eyes still fixed on her wine. "Don't you want us to be together?"

"Of course I do."

"What does that mean, though? Have you even thought about it?"

"It's all I've been thinking about," I confessed. I tried to see her face.

She finally raised her eyes, a strange fire burning in them. "You know what I'm thinking?"

"I have no idea."

She put down her wineglass and took my hands in hers. "I think you should come to Nashville with me."

I felt my breath catch. Then: "Nashville?"

"You can work on tying things up at the farm, take whatever time you need . . . and then meet me there. We can be together, write songs together, chase our dreams together—it's our chance. If things work out, then you can hire more people at the farm or make it larger or raise that grass-fed beef like your aunt suggested. The only difference is that you wouldn't have to be the one actually doing it."

I felt my head begin to spin. "Morgan . . ."

"Just wait," she said, her voice brimming with urgency. "Hear me out, okay? You and I . . . I mean . . . I never thought it was possible to fall in love with someone in just a few short days. I'm not romantic in that, like, hoping-to-find-Prince-Charming kind of way. But you and I . . . I don't know. From the moment we met, it was like . . . we *fit* somehow. . . ."

Clicked like a tumbler falling in a combination lock, I couldn't help but think.

"It was almost like I knew and trusted you from the very beginning. That hasn't ever happened to me, and then the way we made music together . . ." When she paused, her expression was full of hope and wonder. "I've never felt so in sync with anyone." She turned her gaze on me. "You don't want to lose that, do you? You don't want to lose me, do you?"

"No. I want you, and I want us to be together, too."

"Then come with me. Go to Nashville when you can."

"But the farm. My sister . . ."

"You said yourself that the farm is easier now, and you said you have a general manager. And if your sister wants to come to Nashville, bring her. She can probably run her business from anywhere, right?"

I thought of Paige, thought of all the things about my sister that I had yet to admit. "You don't understand. . . ."

"What is there to understand? She's an adult. But here's the other thing." She took a long breath before going on. "You have an amazing voice. You're an amazing songwriter. You have a gift that others only dream about. You shouldn't let that go to waste."

"I'm not you," I demurred, feeling suddenly trapped, needing another excuse. Any excuse. "You didn't see yourself up on that stage."

Her expression was almost wistful. "The thing is, you don't see yourself, either. You don't see what I see. Or what the audience sees. And you also understand that music is something powerful, something that people all over the world can share, right? It's like a language, a way to connect that's bigger than you or me or anyone. Do you ever think about how much joy you could bring people? You're too good to stay on the farm."

Dizzy, I could think of nothing to say, other than the obvious. "I don't want to lose you."

"Then don't," she urged. "Did you mean it when you said that you loved me?"

"Of course."

"Then before you say no, even if you don't want to go to Nashville because I think you should or because we could be together, then maybe think about doing it for yourself." She drew up her legs, kneeling on the couch as she faced me. "Will you do that? At least think about it?"

As she'd spoken, it was easy for me to imagine all of it. Writing songs together, discovering a new city together, building a life with each other. Enjoying life, without the worries and stresses that defined my world now. And she was right about my aunt and the managers being capable of keeping things going. Now that we'd built a rhythm and routine, things were easier, but . . .

But . . .

Paige.

I took a long breath, so many thoughts and impulses racing through me.

"Yeah," I finally said, "I'll think about it."

51.

We didn't speak about it again that night, and I found myself confused and preoccupied. Though I'd expected her to ask how to keep a long-distance relationship going, I was blindsided by her suggestion that I follow her to Nashville.

As we lay together on the couch, I admitted that my dreams of a life in music still flickered somewhere inside me. I also couldn't bear the idea of losing Morgan, and when she began to kiss my neck, we wordlessly migrated from the couch to the bedroom, where our longing for each other was expressed without explanation or doubt.

In the morning I dropped Morgan off at the Don. Instead of going for a run, I showered and spent the next couple of hours walking the beach, mulling everything she'd said the night before. Gradually, I made my way back to her hotel. As I approached, I noticed the beach was unusually crowded, despite the early hour. I thought nothing of it until I realized that it had to do with the girls' recording session.

There must have been several hundred people behind the

hotel, mostly teenage girls. Pulling up TikTok, I realized that all four of them—and their group account—had posted multiple times in the last few days, offering previews of their rehearsals, along with behind-the-scenes footage of them putting on makeup or goofing around in the hotel room. All of it was accompanied by callouts announcing when and where they would perform their next routine and inviting people to attend.

Still, I was amazed by the level of genuine fandom. While I'd known they were popular, for whatever reason it hadn't registered that hundreds of people would actually take time out of their day to attend one of their recordings in person.

I texted Morgan to let her know I had arrived, continuing to marvel at the size of the crowd. After a few minutes she responded, asking if I would be able to help them film, to which I readily agreed.

Noon came and went, but there was still no sign of the girls. The crowd, however, kept trickling in, dozens more making their way down the beach. I scouted the area, trying to figure out the best vantage point from which to record the performance, before realizing that I had no idea where to even start.

I eventually heard a buzz rise from the crowd nearest the hotel. Despite being taller than most of the younger fans, I was able to catch only glimpses of the girls' hair as they milled around on the deck near the sand, probably trying to figure out where to take up positions. Hundreds of phones waved in the air, everyone jockeying to get photos.

The four of them stayed on the deck for several minutes, taking selfies with the fans and signing autographs, while I tried to edge closer. Finally realizing that it was impossible, I went around to the front of the hotel and walked through the interior to reach the pool area. As soon as the girls spotted me, I saw relief on their faces.

"This is crazy!" Morgan exclaimed when I was close. "None of us imagined it would be like this. We weren't sure if anyone would show up, let alone this many people."

"We can't figure out how to clear enough space on the beach for us, either," Stacy fretted.

"Why don't you just perform on the deck?"

"I don't think the hotel will be happy about that. . . ." Maria's brows were knitted with worry.

"You're guests," I pointed out, "so you're allowed to be here on the deck. And it's only three songs, right? It'll be over before anyone at the hotel even knows what's going on."

The four of them conferred briefly, then decided that my idea was the most workable solution. Holly and Stacy set their totes off to the side and returned with two complex cameras, along with tripods that they mounted just off the deck. Maria and Morgan put two of their phones on tripods, as well. Meanwhile, Holly handed me a third camera as she set a boom box in place.

"Your job will be to push the crowd back just a bit and to get some footage of the audience, okay? For B roll, so we can edit it in later. And turn on the music when I give you the signal."

"Got it," I said, taking the camera.

As the girls double-checked their outfits and makeup, occasionally stretching to loosen up, I ushered the crowd a few steps back from the deck. I also asked the people in front to sit, so that people in the back would be able to see, and to my surprise the first few rows lowered themselves to the sand. Meanwhile, Holly told me where to stand and gave me instructions on the kind of shots she wanted—basically a mixture of wide-angle shots and close-ups of the fans. I moved closer to the boom box, while the girls took their positions.

The crowd quieted almost immediately. I pressed PLAY, startled by the volume of the boom-box speakers. At least the girls could be sure that everyone heard the music. I began filming the crowd, observing Morgan and her friends from the corner of my eye. Naturally, the girls were perfectly in sync as they launched into their intricately choreographed routine. As polished and poised as they all were, I felt that I could have been watching the Super Bowl halftime show.

The crowd went crazy, and I captured lots of video of girls try-ing to mimic the moves they liked or losing themselves in the music, inventing moves of their own. In all, Morgan and her friends danced for more than ten minutes.

When they finished, the crowd clapped and cheered, some of the teenagers calling out individual girls' names. "Morgan, over here!" "Stacy, we love you!" I shot video of Morgan and her friends teaching some of their fans various moves while on the deck, but, conscious of the other hotel guests' blocked access to the beach, the girls soon wrapped things up, asking me to collect the equip-ment. I did, grabbing the boom box last. With a quick wave and a thank-you and a flurry of blown kisses, Morgan and her friends retreated through the pool area, with me trailing behind like an overloaded packhorse.

It was midafternoon by the time we ventured out again to the pool area. Snagging chairs on the far side, I rounded up some towels. When the waitress came by, the girls ordered a pitcher of strawberry margaritas, along with five glasses. Apparently, it was time to celebrate.

It was then that I heard my phone vibrating on the small table beside the lounge chairs. Recognizing the name of my general manager, I put the phone to my ear.

Not thirty seconds later I walked away from the girls, the blood draining from my face.

In less than a minute, I felt almost sick, and by the time I hung up, I felt as though my world had come crashing down. I quickly dialed my sister, but there was no answer. The girls must have seen my expression when I finally returned to the chairs, because Morgan jumped up immediately and grabbed my hand.

"What happened? Who was that? What's wrong?"

Lost in my own racing thoughts, I could barely get the words out.

"Toby," I said. "The general manager at the farm. He told me that my aunt Angie had a stroke."

Morgan's hand flew to her mouth. "Oh my God! Is she okay?"

"I don't know," I said. "But I've got to get home. . . ."

"Now?"

"My sister isn't answering her phone."

"So?"

I swallowed, praying that she hadn't answered because she was with my aunt at the hospital. But I couldn't help reliving the past, wondering if the worst was yet to come.

"She hasn't called me, either."

"What does that mean?"

With fear taking root, I could barely process her question. "Nothing good."

In a daze, I kissed Morgan goodbye and ran back to my truck before gunning it to the condo. I tossed everything I'd brought into the truck and was on the highway less than ten minutes later.

In a normal situation, I was eleven hours from home.

I hoped to make it in less than nine.

52.

WITH MY FOOT MASHED ON the accelerator, I sped over the causeway to Tampa, Toby on speakerphone.

"Walk me through it again," I said. "From the beginning."

I'd known Toby all my life, and while he had always seemed unflappable, I could hear the strain in his voice.

"It was Tuesday morning," he said after a beat, "and Angie was in the office when I arrived, just like normal. I updated her on the repairs to the irrigation system—we've been working on that— and then we met with the contractor at the greenhouse to go over the expansion plans. That took about an hour. After that, she went back to the office, and she appeared to be fine. If I'd known or even suspected something was wrong . . ."

"I'm not blaming you," I assured him. "Then what happened?"

"Xavier went to see her right before lunch. There was a problem with the Mopack," he said, referring to the egg-packaging equipment, "and he noticed that something was wrong with her eye. It was kind of drooping, and when he asked her about it, she mixed up her words. He was scared enough to call me, so I hurried over. Right away it was clear there was something wrong with her, so I called for an ambulance. When they arrived, they said she was having a stroke, so they rushed her to the hospital."

"Why didn't you call me?"

"I assumed that Paige told you," he replied, obviously flustered. "I called her right after I called for the ambulance, and she rushed over. She followed them to the hospital, and I know she was there while your aunt had surgery. As far as I know, that's where she's been ever since. I'm sorry."

I realized that I was gripping the wheel so hard that my fingers were turning white, and I tried to force myself to relax.

"Surgery?"

"To remove the clot," he clarified. "That's what Paige said, anyway."

"How's my aunt doing now?"

"I haven't spoken to the doctors—"

"When you've seen her, I mean," I interrupted. "Is she conscious? Is she in ICU?"

"According to Paige, the surgery went well. Angie's not in the ICU. She's awake, but the left side of her face is partially paralyzed, so it's hard to understand her sometimes. And her left arm and leg are really weak."

"Is Paige with her? Right now?"

"I think so."

"When were you last at the hospital?"

He must have heard my anxiety, because his words began to come even more quickly.

"I was there today, right before I called you. I stopped by for half an hour or so. But that was my first visit in a few days."

"Did you see Paige there?"

"No, but where else would she be? She hasn't been home lately. I went over a couple of times and even checked the barn."

"When was the last time you saw her?"

"At the hospital earlier in the week."

I was already speeding, but I accelerated, passing cars in a blur. Though it was dangerous, I used one hand to open Find My Friends on my phone, trying to locate Paige's phone. I saw that hers was at our house and breathed a sigh of relief. A good sign.

Or was it?

53.

I CALLED PAIGE NEXT. It went straight to voicemail.
When I finally reached I-95, I called my sister again.
Same result.
I checked the app. No change.
I drove even faster.

54.

After that, I called the hospital, got the runaround, but finally spoke to a nurse who had just started her shift and hadn't worked since earlier in the week. She didn't have much in the way of helpful information regarding my aunt but promised that someone who knew more would call me back.

The call didn't come for more than an hour. That nurse told me that, as far as she knew, there'd been no recent emergencies but that I needed to speak with my aunt's neurologist for additional information.

Trying to keep my frustration in check, I asked to speak with him. The nurse informed me that he wasn't in the hospital at the present time—it was a weekend, after all—but he was expected at rounds sometime later. She would leave him a message, recommending that he give me a call.

After hanging up, I tried and failed to reach Paige again.

My stomach tightened further.

55.

THE INTERSTATE WAS A HAZY mirage as I left Florida behind and entered Georgia.

Morgan called for the third time; I'd been on the phone the first two times and hadn't answered. After apologizing, I filled her in with what I knew, adding that I hadn't yet spoken to the neurologist.

"I called my parents about what happened," Morgan said. "I asked them about strokes, and they said that if she's not in ICU, she'll most likely survive. But depending on the severity of the stroke, there can be long-term effects."

Like partial paralysis, I thought. "Can those be fixed?"

"I don't know. It sounded like it depends on the original blockage. Apparently, rehabilitation has come a long way in the last few years. I hope you don't mind, but my mom checked out Vidant Medical Center and discovered that it's a primary stroke center, which is really important. It means they'll be able to offer interdisciplinary care even after she's released. She said your aunt is in good hands."

"That was kind of your mom to look it up," I said. "But how did you know my aunt was admitted to Vidant?"

"Google. It's the largest hospital near Washington. It wasn't that hard to figure out."

Even as Morgan spoke, my mind continued to whirl. "The nurses won't tell me anything."

"They're not allowed to. That's the physician's job."

"He hasn't called me, either."

"He will, probably after he finishes his rounds. And depending on how many patients he has, he might call late. That's what my parents do. But what did Paige say?"

I said nothing at first. Finally: "I haven't been able to reach her yet."

"What?" Morgan's voice sounded her disbelief. "Why didn't she call you when it happened?"

That was the question I wasn't yet ready to think about. Instead, I offered, "I don't know."

56.

I STOPPED FOR GAS, then hit the interstate again. From the other direction, headlights appeared as tiny dots in the distance, growing larger as they approached and suddenly vanishing, only to be replaced by others. Overhead, the moonlight was clear and bright, though I was only dimly aware of the passing landscape.

I called Toby again. After my call—maybe because my worries had amplified his—he returned to the hospital, even though he'd visited earlier. He said that he had been allowed to stay only a few minutes, because visiting hours were ending, but that my aunt appeared stable. "She was sleeping," he explained.

"Where was Paige?"

"I didn't see her, but one of the nurses said they thought that she came by earlier. They assumed she went to get something to eat."

"That's great," I said, feeling a sudden surge of relief.

"I also stopped by the house again on my way back," he

added. "The lights weren't on, and her car wasn't in the drive-way."

After I hung up, the relief was strangely short-lived. In the back of my mind, warning bells continued to sound.

My next call to Paige went straight to voicemail again.

57.

BY THE TIME THE DOCTOR finally called, I'd made it through Georgia and was into South Carolina. I was doing 90, praying I wouldn't be pulled over but more than willing to risk it.

"Your aunt had an ischemic stroke," he said. "That's where a clot narrows one of the arteries leading to the brain. The good news is that the blockage wasn't total." He explained the surgery—while I'd imagined something complex, he said it hadn't taken long—and emphasized how critical it was that Toby had called the ambulance when he did. He updated me on her current condition and the medications she was taking, adding that he was confident she'd be released within the next few days.

"What about her paralysis?" I asked.

"That's a bit more complicated," he said, "but the fact that she retains some movement in her arms and legs is a good sign." He went on to discuss potential complications and post-hospitalization rehab, but with my brain still whirling, all I really understood was that right now there was still much he couldn't answer. While I appreciated the honesty, it didn't make me feel a lot better.

"And you've told all this to my sister, right? Paige? She knows what's going on?"

"Initially, yes." He sounded surprised. "But I haven't spoken to her recently."

"Hasn't she been at the hospital?"

"I haven't seen her myself, but sometimes I don't even start my rounds until after visiting hours are over."

I called Toby again, but this time his phone went to voicemail.

It seemed like years before I reached the North Carolina state line.

58.

MORGAN CALLED AGAIN, MAYBE an hour after I crossed into North Carolina.

"Hey," she said, sounding sleepy. "It's a long drive and I know you're upset, so I just wanted to check on you."

"I'm fine." I briefed her on what the doctor had said, or as much of it as I could remember.

"How far away are you now?"

"Two hours or so?"

"You must be exhausted."

When I didn't answer, Morgan went on. "What did Paige say?"

"I still haven't been able to reach her."

Silence stretched out over the line, to the point where I wondered if we'd lost the connection. Finally: "Is there something you're not telling me, Colby?"

For the first time since I'd known her, I lied.

"No."

I could tell she didn't believe me. After a beat, she said only,

"Keep me informed, okay? I'm going to have my phone with me all night. You can call me no matter how late it is."

"Thanks."

"I love you."

"Love you, too," I responded automatically, though my mind remained elsewhere.

59.

Southeast of Raleigh, while still on the interstate, I knew I had a decision to make. I could keep going a little farther and take the highway that led to Greenville and Vidant. Or I could take a different highway, one that led back home.

I doubted visitors would be allowed into the hospital at this hour, but even if they would allow me in, my gut told me that I needed to head home first.

Just in case.

60.

I FOLLOWED THE HIGHWAY I'd driven thousands of times, only half aware of the turns I was navigating. Lightning flickered in the distance, remnants of a passing storm. As I eventually neared Washington, it was coming up on eleven, and I could feel the tension building in my shoulders and my neck.

After exiting, I made the final turns, one after the next, until reaching the gravel road that separated one side of the farm from the other. The moon had drifted below the horizon and the gravel was slick from a recent downpour. In the darkness, it was difficult to make out the shape of the blackened house, but I thought to myself that it looked as deserted as Toby had said.

As I neared, however, I realized that wasn't wholly correct; there was a faint light from the kitchen, barely noticeable through the bushes, which would have been easy to miss.

I wheeled into the drive, going so fast that I had to slam on the brakes, the truck sliding in the mud-slicked dirt. I jumped out, splashing in a puddle, and noted the absence of Paige's car even as I raced along the path that led to the small front porch.

I burst through the door, and a single glance in either direction was enough to confirm my worst fears. I tore through the bottom floor, searching everywhere, then finally bounded up the stairs, horror taking hold.

I found Paige on my bed, looking at first as though she was sleeping. I shouted her name as I rushed toward her, loud enough to wake her, but there was no response. A bone-deep chill flooded my body when I saw an empty prescription bottle on the bed beside her—and other scattered prescription bottles on the floor—and I began to scream.

61.

HER CHEST WAS BARELY MOVING, and I couldn't find a pulse when I checked her wrist. I put my fingers over her carotid artery and felt something thready and weak. Her face was gaunt and deathly pale, and after grabbing the prescription bottle and shoving it into my pocket, I scooped her into my arms and carried her down the steps. Unsure whether she would last long enough for an ambulance to arrive, I hurried to the truck, buckling her slumping body into the passenger seat.

I backed out with the engine roaring, then gunned it down the gravel road. As soon as I reached asphalt, I pressed the emergency button on my phone.

My call was answered by the dispatcher right away, and I explained what I knew. I recited my name and my sister's information and said that I was rushing for the hospital now. I told them the name of a physician I knew from Vidant. The woman on the other end reproached me for failing to call an ambulance; ignoring the comment, I pled with her to let the emergency room at

Vidant know I was coming. Then I disconnected immediately, focusing all my energies on the road.

The speedometer occasionally inched into the red, but thankfully there was little traffic at this time of night, even in Greenville. I slowed when I saw a red light and made sure the intersection was clear before rolling through it, adding to a long list of driving infractions. Throughout the ride, I kept shouting at Paige, trying to wake her, but she remained slumped over in the seat, her head bowed. I didn't know whether she was alive or dead.

At the emergency room, I again scooped Paige into my arms, carrying her through the electronic doors as I called for help. There are emergencies and then there are *emergencies*—I think everyone in the waiting room knew this was the latter—and a minute later, an orderly appeared from behind closed doors with a gurney.

I laid Paige down and walked alongside as the gurney began moving toward the back. Repeating to the nurse what I'd said to the dispatcher, I handed over the empty prescription bottle. A moment later, the gurney disappeared behind locked doors, and I was told to return to the waiting room.

Then, like a switch had been pulled, the world descended into slow motion.

Others in the waiting room had settled back down after the commotion I'd caused, reverting into their own worlds. I was told I had to sign in for Paige and stood in a slow-moving line, until finally reaching the window. I sat and filled out forms, detailing Paige's medical and health-insurance information. When finished, I was instructed to take a seat.

In the aftermath of flooding adrenaline, I practically collapsed into a plastic chair, feeling disoriented. There were men, women, and children of every age, but I was only distantly aware of them. Instead, I thought of all that had happened. I wondered if I'd made it to the hospital in time and if Paige would live. I tried to imagine what was being done to help my sister, tried to imagine the orders a doctor was calling out, but couldn't picture a thing.

I waited, then waited some more. Time continued to slow. I'd check the time on my phone, sure that twenty minutes had passed, only to realize it had been just five. I tried to distract myself with the internet and learn what I could about overdoses, but there was little about the drug I thought she'd taken other than warnings and prompts that immediate treatment at a hospital was necessary. Sometime later, I thought about calling Morgan but wasn't sure what I'd be able to tell her, because I had no answers. Seated opposite me was a woman who was knitting, her movements hypnotic.

Saturday night—or technically, Sunday morning, I suppose—was a busy one at the emergency room. People continued to stream in and out every few minutes. When I had waited for what felt like an intolerable length of time, I approached the admissions window again and begged the nurse to tell me what was happening with my sister. In my mind's eye, I imagined her intubated while the doctors performed dark magic to keep her alive. The nurse said she'd see what she could find out and would let me know as soon as she did.

I returned to my seat, frightened and angry, exhausted and tense. I felt like crying; in the next instant, I wanted to break something. I wanted to kick through a door or window, and then suddenly I felt like crying again. How, I wondered, was it possible for everything to have gone so wrong in such a short period of time? And why hadn't I been told anything?

I wanted to be angry at Toby. He'd told me that my sister was at the hospital earlier, and because I'd believed him, I hadn't sent him back to the house. By the time I realized that I needed him to do just that, he wasn't answering his phone. Had he answered, he could have gotten Paige to the hospital sooner. Had he answered, he might have prevented the overdose in the first place.

But it wasn't his fault. It was the nurses who'd been mistaken about seeing Paige earlier, but, honestly, I knew it wasn't their fault, either. All of this was my fault. For going to Florida. For not calling every day, even though part of me knew I should have. And as my anger turned inward, I realized I hated myself, for had I been at home, my sister would be alive and well.

I continued to wait. Meanwhile, the rest of the world persisted in its ordinary routines, though nothing felt normal to me. Names were called, and one by one, patients vanished behind the doors. Often, family members or friends accompanied them; sometimes they didn't. Some eventually emerged; others remained hidden in the bowels of the hospital. A child who wouldn't stop crying was brought in and seen immediately. A man with a homemade sling had been waiting even longer than I had.

More hours passed. When there was still no word about Paige, I checked with the nurse again. Again, she said she'd let me know. I returned to my seat, aching with fatigue but knowing that sleep was impossible. An hour before dawn, a nurse finally came to fetch me, and I was led to the back. Because Paige had been admitted and transferred elsewhere, I couldn't see her, but I was introduced to a harried physician who looked barely older than I was.

Her expression was serious, and she admitted it was still too early to know whether Paige was going to make it; she added that she'd had to request the help of another critical-care specialist to even ensure that Paige survived as long as she had. The next few hours would be crucial, she said; until then, there wasn't much more she could tell me. At the end, surprising me, she placed a sympathetic hand on my shoulder before returning to her duties.

62.

I CHECKED INTO A NEARBY hotel. Not only was I too worn out to make the drive, but being surrounded by the chaos of the house would conjure up images of Paige's activities during the past week, and I didn't have the strength or energy to face them.

In the hotel room, I drew the shades and fell asleep immediately, only to jolt awake a few hours later.

Paige, I thought.

Aunt Angie.

I showered and dressed in clean clothes, then made the short drive to the hospital. In the emergency room, I asked about Paige, but the shifts had changed, and it took almost half an hour for me to learn the location of the room to which she'd been transferred. But the nurse could offer me no additional information.

At the main visitors' desk, I learned where I could find my aunt, but I decided to check on my sister first. When I finally reached Paige's room, I found her intubated and hooked to a slew of machines and IV bags, unconscious. I kissed her cheek, whispering in her ear that I'd be back, then wound my way to another wing and floor of the hospital.

Aunt Angie was awake and hooked to only an IV, but the left side of her face sagged, and that side of her body appeared strangely limp and inert. Nonetheless, half of her mouth lifted at the sight of me, her eyes glistening as I scooted a chair close to the bed so we could talk. Trying to keep things easy and light, I told her about Morgan and the trip to Florida while she nodded, almost imperceptibly, her left fingers twitching from time to time, until she finally dozed off. Then I returned to Paige's room.

As I held my sister's hand, I stared at the numbers on the digital machine, unsure whether they were normal or worrisome. I went to the nurses' station and asked to speak to one of her physicians, but no one was available, since morning rounds had already been completed.

I found the silence of Paige's room oppressive. Instinctively, I started to chatter inanely, regaling her with the same lighthearted stories that I'd told my aunt. She didn't stir, nor did she register any awareness of my presence.

63.

Stepping outside the hospital, I called Morgan from the parking lot. She answered on the first ring, and I updated her on my visit with my aunt. I couldn't summon the courage to tell her about my sister. Nor did Morgan ask; somehow, she sensed that I wasn't ready to talk about Paige just yet.

"How are you doing?" she asked, sounding genuinely worried. "Are you holding up?"

"Barely," I admitted. "I didn't sleep much."

"Do you want me to come?"

"I couldn't ask you to do that."

"I know you're not asking," she said. "I'm suggesting it."

"I thought you were supposed to fly home today."

"I am. I'm almost packed, and we'll be heading to the airport in an hour or so."

"Okay, good," I murmured.

"I went by Bobby T's last night," she added. "I told Ray what happened. I wasn't sure that you remembered."

"Thank you—you're right, it totally slipped my mind," I admitted. "Was Ray upset?"

"I think that's the least of your worries right now, but he said he understood."

"Okay," I said, my mind suddenly flashing to Paige. After a prolonged silence, I heard Morgan's voice again.

"Are you sure you're all right, Colby?"

64.

AFTER HANGING UP, I returned to my aunt's room. She was sleeping when I got there, and I let her rest. When she woke, I helped her sit up and cautiously fed some ice chips into the right corner of her mouth, making sure she was able to swallow. Her speech was distorted, as if her tongue were an unfamiliar presence in her mouth, but with some effort she was gradually able to recount what happened.

When she had gone to the office that day, she noticed that the fingers on her left hand felt oddly numb, and then her vision started to blur. The room spun and tilted, she said, making it impossible for her to keep her balance. That was when Xavier came in. For some reason, he couldn't understand what she was saying. Not long after that, Toby arrived, then Paige, and they couldn't understand her, either. She suspected she was having a stroke—she'd seen the signs on some medical drama on television—but she had no way to tell them, which made it even worse. The entire time she was being loaded into the ambulance, she fretted over whether the effects would be permanent. I gave her left hand a soothing squeeze; her fingers curled but there was hardly any strength.

"You'll be good as new soon," I assured her, trying to sound more confident than I felt. I told her nothing about Paige.

"I don't want to be paralyzed," she mumbled, the last word almost unintelligible.

"You're going to recover," I found myself saying.

When she finally dozed off, I went back to Paige's room.

Then I visited my aunt again, and that was how I spent the rest of the day. Going back and forth from one room to the other.

In all that time, Paige never regained consciousness.

65.

Right before I left the hospital for the night, I finally managed to connect with the physicians. First up was my aunt's neurologist, to whom I'd spoken on my drive back from Florida.

While the stroke was serious, he reiterated that it could have been much worse. Based on her recovery to that point, he still planned to release her in a couple of days but said she would likely need assistance once she got home, since walking, dressing, and other basic activities would be difficult. If I couldn't do it—or if another family member couldn't—it was recommended that I hire a home-healthcare worker. He added that after her release, she would also need extensive physical therapy and that he was already making arrangements for just such care. Despite all of that, he remained relatively positive about her prognosis.

I next met with the critical-care specialist who'd been called in to help treat Paige while she was in the emergency room. I was lucky to speak with him in person, as he'd returned to the hospital only by chance to retrieve something he'd forgotten, and the nurse pointed him out to me.

"It was touch-and-go for a while," he admitted, echoing what the other doctor had warned me about. Though prematurely graying, his alert gaze and youthful energy suggested he was only in his early forties. "Since she's still unconscious, it's hard to know the full extent of any possible impairments," he qualified, "but now that her vitals have begun to improve, I'm hoping for the best."

Until that moment, I realized, I'd been expecting the worst.

"Thank you," I said, exhaling.

Suddenly ravenous, I stopped at a drive-thru to pick up some cheeseburgers and fries, wolfing everything down on the short drive to the hotel. Again, I fell asleep almost immediately, too tired even to remove my clothes.

66.

I slept for more than twelve hours and woke feeling almost human again. I showered, had a huge breakfast, and returned to the hospital.

I went directly to my sister's room but, strangely, found it empty. After a few moments of panic, I learned that she'd been transferred to another floor. When the nurses explained why, I understood, but my heart filled with dread as I made my way there.

When I arrived at the room, she was awake and no longer intubated. Her face was still sunken and gray, and she seemed to be struggling to bring me into focus, as if willing me into existence. Finally, she cracked a weak smile.

"You cut your hair," she said, her voice so soft I had to strain to make it out.

Though I'd known it was coming, I nonetheless felt something plummet inside me. "Yeah," I lied.

"Good," she said through dry, cracked lips. "I was just about to fly home and cut it myself."

Her old joke, I thought. Though I knew she was trying to be funny, I couldn't help eyeing the restraints on her wrists. I took a seat beside her and asked how she was feeling.

Instead of answering my question, she frowned, visibly confused. "How did you find me?"

As I searched for an answer to soothe her rising anxiety, she shifted in her bed. "Did he send you?" She scanned my face. "Gary, I mean?" Twisting the sheets in her bony hands, she went on: "I had to plan for months, Colby. You don't know how bad he got. He hurt Tommie. . . ."

And then she launched into a story that I'd suspected would be coming. As she rambled, her agitation grew, until her shouts and the rattling of her bed rails began to attract the attention of a nurse, who came into the room. The nurse told me over my sister's strenuous pleas that the psychiatrist wanted to speak with me.

Not any psychiatrist. Paige's psychiatrist, a man I knew well.

He arrived within twenty minutes and led me to a room where we could have a private conversation. I told him everything I knew. He nodded as I described my inability to reach Paige, the frantic drive home, and the state of the house when I arrived, but he sat up sharply when I told him about my aunt. He hadn't known she was in the hospital, but now I could see him putting all the pieces together in the same way I had.

He recommended that I avoid visiting Paige for the rest of the day, maybe even the day after that, and told me why. I nodded, understanding and accepting his reasoning. After all, none of this was new.

Afterward, I went to my aunt's room and finally told her about Paige. Her eyes welled with tears, and I saw the same anguished guilt in her expression that I felt, the same helplessness.

When I finished, she pinched the bridge of her nose, then wiped away her tears.

"Go home," she said, fixing me with a stern glare. "You look exhausted."

"But I want to stay," I protested. "I need to be here."

She forced a lopsided scowl, only half of her face cooperating. "Colby, you need to take care of yourself right now."

She didn't bother to point out how pressed I would be at the farm for the next few weeks or that I'd be no good to either of them if I collapsed. We both already knew those things.

67.

At the hotel, I repacked my things, feeling like my days in Florida were a distant dream. As I drove home, I could still feel lingering tension in my neck and shoulders, and memories of Paige's terrified pleas as I left her hospital room only made things worse.

I exited the highway in Washington and eventually reached the gravel road that led to the farm. I scanned both sides of the road, noting the farmworkers in the fields and vehicles parked near the office and the egg-packaging facility. From outward appearances, it seemed as though nothing had happened, yet all I could think was that everything had been irrevocably altered.

When I saw the house in the distance, I swallowed my dread at the thought of having to go inside. But as I turned in to the drive, I made out a petite figure sitting on the porch, a small carry-on suitcase and a tote beside her. I blinked to clear my vision, but it wasn't until I pulled to a stop and saw her wave at me that I realized it was truly Morgan.

Stunned, I climbed out and approached her. She was dressed

in jeans, boots, and a white sleeveless blouse, her long dark hair cascading over her shoulders. A hundred memories and sensations rushed to the surface, leaving me dazed. "What are you doing here?"

"I was worried about you," she said. "You didn't sound too good on the phone and then I didn't hear from you after I got home last night, so I booked the earliest flights I could for this morning and called an Uber from the airport." She stood, shifting nervously from foot to foot. "Are you mad at me?"

"Not at all," I said, reaching out to touch her arm, my fingertips lingering on her wrist. "How long have you been waiting?"

"Not long. Maybe an hour or so?"

"Why didn't you tell me you were coming?"

"I left a message," she countered. "Didn't you get it?"

Pulling out my phone, I saw the voicemail notification. "I didn't check. And I'm sorry for not calling you. I just couldn't."

She ran a hand through her hair and nodded. In the silence that followed, I knew my words had hurt her.

I avoided her gaze, hating myself for yet another reason. "How did you know I'd be here?"

"It was either here or the hospital." She shrugged. "The hospital was closer to the airport, but I don't know your aunt's last name, so I wasn't sure I could even find you. So here I am. But I still can't tell if coming was a good idea." She hugged her arms to her body.

"I'm glad you're here," I said, moving closer and pulling her toward me. When I felt her body against my own, the emotions I'd been suppressing since my return suddenly engulfed me. I choked out a ragged sob as Morgan clutched me tight, whispering that everything would be okay. I'm not sure how long we stood that way, but in the comfort of her embrace, my tears finally subsided.

"I'm sorry," I began, pulling back, only to have Morgan cut me off with a shake of her head.

"Don't ever apologize for being a human being. Your aunt had a stroke—it's got to be terrifying." She stared up at me, searching my eyes. "You still love me, right?"

"More than anything."

She rose to her toes and kissed me. Reading the lingering anxiety in my expression, she apparently decided to wait until I was ready to share any updates. Instead, she swept her arm toward the fields. "So, this is it, huh? The farm?"

"Yeah." I smiled as I watched her study the surroundings with open curiosity.

"It doesn't look like I imagined."

"What did you imagine?"

"I'm not sure. I've never been to a farm, so I walked around a bit while I was waiting for you. I think I saw those prairie schooners you told me about."

When she pointed, I followed her gaze. "That's them," I confirmed. "And behind them is the greenhouse. It's where we start the tomatoes before they go in the field or where we grow them in the winter."

"It looks huge."

"And growing," I added. "We keep having to expand it."

"Is all of this yours and your aunt's?" she asked, spinning around.

"Most of it."

She nodded, remaining quiet. Then: "How is she?"

I described my latest visit with Aunt Angie and also the unknowns of her condition.

"Well, that's positive overall, right?" she asked, squinting up at me. "That she'll be released soon, even if she's going to need help?"

"It is," I conceded. "But there's something I haven't told you."

She tilted her head, but her gaze didn't stray from mine. "You mean about Paige."

I nodded, wrestling with how to begin. Finally, I took her hand and led her to the barn. As we walked, I could sense Morgan's curiosity, but I said nothing. Instead, I lifted the latch and opened the barn door, sunlight spilling across the concrete floor that I'd poured years earlier. I flipped an industrial switch, and the overhead lights came on with a buzz, so bright they almost hurt my eyes.

Half of the barn was used for storage of the kind of items I assumed most people kept in garden sheds—a wheelbarrow, lawnmower, buckets, garden implements, things like that. The other half was used by Paige as her work area. At first glance it appeared chaotic, but I'd seen her quickly find anything she needed. Her own opinion was that art studios should always be a bit cluttered.

A cluster of tables in the shape of a U constituted much of Paige's actual workspace; behind them in the corner was another table. Plastic bins filled with small pieces of colored glass lined the shelves along the back wall. Dozens of larger pieces of glass were stacked upright like books; on other shelves were boxes containing lamp stands she ordered from an artisan in Virginia, who crafted them from original Tiffany designs. Two lampshades, both nearly finished, sat on the main table; one of the other tables was where she cut the glass. Wooden boxes atop a third table housed a mix of glass-cutting tools, markers, copper tape, flux, and solder, along with anything else she might possibly need, everything within easy reach.

I led Morgan that way, watching as her gaze flitted from one spot to the next, trying to figure out the workflow. Surveying the main table, I knew that even someone unfamiliar with the artisanal craft could see the quality of the workmanship on display. I watched as Morgan leaned closer, examining the lampshades, studying the intricate detail.

"Like I told you, she's incredibly talented." I pointed out the plastic molds that the lampshades were being constructed around. "Before she makes the lamp, she has to cast the mold perfectly, so that once the lampshade starts coming together, it retains the precise shape she wants." Moving toward the adjoining work-table, I tapped one of the pieces of cut glass. "Usually, you're al-lowed a tiny bit of leeway when you solder the pieces together, but because she treats the lamps as art—and because people pay top dollar for them—she'll cut and recut the glass until it's abso-lutely perfect. She does the same when she wraps the edges with copper tape, and then again when she solders. Take a look."

On the table lay dozens of pieces of cut glass, some already finished with copper tape, on a cardboard schematic that showed the design and pattern. Morgan lined up a few pieces of the glass as though putting together a puzzle and smiled when she real-ized that each piece of glass fit precisely.

"Over there," I said, pointing to the table separate from the rest, "is where she runs the business side of things." Her laptop computer stood open, along with an overflowing wire inbox, a stack of notepads, a coffee cup filled with pens, and a half-filled water bottle. Beside the work desk stood some mismatched file cabinets piled high with assorted books, ranging from the history of stained glass to coffee-table photo collections of Tiffany lamps. "The cabinets hold copies of all the original Tiffany designs, in-formation on her clients, and specific work details on the lamps she's already created and sold. I think I told you she's built a good business, but I probably underplayed that. She's one of the few people in the country who do this, and she's far and away the best. You can find her work in some of the most beautiful and expensive homes in the country and as far away as Europe. Which is kind of crazy when you think about it, since she's lived most of her life right here on the farm, except for the few years she was married. The local guy she learned from was competent at stained glass, nothing more—he mainly did windows or pieces that hang in windows, and he worked with lead, not solder—so she taught herself all of this. And then figured out how to identify customers, market and promote her work. Without her, I don't think the farm would have made it. Most of the money we needed for the early changes actually came from her. She gave it to us without a second thought."

Morgan studied the workshop thoroughly before her eyes swung back to me.

"Why are you showing me this?"

"Because I told you that she was smart and talented and generous. I don't want you to forget those things. Just like I don't want you to forget that she's my best friend in the world, or that we play games or watch movies at night, or that she's an excellent cook. Or that she was the one who pretty much raised me. I don't know who I would have become without Paige."

"I never doubted any of those things," she said.

I smiled, feeling the weariness of the last few days. "You will."

"I don't understand . . ."

I lowered my gaze, extending my hand again. "Come with me."

I closed up the barn and led Morgan toward the house, pausing at the front door. "She painted the door red, by the way. I thought it was silly, but she told me that early on in America, a red door meant that visitors were welcome. Like if they were traveling on horseback, it would be a place they could spend the night or get something to eat. That's what she thinks a home should be."

I steeled myself before reaching for the knob, then finally opened the door. I gestured for Morgan to step inside, noting that her gaze swept from left to right. I slipped past her, walking toward the kitchen. In the silence, I heard her tentative steps as she followed.

In the air was the odor of burned and spoiled food mixed with the faint residue of fresh paint. In the kitchen, dishes were piled high in the sink and on the stovetop and atop the table. There was a plate of chicken drumsticks, charred on one side, raw on the other; on another plate was raw hamburger, already spoiled. There was a pot of soaking beans on one of the stove burners. There were unfinished meals on the table, next to a container of milk that had turned rancid. In a dirty mason jar with a large dirty spoon beside it, I saw what appeared to be a dead tadpole. All the drawers and cabinet doors stood open. The walls of the kitchen were yellow, but the paint job had been hasty and sloppy, with smears on the cabinets and countertops and splashes on the floor. Kitchen utensils were splayed everywhere, and in front of the sink was a pile of detergents, cleansers, sponges, and other items that had obviously been pulled out in haste. Dead flowers sat in a jelly jar, and I saw Morgan startle at the bloodstains on the counters. On the table, strangely, was a drawing of a house; though in crayon, it was surprisingly good, and it reminded me of the place where Paige had lived in Texas. Picking our way to the pantry, we surveyed the cleared shelves and items stacked on the floor. She said nothing as we walked to the living room— I wordlessly pointed out the emptied closet in the hallway as we passed—but noted with obvious shock the cockeyed cabinet and half-painted wall, rotting apple cores on the rug, toppled stacks of DVDs and books and albums and a pair of Paige's shoes and other odds and ends heaped everywhere. The television was on the floor, and as I used the remote to check that it was still working, I saw that it was tuned to the cartoon channel and turned it off. Touring the back porch, we observed that almost everything except a drill and saw had been removed from the shelves and placed on the floor, just like in the pantry.

We eventually climbed the stairs to the second floor where I absently motioned toward the contents of the linen closet heaped in the hallway. In my room, there was a stack of children's clothing and a smallish pair of sneakers, along with a book I'd saved from childhood called *Go, Dog. Go!* On the nightstand was an Iron Man action figure I'd never seen before. For whatever reason, my pillowcase looked as though it had been dragged through the mud, and Morgan's eyes widened when she saw a pile of bloody Band-Aids on the floor of my bathroom, along with more dried blood on the counter.

Paige's room was far worse than mine. As in the kitchen, all the drawers and the closet doors were flung open, and her clothing and personal effects had been strewn everywhere. On the floor of the closet—as though placed for emphasis—was a box containing my sister's favorite shoes, the Christian Louboutin pumps that her husband, Gary, had once given her for her birthday.

In the bathroom, Morgan gasped at the sight of a bloody T-shirt crumpled on the floor, as well as a wig and an Ace bandage that lay uncoiled on the countertop.

"I can't stay inside," I muttered. "It's too painful."

Turning on my heel, I hurried down the stairs and out to the front porch again, where I sat in one of the rockers. Morgan followed close behind, lowering herself into the other one. Leaning forward, I clasped my hands in front of me.

"I know you're wondering what you just saw," I began. "I

mean . . . it looks . . . crazy, right? But as soon as I got here, I knew exactly what it meant. I found Paige upstairs. She had overdosed on sleeping pills and barely survived. This morning was the first time I was able to speak with her."

Morgan paled slightly. "Was it an accident?"

"No," I said, feeling the weight of my words. "And it's not her first suicide attempt."

Morgan covered my hand with her own. "I'm so sorry, Colby. I can't imagine how you're dealing with everything right now."

I closed my eyes for a long moment before opening them again. "I understand that you have questions, but there's a lot I just don't know right now. Like . . . Paige's hand was burned when I found her, but I don't know how that happened. I don't know why the house looks the way it does. I don't know why she didn't call me about my aunt. Once I'm able to have a lucid conversation with her, I'm sure I'll get some answers, but she's not there yet. When I saw her this morning, do you know the first thing she said to me?"

"I have no idea."

"That she was glad I'd cut my hair. She said that if I hadn't, she would have flown home and cut it herself. And then she wanted to know how I found her."

Morgan's expression was uncertain.

"She thought I was still in high school," I clarified.

"I don't understand," she said with a frown.

I swallowed. "My sister is bipolar. Do you know what that is?"

"You mentioned that you thought your mom was, but I don't know much about it."

I brought my hands together. "Bipolar is a mood disorder that causes alternating periods of mania and depression. In the manic phase, Paige barely eats or sleeps and runs on nervous energy.

Then, after the mania passes, depression sets in, and that's just what it sounds like. There's a lot of crying and a lot of sleeping, and dark, dark thoughts intrude. Sometimes she becomes suicidal."

"And that's what happened?"

"Kind of," I said. "With Paige, there's more. She has bipolar 1, which is an even more severe form of the illness. Every now and then she experiences a psychotic break, complete with delusions and hallucinations. That's why she thought I was still in high school. It's also the reason her psychiatrist recommended that I not visit her again until she's stabilized."

"But you're her brother. . . ."

"She's in restraints, Morgan. If this episode is anything like the last one, she imagines she's new in town and on the run from her husband. The last time it happened, she was also convinced her son, Tommie, had been abducted. But none of that is true." I rubbed my eyes, infinitely weary. "She's even calling herself Beverly again."

"Beverly?"

I sighed, hating the biology and genetics my sister inherited, hating that I hadn't been at the farm when she needed me most.

"It's her first name, but after my mom died, she started using her middle name, Paige. That's how everyone knows her. The only time I ever hear the name Beverly is during times like these."

"Isn't there any medication that can help her?"

"She's on medication. Or she's supposed to be, anyway. I'm not sure whether the medication stopped working or whether she forgot to take it in the midst of the crisis with my aunt, but . . ." I turned to her, spreading my hands out before me. "I know what you're thinking, and trust me when I say I understand how scary the words *psychotic break* sound. But please keep in mind that in those periods—like now—Paige isn't really dangerous to anyone but herself. Do you know anything about bipolar psychosis? Or delusions and hallucinations?"

When she shook her head, I went on.

"A delusion is a faulty but unshakable belief system. For example, like I said, in her last episode she truly believed she was on the run from her husband, Gary, who was trying to take Tommie away from her and eventually did. As far as hallucinations go, hers are both visual and auditory. In other words, she also believed that Tommie was with her. She saw and spoke to him just the way you and I are interacting now. It felt that real to her."

I could see Morgan struggling to absorb this information. "That almost sounds like schizophrenia."

"The conditions are different, but sometimes they share the same symptoms. Delusions and hallucinations are rarer for those with bipolar, but they can be triggered by a bunch of different things—acute stress, sleep deprivation, lack of medication, sometimes marijuana. Anyway, once the mania begins to wane, it becomes more and more difficult for Paige to maintain the delusion, and the depressive phase sets in. Sometimes it's just too much for her mind to handle, which, in her case, spirals down into suicide attempts. There's a lot more to all this, but that's a general overview."

She was silent for a while, digesting, before she realized the obvious.

"You never told me that she had a son."

"Tommie," I said, nodding.

"Where's he now? Does Gary have custody?"

I expelled a breath. "Gary and Tommie died over six years ago in a car accident."

Morgan covered her mouth in shock. "Oh my God . . ."

"Tommie was only a toddler at the time," I said, my voice soft. "It was one of those stupid things, another car running a red light. The guy wasn't drinking; he was just distracted by his phone. Not long after their funerals, Paige had her first psychotic break. We found her in Arkansas, after we got a call from the sheriff. She'd been arrested for vagrancy. I guess my aunt had sent her a letter with a return address and Paige had it in her bag, which was good, because she had no other identification with her. The sheriff made it clear that she needed medical help, so my aunt and I drove out to get her. Her psychiatrist—the same one I met with this morning—was the one who eventually diagnosed her and got her on the appropriate medicines. Once she was stabilized, she agreed to move back to the farm, and I set her up with a workshop in the barn."

"Where does the delusion come from? I mean, if there's an answer to that."

I shrugged, knowing I barely understood it myself. "As far as I can tell, she mixes up bits and pieces of her past into her delusions; she fits everything she sees into the story she's currently telling herself, and there are usually grains of truth in all of it. For instance, I know that she and Gary were having serious troubles in their marriage, to the point that they'd separated. I'm sure her illness had something to do with it, since it wasn't being treated at the time, but anyway, Gary was temporarily awarded full custody, and he wanted to make it permanent. He also worked for the Department of Homeland Security, though in his case it was for FEMA, not any security or anti-terrorism branch. As for the specifics of this particular episode, I really can't tell you. Some of the things she was ranting about in the hospital this morning echoed delusions from her last episode, but others didn't. Like . . . she swore that Gary must have gone to John Small Elementary

School, which is where both of us, not Gary, went to school when we were little, so that part didn't make sense. Until she fully stabilizes, I won't know for sure."

"And you said she's attempted suicide before?"

I nodded, feeling a wave of hopelessness wash over me. "On our way back from Arkansas, she tried to jump out of the car while we were on the highway. In the end, we had to use duct tape to keep her from trying again. Her second attempt happened a couple of years after she'd moved back to the farm. In that instance, her medication had stopped working, and we didn't realize that she had begun self-medicating with weed. I woke one morning to discover that she'd run off in the middle of the night. She took buses and hitchhiked halfway across the country, but fortunately, in that case, she had her phone and I was able to track her with Find My Friends. I eventually found her in a diner near a bus station. She had a cup of hot water and was using packets of ketchup to make tomato soup. She was still in her manic phase and didn't recognize me, but when I offered her a ride, she accepted. For whatever reason, she thought I sold carpets for a living. In the truck on the way back, she began sleeping more and crying more, and when we finally stopped at a hotel for the night, she tried to jump from the balcony. I should have known it was coming, but I'd gone to use the bathroom for just a minute. I caught her when she was halfway over the railing. Had I not found her when I did, had she been alone that night, I don't . . ."

After trailing off, I could see her trying to grasp it all. "It's a good thing she had Find My Friends turned on so you could find her," she said.

"Believe me, I make sure she keeps it on, and I checked it while I was driving home. Not that it did me much good this time."

"Is she going to recover?"

"Physically, yes, once she's stabilized. But it'll be really hard for her emotionally for a while, because she'll remember most of what she did and everything she was thinking, and a lot of it won't make sense even to her. She feels a ton of shame and guilt about that, and it's going to take her a while to forgive herself. I sort of get it," I admitted, running a hand through my hair. "When I was walking you through the house, it felt like I was wandering into her mind and seeing how broken it was. . . ." I could hear my voice dwindling. "I know how awful that sounds."

Morgan shook her head in sympathy. "It sounds like she's sick and she can't help it."

"I wish more people thought that way."

"Is that why you didn't tell me about her? Because you were afraid of what I'd think?"

"It's not my story to tell," I countered. "And you've got to understand: This—what's happening now—isn't who she usually is. The vast majority of the time, she's just my incredibly gifted and witty and generous sister who cooks a great meal and makes me laugh. I didn't want you to think of her as my mentally ill or crazy sister. But I knew that no matter what else I said about her, as soon I said *bipolar* or *mentally ill,* or *prone to psychotic breaks* or *occasionally suicidal,* those labels would have been front and center, because you haven't met the real her."

Morgan gazed out over the distant fields, no doubt thinking about everything I'd told her, and for a long time neither of us said anything. "Paige has had such a hard life," she whispered.

"No question," I agreed. "She was dealt a really unfair hand."

"It's not easy for you, either," Morgan observed, turning back to me.

"Not always."

She gently squeezed my shoulder. "You're a good brother."

"She's a great sister."

Dropping her hand to cover mine, she seemed to come to a resolution of sorts. "Do you know what I think we should do? If it's all right with you, I mean."

I raised an eyebrow.

"I'd like to help you clean up the house. You shouldn't have to do that by yourself. And after that, I'll make you dinner."

"It doesn't look like there's much food in the house."

"We can go grocery shopping," she responded, undeterred. "I'm not a great cook, but my grandma taught me at least one foolproof dish, and I think I can pull that off."

"You won't find much in the way of specialized ingredients around here," I cautioned.

"As long as I can find rice noodles and soy sauce, I can improvise the rest," she said with a shrug. "And wait until you try my grandma's *pancit bihon*. Fried noodles are the ultimate comfort food, trust me."

"Okay," I said, forcing a smile, though it was the last thing I felt like doing.

Rising, we headed inside, but I found myself stopping just beyond the threshold, too daunted by the chaos to even know where to begin. However, in take-charge fashion, Morgan merely stepped around me and made straight for the kitchen. Kneeling before the pile in front of the sink, she called out, "All this goes underneath, right? Is there anything particular I should know? Like dish soap on the left or whatever?"

When I shook my head, she started putting things away. Her initiative prodded me into action, and I cleared the table, scraping food into the garbage. I dumped the beans and half-burned chicken and spoiled meat, as well, along with a dozen wads of used plastic wrap and the mason jar and jelly jar and anything else I could find to discard. When I hauled the bag out to the garbage can, I opened the lid and saw all the food that Paige had thrown away. I simply put the bag in and closed the lid, wondering again what she'd been thinking. By the time I returned, the pile on the floor had been cleared, with the dishrags in a pile. Morgan had also gathered up all the scattered kitchen utensils and placed them in the sink. She was already filling the basin with water.

"I couldn't find the dishwasher."

"That's because there isn't one."

She smiled. "In that case, do you want to wash or dry?"

"Either."

"I'll wash," she said, and little by little we worked through all of it. I noticed that she knew not to use soap on the cast-iron skillet, running it under hot water and scrubbing until it was clean instead. She asked if there was any vegetable oil.

"There was," I answered, "but Paige threw it away."

Knowing enough not to ask why, she handed the skillet to me to dry before soaping a dishrag and wiping down the counters and stovetop. Oddly, I noticed the oven was as clean as I'd seen it in years. Spotting an old backpack of mine in the corner, I opened it to find half a dozen peanut butter and jelly sandwiches mashed together, along with a couple of apples. Dumping the contents into the garbage, I tossed the backpack into the pile of dishrags on the floor and brought everything to the back porch, depositing the load in the washer. The sight of empty shelves outside only spurred more questions.

Next was the pantry, which didn't take long to reorganize. Morgan would hand me something and I'd put it where it belonged; we repeated the routine on the back porch. Restoring everything in the closet went fairly quickly, too, and in the living room Morgan helped me move the cabinet back in place before I put the television, antiquated DVD player, and streaming devices where they belonged and reconnected everything. Morgan threw the apple cores into the garbage and handed me albums and books and DVDs in neat stacks while I put them away. The half-painted wall still looked ridiculous, as did the messy paint job in the kitchen, but for now the downstairs was serviceable.

"If you're wondering why she painted, I have no idea. She just painted these walls maybe a month ago. She loves Hermès orange and swore the kitchen would look fabulous. Same thing with the wall here."

"I'm sure she had her reasons," Morgan said, which was the nicest possible thing she could have said.

Upstairs, we refolded and put away the items from the linen closet, cleaned my bathroom, and I scooped up the children's clothes and my pillowcase, leaving the pile at the top of the stairs for the time being. In Paige's bedroom, I hesitated, somehow reluctant to intrude in my sister's personal space. Morgan had no compunction, however; she immediately started sorting through piles of clothing and folding them. "I'll fold and you put away," she instructed. "And maybe hang whatever's on a hanger back in the closet, okay?"

I wasn't sure where all of it belonged, but I did my best. In the bathroom, I scooped up the bloody shirt, knowing that it would end up in the garbage, and carefully inspected the wig, trying to imagine why Paige would have felt the need to wear one.

"She dressed as a flapper for Halloween a couple of years ago," I mused, spinning the wig around on my hand. "This was part of her costume."

"Hey, I dressed as a flapper last year!" Morgan chirped, spraying the bathroom sink and countertops with cleanser. "Great minds think alike."

I had to admit that it was a lot easier to clean with her help. Alone, I would have scrutinized every item, trying to figure out how it fit into the delusion, but Morgan simply kept moving forward until each task was completed. By the end I felt, if not quite whole, reassured that everything would eventually return to normal.

"Is there a decent-sized supermarket nearby?" Morgan said, washing her hands at the kitchen sink.

"There's the Piggly Wiggly." I shrugged. "But, really, we can go out if you'd rather rest after all this work. . . ."

"You cooked for me in Florida, so it's my turn," she said.

At the Piggly Wiggly, Morgan miraculously managed to find a package of rice noodles in the Asian food section, along with a small bottle of soy sauce. Adding garlic, frozen shrimp, chicken breasts, cabbage, and a few vegetables to the cart, along with a dozen eggs, she triumphantly pulled up to the beverage aisle and threw a six-pack of beer into the bottom of the cart.

Back at the house, she got busy in the kitchen, washing and chopping vegetables and starting a pot of water to boil on the stove. Pulling out a large skillet, she made a shooing motion in my direction. "Leave me alone in here. Go sit on the porch with a beer and relax," she instructed, in a voice that brooked no disagreement.

Pulling a beer from the six-pack, I grabbed my guitar from the truck and settled into one of the rockers out front. I fiddled around with whatever chords came to me as my mind wandered over the last few days. Every now and then I'd stop to take a sip of beer, feeling the beginnings of a melancholy ballad take shape.

"That's pretty," I heard Morgan say from behind me. I turned to see her standing at the screen door, her hair tied back in a ponytail with a rubber band. "Is it new?"

I nodded. "Yeah . . . but I'm not sure what it is yet. And I'm sure I'll need help with the lyrics, since you're so good at those all-important hooks."

Morgan brightened. "After dinner," she promised. "Food in fifteen minutes," she called over her shoulder as she returned to the kitchen.

The smells wafting through the screen door were making my mouth water, and the crackling sound of frying garlic and onions eventually made me lay down my guitar and wander back into the house. Morgan was stir-frying the shrimp, chicken, and vegetable mixture in a heavenly mix of soy sauce, black pepper, and other spices, all the while keeping an eye on the quick-cooking rice noodles.

"You can set the table," she said, swiping absently at a tendril of hair that had escaped her ponytail.

I set two places, cracked open two cold bottles of beer, and put them next to the plates just as Morgan set down a huge platter of fried noodles garnished with limes and hard-boiled eggs.

"Wow," I said. "Kinda puts my chicken dinner to shame."

"Don't be silly," she said, taking a seat across from me. "This is the easiest dish in the world, although it really hits the spot." She raised her own bottle of beer. "To family," she said.

We clinked bottles and took sips before digging into our fragrant plates of food. I think Morgan knew I needed a distraction from thinking about my aunt or Paige, so she regaled me with stories of her family trips to Manila and her grandma's attempts to teach her how to cook. "I wasn't a very good student," she said, laughing. "Once I caused a small fire while I was trying to use the wok, but I did learn one or two things." She popped a shrimp into her mouth and washed it down with another sip of beer. "My grandma finally told my dad that it was a good thing I was smart, because no one would marry me for my cooking."

I leaned across the table and kissed her. "I love your cooking," I said. "And everything else about you."

Morgan went on to tell me about her last day with her friends at the Don CeSar. While she admitted that my sudden departure put a bit of a damper on their last afternoon, what made it worse was a group of guys who monopolized the chaise longues next to theirs at the pool and spent the entire time badgering them to meet up later.

"It was irritating. All we wanted was a peaceful last afternoon together in the sun."

"Did you end up going out on your last night?"

"We did, and thank God we didn't run into those guys. But we weren't out late. Everyone was kinda tired. It was a big week for all of us."

"Fun though, right?"

"I can't speak for them, but I was living in dreamland."

I smiled. "How did your parents react to you leaving again as soon as you got home?"

She made a face. "I didn't tell them until after I booked the flights, and while they weren't thrilled, they didn't try to stop me. I should mention, though, that as soon as I got home, my mom sat me down and tried again to convince me to take that music-teaching job in Chicago instead of going to Nashville."

I made sympathetic noises as I stood and cleared the table. Together, we did the dishes, by now in practiced rhythm. As I put the last of them away, she nodded in the direction of the porch. "Let's sit outside for a while. I want to help you keep tinkering with that song you started."

We settled ourselves in the rockers then, absorbing the smells and budding scenery of the late-spring evening. The air was balmy, and the stars were scattered in the sky like handfuls of loose crystal. From the small creek beyond the barn, I heard the night chorus of frogs and crickets. The moon lent the landscape a silver sheen.

"It's beautiful here," Morgan breathed, taking it all in. "And"—

she interrupted herself with a laugh—"I was going to say it's quiet, but it's not. The sounds are just different than back home. Or even in Florida, for that matter."

"It's called living in the boondocks."

"It's not that bad. I was able to get an Uber in Greenville, after all, and it was a real car and everything." She leaned her head back against the rocker. "Earlier, when I was listening to you working on the song, my thoughts kept returning to our week together. I know you're channeling a lot of stress and worry right now about your sister and your aunt, but when you're writing a ballad, the song needs to come from a memory of happiness or it's not going to work. Sadness is powerful, but it has to be earned, you know? So I was thinking the first line of the song could be something like this. . . ." She drew a deep breath, then sang the opening few bars: "There's a place that I know, where only you and I can go . . ."

I instantly knew she was right. "Anything else?"

"It's your song, not mine. But since you asked . . ." She grinned, arching an eyebrow. "I think the opening should be more complex, instrumentally speaking. Like orchestral, even. A big romantic sound."

I reached for my guitar. "Since you think this should be a song about us, right?"

"Why not?" she asked. "And we should probably get going on it, since I'm leaving tomorrow."

"So soon?"

"I can't stay. I have to spend a little time with my family before I leave for Nashville next week. And there's so much to do in Nashville. I've got to furnish my apartment, set up a bank account, get utilities turned on, things like that. Anyway, you've got a lot on your plate right now, and I'd just be a distraction."

Though she was right, I felt a ripple of sadness at her words; I didn't want to think about that yet. Instead, I strummed the opening chords to the song. Then, in a flash, I knew what it needed. I started over, and Morgan's gaze leapt to mine in recognition. As soon as she sang the opening line, the following line came almost automatically. Wanting to be sure, I played the first stanza a second and third time, already feeling the song take flight.

We worked as we had in Florida, seamlessly, with an unspoken give-and-take. As I tweaked and adjusted the melody, Morgan kept adding to the lyrics, turning the ballad into one of hope and love and inevitable loss. It was she who came up with the chorus, which struck me as undeniably right:

Hold on to Dreamland
Forever, not just today
Someday Dreamland will be ours
Hold fast, don't fall away

By the time we finished the first draft, the moon had traversed the sky and a hush had fallen over the fields. I put away my guitar and led her upstairs to the bedroom. When we made love in the darkness, I felt as though our every touch and movement were choreographed. She seemed to anticipate each breath I drew, and the sounds of her voice merged with mine in the stillness of the room. Afterward, we lay together without speaking, Morgan pressed up against me, her breaths slowing until she fell asleep.

But for me, sleep wouldn't come. Restless, I rose from the bed and threw on a pair of jeans and a shirt, then crept downstairs, where I sat at the small kitchen table, still trying to make sense of all that had happened in the last ten days. When my thoughts turned to Morgan, my life felt complete; when I thought of Paige, the life I truly wanted felt as if it would always be out of reach. I sat with those contradictory feelings, alternately at peace and in turmoil, until the light of dawn seeped through the windows. When it was bright enough, I found some paper and a pen, and I scribbled out the lyrics that we'd written the night before.

In the truck were the bags I had yet to unpack from my trip to Florida, and I walked barefoot through grass damp with morning dew. I fished out my pair of Vans and made a trip to the grocery store for coffee, along with eggs, bread, milk, and a few other items, remembering at the last minute to grab a box of green tea. I was sipping coffee at the kitchen table when Morgan finally wandered down the stairs. When she saw me at the table, she covered her mouth.

"I'd kiss you, but I haven't brushed my teeth yet."

"I haven't, either."

"Then you can't kiss me yet, either."

I smiled. "Would you like coffee or tea?"

"Tea would be great if you have some."

I added water to a teapot; when it whistled, I poured the hot water into the cup and added a bag, bringing it to her at the table.

"You were up early," she said. "Almost like you're a farmer."

"I couldn't sleep."

She reached over, taking my hand. "I hate that you're having to deal with all this."

"Me, too."

"Is your aunt going to be released today?"

"Probably tomorrow or the day after that."

"How about Paige?"

"That'll be longer. It might take a few days until she's stabilized. What time are you leaving today?"

"Two? Which means I should probably be at the airport by one."

With travel time, I realized, we had only a few hours left together, and more than anything, I didn't want to spoil them. "Do you want breakfast?" I asked. "I can make eggs and toast."

"The tea is fine for now. I'm not all that hungry yet. But you know what I'd like to do after I shower and brush my teeth?"

"Kiss me?"

"Of course," she said with a smile. "But I'd also like to see the farm, so I can put actual images to your descriptions of things."

"Sounds good."

"And maybe get a photo of you on a tractor. Or maybe even a video of you driving one so I can text it to my friends."

I had to laugh. "Whatever you'd like."

68.

AFTER SHOWERING, I WAITED for her on the front porch. In the distance, I saw Toby's truck parked near the office and caught sight of the sprinklers irrigating the fields. Some workers were already working in the tobacco fields while another group was carefully bringing baskets of eggs into the processing facility for inspection and packaging. The activity reminded me of how much time it was going to take me to catch up—especially with my aunt out of commission. I pushed my worries to the side and wandered to the barn instead.

At Paige's work desk, I sifted through the piles of paperwork, searching for the order she was working on. I'd need to call the customer to explain that there'd been an emergency and that the order might be delayed, but, unable to figure it out, I left the barn, wondering when Paige would be coherent enough to tell me.

By the time I got back, Morgan was in the kitchen, heating more water for her tea. Soaking up the sight of her, I remembered how she'd felt in my arms last night, and moving her hair aside, I kissed her on the back of her neck.

After she finished her second cup, we set out on our tour. I let her walk through one of the prairie schooners, past the clucking chickens, then showed her the facility where we checked and packaged the eggs. I guided her through the greenhouse, then showed her the facilities where we readied the tomatoes for shipping and the warehouse where we dried the tobacco leaves. We stopped by the main office—I called it *paperwork central*—and strolled through the tomato and tobacco fields, before I finally allowed her to shoot video of me driving a tractor. Aside from Toby, the workers went about their business, offering nothing more than a good morning or wave from afar, but I nonetheless felt their curious glances. It took me a little while to realize it was probably the first time any of them had seen me walk around the farm with a woman other than my aunt or my sister. Michelle had never been interested in the specifics of my daily life.

We had an early lunch at a place called Down on Main Street, in the heart of the waterfront district. Though the food was appetizing, I was too tense to eat, and I'm pretty sure Morgan felt the same way, since she mainly picked at her salad. Afterward, we strolled hand in hand toward the waterfront, with its gorgeous views of the Pamlico River, the water glittering beneath a cloudless sky. In the middle of the river, a sailboat rode the gentle breeze, moving slowly, as though in no rush to go anywhere at all.

"Have you given any more thought to coming to Nashville with me?" she asked, stopping to face me. "I mean, I know I shouldn't even be talking about this right now, and I understand that it might be a while before you could get there, but you never really answered me."

In the glinting sunlight, I could see tiny flecks of hazel in her eyes, something I'd never noticed. "I don't think I can. I don't see how I can leave my aunt and my sister when they need me most.

I left for three weeks and look what happened." They were some of the most painful words I'd ever said in my life.

"Yeah," she said. Her eyes looked wet. "That's what I thought. But you'll come visit me, right? After I settle in?"

I hesitated, wishing we could talk about anything else, wishing that so many things in my life were different.

"I'm not so sure that would be a good idea. . . ." I offered, trailing off.

"Why wouldn't it be a good idea? Don't you love me?"

"Of course I do."

"Then we'll do the long-distance thing. In this day and age, it's easy. We can FaceTime, we can visit each other, we can call and text. . . ."

She reached up to turn my face to hers, and I responded by tucking a strand of hair behind her ear. "You're right. We can do those things. I just don't know if we should."

"What on earth are you talking about?"

I brought my lips together, wishing more than anything that I didn't have to say the words that I knew would be coming next. "When I was at the hospital, I had a lot of quiet time to think about you and me and the future, but no matter how I tried to imagine it, my thoughts kept circling back to the idea that, from now on, we're going to be living in two very separate worlds."

"So what?"

"Those worlds won't ever come together, Morgan, which means that it would *always* be long distance for us. You're going to Nashville, and as for me, I can't leave my aunt. I can't leave Paige, and as far as the farm, it's the one thing I know I'm good at. It's what I do."

"But you have gifts as a singer and songwriter that you can't ignore. You saw the crowds at your shows in Florida. You saw how people reacted to what you were doing. . . ." Morgan's voice was edged with irritation.

"Even if that's true, it doesn't matter. Who would take care of my family? You and I are different, and what does that mean for us in the long run? Do we stay together with the knowledge that we'll lead mostly separate lives, where we can only see each other every now and then? And if so, for how long? A year? Five years? Forever? Long-distance relationships work when they're temporary, but with us, it would never change. I'm stuck here, maybe permanently, but you have your whole life in front of you, and the world is waiting for you. And, most importantly, is that the kind of relationship that you want? One where we barely see each other? You're only twenty-one. . . ."

"So you're breaking up with me? You just want to end it?" As she asked, I could hear the crack in her voice, could see the tears beginning to form in her eyes.

"It was never meant to be," I said, hating myself and hating the truth and feeling as though I was letting the best part of me die. "Your life is going to change, but mine can't. And that's inevitably going to change things between us—even though I do love you, even though I know I'll never forget the week we had together."

For the first time since I'd known her, Morgan seemed at a loss.

"You're wrong," she finally bit out, swiping angrily at a tear that had spilled onto her cheek. "And you don't even want to try."

But I could tell that she was thinking about my aunt and Paige and the farm and understood what I'd said. She crossed her arms and stared out over the water, unseeing. I reached into my pocket and pulled out the piece of paper I'd scribbled on that morning.

"I know I have no right to ask anything of you," I said. "But please take our song and make it famous, okay?"

She reluctantly took the paper and glanced at it, while blinking back the tears that kept threatening to overflow.

There's a place that I know
Where only you and I can go
Far from the darkness of the past
Where love can bloom at last

Hold on to Dreamland
Forever, not just today
Someday Dreamland will be ours
Hold fast, don't fall away

In my mind we're living there
In that place we're meant to share
No more talk of what we owe
Just what our hearts already know

In Dreamland, down in Dreamland
Hold fast, don't fall away . . .

She didn't finish but slipped the page into her purse, and for a long moment we simply stood together in the small town I knew I'd never escape, a place too small for Morgan's future. I put my arm around her, watching as an osprey took flight over the lapping waves. Its simple grace reminded me of Morgan paddling through waterways in a place that already seemed far, far away.

After a while, we made our way back to the truck and drove to the Greenville airport. A handful of cars idled in front of the small terminal, unloading passengers, their hazard lights flashing. I pulled the truck in behind them and reached for her bag.

Morgan slipped the tote over her shoulder as I rolled her luggage to the entrance.

My stomach was in knots as I buried my face in her hair. I reminded myself that I had spoken the truth. No matter what plans we made or how hard we both wanted things to work between us, Morgan would leave me behind someday. She was destined for great things, and she'd eventually find someone with a life more in sync with hers, something I knew I could never offer her.

Still, I understood that I'd hurt her deeply. I could feel it in the way she clung to me, in the finality with which she pressed her body against my own. I knew that I would never love another woman in the same way I loved her. But love, I realized, wasn't always enough.

When we separated, Morgan met my eyes.

"I'm still going to call you," she said with a catch in her voice. "Even though I'm furious at you."

"All right," I said, my voice hoarse.

She reached for her bag and adjusted the tote strap on her shoulder, then forced a brave smile before heading into the terminal. I watched the electronic doors open and shut as she passed through them and, shoving my hands into my pockets, I started back toward the truck, aching for her, and for me. As I slid behind the wheel, I recalled what Paige had once said about love and pain being two sides of the same coin and finally understood exactly what she meant.

Turning in to traffic, I tried to picture Paige and my aunt as I'd last seen them, feeling a heaviness settle in my chest. As much as I loved them, I knew that somehow they'd also become my prison.

EPILOGUE

Colby

THOUGH MORGAN AND I stayed in touch, the calls and texts diminished over time. In the end, it had more to do with her than with me. In the weeks following Morgan's move to Nashville, I'd struggled to manage the farm while overseeing Paige's and Aunt Angie's recovery. By late autumn our life had settled a bit, but by contrast, events overtook Morgan's life like a boulder gathering speed and power as it rolled downhill. The changes that followed the igniting of her music career left me stunned; it reached the point that when I left a voicemail, she sometimes couldn't return my call for two or three days. It was fine, I told myself—as I'd told her, I didn't think we should try to make the long-distance thing work, since it would inevitably come to an end. Instead, when we finally connected—often while she was in airports or between meetings, or during recording breaks—I would listen with interest and pride as she relayed the latest developments in her meteoric professional rise.

Even in her wildest dreams, she couldn't have planned the path her career had taken. Upon arriving in Nashville, she'd spent time in a recording studio and, with demos in hand, met with the handful of managers she'd mentioned to me, all of whom showed mild to moderate interest. At the casual encouragement of one of those managers ("Why not?"), she'd posted the video of her performance at my show to her social-media accounts. It had been edited exceptionally well by her friends, intercutting footage from her recording the song at the studio with scenes from Bobby T's and clips of Morgan dancing on TikTok. Interest in the song sparked among some key influencers—including a few admiring stars with huge followings—erupting into an inferno. Within weeks, it was viewed tens of millions of times online, and she quickly released another video, in which she performed "Dreamland." Naturally, her social-media following exploded, as well, and she was soon being courted by the most prominent managers and recording labels in the industry. "The new Taylor Swift" was how she was often described, drawing comparisons to female megastars like Olivia Rodrigo, Billie Eilish, and Ariana Grande.

The manager with whom she ultimately signed was admittedly a marketing genius, and he built on the early momentum, immediately packaging Morgan in a way that made her seem like an already established star. She started getting play on the radio, and a formal publicity campaign was launched that took her from city to city, with appearances on talk shows in New York and Los Angeles. Her face appeared regularly in stories about celebrities, and by the time she performed on *Saturday Night Live* in November—where she was introduced as a *global phenom*—it seemed to me as though everyone in the world had heard of her. Somehow, between all of that, she managed to find time to begin recording an album. Produced by huge hitmakers, it featured songs written by her as well as collaborations with the hottest hip-hop, pop, and R&B stars in the business.

Originally, she told me, there'd been discussions of her going on tour and opening for one major act or another, but when she released a third song on social media after her appearance on *Saturday Night Live* and in advance of her debut album drop, the song went to number one on the charts. Now there was talk of others opening for her solo tour next autumn, which was already at thirty cities in North America and counting.

She was caught up in a cyclone, so it wasn't surprising that we were in touch less frequently. And whenever the ache of missing her became too great, I reminded myself of what I'd said on our last day together.

As for me, I hired an aide to help with my aunt after her release from the hospital; she not only helped Aunt Angie around the house but shuttled her to and from her physical-therapy appointments. The paralysis on her left side had been slow to improve; it wasn't until Halloween that she was confident enough to finally send the aide on her way. She still limped, her left arm remained weak, and her smile was crooked, but she was back to running the office full-time and even got around the rest of the farm with the help of a four-wheeler. The farm, more than Paige or me, remained the center of her life.

And Paige . . .

It took her six days to fully stabilize again, after which I eventually pieced together the timeline of her crisis. As I'd suspected, she raced to the hospital when my aunt was admitted, leaving her meds and her phone behind in her haste, which was the reason she hadn't called me as soon as it happened. And although she swore she kept intending to retrieve her meds from the house, my aunt's condition was too serious for her to feel comfortable leaving the hospital without any family members present. Within a couple of days, the chemicals in her brain began to cause misfires, affecting her perception; not long after that, the sudden withdrawal of her medication distorted her reality. Among other things, she was convinced that she'd called and spoken to me about my aunt's condition, not once but two or three times; it wasn't until I showed her my call log that she accepted that she'd imagined entire conversations. After that, her memories were fuzzy and incomplete until the delusion set in; she remembered walking out of the hospital but didn't recall smoking weed, even though her blood tests showed a high level of THC.

After her release, she didn't want to talk about it for a long time. As I'd known she would be, she was deeply ashamed and embarrassed. Nearly a month passed before I was able to get the whole story. It became apparent that she'd incorporated some elements from her previous psychotic episodes into the new de-lusions, including the bus rides and hitchhiking and the diner where she added ketchup to a cup of hot water. She explained why the house was in shambles and admitted she'd taken the guns that I kept beneath my bed and buried them near the creek. She vaguely remembered buying the Iron Man action figure from a store near the hospital; she'd intended to give it to my aunt to boost her spirits by making a joke about how tough she was. But the hardest parts for her to talk about, the ones that seemed absurd even to her, were the obvious ones: How could she not have recognized her own home? How could she not have recognized Toby, a man she'd known for most of her life, when he'd come to the house? She had no answer to those questions, just as in the past she'd had no answer to why she didn't recog-nize me. As far as the rest of her delusions, we'd already lived through most of them, and neither of us felt the need to rehash the painful details.

I dug up the guns, then cleaned and oiled them, thanking God that I'd long ago equipped them with external trigger locks and always kept the keys with me, which made them impossible to fire unless the locks were removed. After Paige's first suicide attempt and even before she'd left the hospital, I'd taken no chances. Still, to be doubly careful in the future, I purchased a gun safe, as well, and stored them there. I also repainted the walls and cabinets in the kitchen, along with the living room, before she was released from the hospital. Orange and burgundy, the colors she'd chosen not too long before.

Once she was home, getting back to work was a necessary distraction, and thankfully, her business hadn't suffered. Still, it was a few months before she began to seem like her old self. Though she still cooked dinner for us a few times a week, she often averted her eyes while we ate, and there were times I found her crying quietly on the porch.

"I hate that I'm broken," she said on one of those occasions. "I hate that I can't even control what I think."

"You're not broken, Paige," I soothed, taking a seat beside her and reaching over to stroke her arm. "It was only a few crappy days in the scheme of things. Everyone has them."

Despite herself, she laughed. "The difference is that my bad days are really, really crappy compared to most."

"I can't argue with you there," I agreed, and again she laughed, then grew serious.

"Thanks," she said, turning toward me. "For saving my life. Again."

"You saved me, too."

I eventually told her about my trip to Florida and Morgan, leaving nothing out. It was around the time that Morgan had posted the first video of her performance at Bobby T's on social media, and Paige—like everyone—was floored by her talent. When the video ended, she turned to me, eyebrows raised.

"And she thought *you* were good?"

I laughed at that—Paige actually loved when I sang. But she

was also sensitive to how hard it was for me to watch Morgan drift further away over the next few months. I know Paige spotted the photograph plastered all over the gossip sites a couple of weeks before Christmas—a paparazzi shot of Morgan walking hand in hand with a famous young Hollywood actor. Paige loved to follow celebrity gossip, but she was careful not to mention the photo to me. Still, I would have had to be living under a rock to miss it.

I'm not going to say that seeing the photo didn't hurt me, just as I'm not going to say that I was shocked. And though our lives had diverged just as I'd predicted, I never forgot the decision I'd made on the night that Morgan and I first made love, when I resolved to make changes in my own life so I didn't end up like my uncle. While that had to wait until I knew my aunt and Paige were going to recover, I like to think I kept my promise. I'd been able to make it to the coast to go surfing four times since my trip to Florida, and I set aside times on Fridays and Sundays to do nothing but play or write music, no matter how much work remained unfinished. I reconnected with a few old friends and met up with them on the occasional weekend night, even if it still sometimes felt like *Groundhog Day*.

I'd also made an effort to relax my routines from time to time, which is why I decided to change the brake pads on my truck one Tuesday morning, despite the long list of other things I should have been doing. While basic vehicle repairs might not sound like fun to most people, I enjoyed it; unlike practically everything else at the farm, it was a task with a definite finishing point. In a world where nothing ever stops, actually completing something can be very gratifying.

Thankfully, the temperature was mild that afternoon, and I pushed up the sleeves of my work shirt as I thought through the steps of the repair. But fate is a strange thing: Just after I turned on the radio in the cab and readied myself to slide under the truck, Morgan's voice soared out of the car speakers. It was "Dreamland," which by then I'd probably heard a hundred times. Still, I had to admit that the song always made me stop in my tracks. Her voice was resonant and heartbreaking. She'd changed parts of the lyrics to add the wonderful hook I'd known she'd find, and I allowed myself the briefest of memories of her sitting on the porch that day.

It was about then that I heard a car approaching from the distance. I squinted, trying to make it out, and was surprised when it slowed, then pulled into the drive, coming to a stop behind my truck.

From the back seat, Morgan got out. For a moment I couldn't move, and it was only when the Uber started backing out that I unfroze.

"What are you doing here?" I stuttered.

She shrugged, tossing a length of hair over her shoulder, and I wondered how it was possible that she'd grown even more beautiful since the last time I'd seen her.

"I came to visit you, because I was tired of waiting for you to visit me."

Still trying to process her sudden appearance, I couldn't say anything else for a few seconds. "Why didn't you tell me you were coming?"

"And ruin my Valentine's surprise? I don't think so."

Leaving her luggage behind, she walked into my arms as though it was the most natural thing in the world, like we'd never stopped holding each other.

"It's not Valentine's Day," I mumbled into her hair, feeling her body against my own.

"It's close enough. I'm going to be in L.A. on the actual day, and this is the best I could do."

When we separated, I saw a familiar mischievous glint in her eyes.

"I thought you were seeing someone," I said, trying to sound casual as I mentioned the actor's name.

"We went out a couple of times, but it just wasn't right." She waved a hand dismissively. "He was lacking that special something, you know? Like . . . when we were together, I kept thinking about the zombie apocalypse and wondering whether he could grow food and fix trucks and all that other survival stuff."

"Yeah?"

"We love what we love, right?"

I grinned, relieved that she didn't seem to have changed in the slightest.

"Right," I said. "But I still can't believe you showed up like this. You've got so much going on."

"And you don't?"

"It's different."

"Everyone is busy, because life is busy for everyone. I also came here to tell you something."

"What's that?"

"Do you remember that big speech you made on our last day together? You know, when you were pretty much trying to end things between us while doing your best to sound all noble?"

Though I wouldn't have described it that way, I nodded, still unable to stop smiling.

"I've been thinking about that a lot, and I've now come to the conclusion that you were a hundred percent wrong about pretty much all of it."

"Oh yeah?"

"Like I told you then, I was angry. I wouldn't have expected a nice guy like you to be such a heartbreaker. But I'm finally over it, and I decided to give you another chance. So, from now on, we're going to try it my way." She fixed me with a stern gaze. "The long-distance thing, I mean. Where I visit you and you visit me, and in between we text and call and FaceTime each other because, as of now, we're a couple again."

As soon as she said the words, I knew they were exactly what I'd wanted to hear.

"How long can you stay?"

"Only a couple of days, but I have some free time next month. That'll be your turn to visit me."

My mind flashed to Paige and my aunt, but I suddenly knew with certainty that I would somehow make it work.

"Yes, ma'am," I said.

"Now tell me that you love me. You stopped texting that to me a few weeks ago, and I didn't like that, either. But I've decided I'll forgive you for that, too."

"I love you, Morgan," I said, the words coming easily.

Rising to her toes, she kissed me, her lips as soft as I remembered.

"I love you, too," she whispered. "Let's make the most of these next couple of days, shall we?"

The turn of events was so dizzying that it was difficult for me to grasp what was happening.

"What did you have in mind?"

She surveyed the surroundings, then settled her eyes on me. "You know what I'd like to do first? Before anything else?"

"I haven't the slightest idea."

"I'd really love to meet your sister."

"Paige?"

"I want to get the real scoop on what you were like as a kid. I'll bet she has some interesting stories. I also want to tell her thank you."

"Why?"

"You told me she raised you, and I love who you turned out to be. Why wouldn't I thank her?"

It was my turn to kiss her then, if only because I knew she really, truly understood me. When I pulled back, I allowed my hand to linger on her hip.

"Let's go up to the house," I said, taking her hand. "I'm sure Paige would love to meet you, too."

ACKNOWLEDGEMENTS

LIKE SO MANY PEOPLE around the world, I have spent the last couple of years in relative isolation due to Covid. And as for so many others, the period of enforced distancing caused me to reflect deeply on the nature of my relationships. Some of those relationships atrophied in this era of crisis; others flourished and grew deeper. Remarkably, some fresh new connections emerged, as well, mirroring the shifts in priorities and desire for change that millions of people experienced during the Great Pause.

One enduring relationship has remained and, if anything, grown even deeper during these recent years: my friendship and collaboration with my longtime literary agent and producing partner, Theresa Park. T, at twenty-seven years and counting, our close partnership stands as one of the most important and constant in my life. Together with the leaders of my first-class team at Park & Fine—to whom I've dedicated this novel—you've helped me sustain a career that has defied even my own expectations. But even more meaningful has been the decades-long journey that we have shared as friends and fellow travelers on the road of life.

Among the new relationships that I embarked on during the pandemic is my professional affiliation with Penguin Random House. I am immensely grateful to Madeline McIntosh for midwifing my introduction to the PRH family, and to Gina Centrello for making such extraordinary efforts to ensure that I was comfortable in every way. Kara Welsh and Kim Hovey, it's been a pleasure to get to know you—and I now understand how your division runs with such professionalism, efficiency, and grace. Your long experience and relentless pursuit of excellence are surely responsible for your unparalleled roster of bestsellers, and yet your leadership style always feels deeply humane. To Jennifer Hershey, whose meticulous oversight of every detail of this book's publication ranged from the broadest strategic initiative to the tiniest quibble in page proofs, I wish to convey deepest thanks and genuine admiration.

To Jaci Updike and her unparalleled sales team, you have my heart and soul (remember that I always will be a sales rep at heart!). It is an honor to have my books sold by such outstanding professionals.

In marketing, Quinne Rogers and Taylor Noel bring originality, dogged persistence, and fierce ambition to their jobs; it's rare to find an ardent sense of possibility and limitless ambition in the genteel world of publishing, and yet they bring that to their work every day. Similarly, in the world of publicity, I cannot imagine greater dedication and passionate advocacy than that delivered by Jennifer Garza, Karen Fink, and Katie Horn.

The sophistication and innovative strategies of the PRH audio division stem directly from its stellar team: Ellen Folan, Nicole McArdle, Karen Dziekonski, Dan Zitt, and Donna Passannante.

I look forward to lots of high-quality audio versions of my books in coming years.

Of course, the book you are holding in your hand or reading on your device could not exist but for the detail-oriented, deadline-driven, and technologically savvy production folks who work around the clock to deliver a flawless and beautiful product: Kelly Chian, Kathy Lord, Deborah Bader, Annette Szlachta-McGinn, Maggie Hart, Caroline Cunningham, Kelly Daisley, and David Hammond. You all take such pride in your work and it shows.

Last in my thanks to my new PRH team, but definitely not least: the inspired art directors Paolo Pepe and Elena Giavaldi, who created the gorgeous new look of this novel. The magic you bring to this process holds me in awe.

I owe the success of my career-spanning novels, feature films, partnerships, and social media to the loyal (and sometimes long-suffering) team who continues to manage and oversee all of my business and public-facing endeavors. In the world of film and TV, my close friend and wizard-like agent, Howie Sanders, at Anonymous Content: Howie, I continue to marvel at your instincts on timing, story, and the marketplace; I treasure your unflagging decades-long friendship more than I can say. As my entertainment lawyer and fierce, tenacious advocate, Scott Schwimer never gives up on the best possible terms or on me as a friend; Scottie, I hope you know that you remain close to my heart through all the ups and downs of our respective lives. To my new partners and friends at Anonymous Content, CEO Dawn Olmstead and producer and manager Zack Hayden, I'm grateful for your support and vision for our creative future. On a related note, I can hardly overstate my excitement at the prospect of working with Peter Cramer, Donna Langley, and Lexi

Barta at Universal Pictures on a slate of new projects based on my books—thank you for betting on the stories I write and for bringing such enthusiasm and energy to our collaboration.

My publicist Catherine Olim at Rogers & Cowan has guided me through the best of times and the worst of times, with pragmatic yet savvy instincts; Catherine, you never hesitate to tell me the truth and I prize your forthright opinions, which always come from a place of love and protection. LaQuishe Wright ("Q") is hands down the most brilliant, supportive, and sophisticated social-media manager in the entertainment business—and also a trusted friend whose integrity is beyond reproach. Mollie Smith, you practically invented my Web presence and fan outreach—without you I wouldn't know how to connect with my readers. Your insights and patience with all of the changes and developments in my career over the past decades have been a stabilizing force for me. In Theresa's office at Park & Fine, Charlotte Gillies has proven indispensable at managing all the logistics, scheduling, contracts, and payments that Theresa oversees, constantly liaising with my entire team. And where the nuts and bolts of earning a living are transformed into numbers I can understand, Pam Pope and Oscara Stevick, my faithful and rigorous accountants, reign supreme—thank you, old friends, for shepherding me to a place of order and security.

Of course, my working life as an author is profoundly intertwined with the personal and community relationships that sustain me: My children, Miles, Ryan, Landon, Lexie, and Savannah; Victoria Vodar; Jeannie Armentrout; Tia Scott Shaver; Christie Bonacci; Mike Smith; Buddy and Wendy Stallings; Angie, Linda, and Jerrold; Pat and Bill Mills; Todd and Gretchen Lanman; Lee and Sandy Minshull; Paul Minshull; Eric and Kin Belcher; Tony and Shellie Spaedy; Tony Cain; Austin and Holly Butler; Gray Zuerbregg; Jonathan and Stephanie Arnold; David and

Morgan Shara; Andy Sommers; David Geffen; Jim Tyler; Jeff Van Wie; Paul DuVair; Rick Muench; Bob Jacob; Chris Matteo; Pete DeCler; Joe Westermeyer; Dwight Carlblom; David Wang; Missy Blackerby; Ken Gray; John Hawkins . . . and my gratitude further extends to my family, as well: Monty, Gail, Adam and Sean, Dianne, Chuck, Todd and Allison, and Elizabeth, Sandy, Nathan, Josh, Mike and Parnell, Matt and Christie, Dan and Kira, and Amanda and Nick . . . and, of course, all of *their* children.

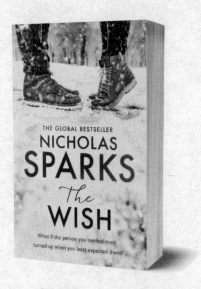

THE GLOBAL BESTSELLER
NICHOLAS SPARKS
The WISH

What if the person you needed most
turned up when you least expected them?

**What if the person you needed most,
turned up when you least expected them?**

Maggie hasn't told this story in years. More than two decades ago, she
fell in love. She was sixteen and far from home, waiting to give her baby
up for adoption. Bryce showed Maggie how to take photographs and
he didn't judge her for the way her belly swelled under her jumper. They
had the perfect first kiss. Theirs was a once-in-a-lifetime kind of love.

Now, as Maggie sits by the Christmas tree in her gallery telling her story,
surrounded by the photographs that made her famous - the photographs
Bryce never saw - her new gallery assistant asks her a question.
If she had one wish, what would she wish for this Christmas?

Maggie always thought she knew the answer to that question.
But before she can say 'I'd go back to that winter with Bryce', she stops
herself. It is all she has ever wanted but suddenly here, on this dark night
under the twinkling stars, there is something else she wants. She wants
to find her baby.

OUT NOW

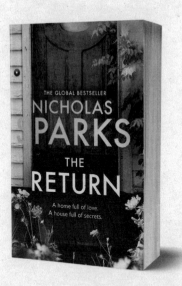

THE GLOBAL BESTSELLER
NICHOLAS PARKS
THE **RETURN**

A home full of love.
A house full of secrets.

**Trevor Benson never intended to return to North Carolina.
But here he is, back where it all began.**

Trevor found himself unable to resist the call home when he
inherited a tumbledown cabin from his grandfather. He's come
back to live the simple life but nothing here is simple.

There's Callie, the sullen local teenager who seems to know more
than she should about Trevor's grandfather's death. And there's
Natalie, the deputy sheriff intent on making a point and lingering
in Trevor's mind long after she's left his porch.

In a bid to unravel Natalie and Callie's secrets and to find out
what really happened to his grandfather, Trevor is about to learn
more than he's bargained for - that sometimes, in order to move
forward, we have to return to the place where it all began.

OUT NOW